CATS' EYES OF MUCH MEDDLING

Pauline Potterill

Pobo

INTRODUCTION

In this, the third of the Much Meddling novels, Emily is wondering what she can do to entertain her children during the long summer holiday. However, before it has even begun, the mysterious Catolith appears. Unnervingly, it seems the girls were expecting it.

More mystery and romance, as the inhabitants of Much Meddling go about their lives.

What are the children up to in the woods with an axe? Why are the older inhabitants so disapproving of the vicar's new housekeeper? Who is the secretive stranger and what does he want?

As the children cope with what the Catolith has brought, Emily discovers what the Cats' Eyes have to reveal.

Cats' Eyes of Much Meddling

Summer

CHAPTER ONE

I t was on the last day of the summer term, as the triplets tumbled from their school bus, that a large tortoiseshell cat was spotted strolling along the wall of Wishing Well Cottage. What was notable about the cat, other than its fabulous colouring, was its lack of a complete tail. What remained, was kinked and, as the cat retreated, very much resembled a question mark.

Seeing the cat, the girls stopped in their tracks and looked at one another. No words were spoken, but their eyes narrowed. Deep in thought they marched the few metres to the cottage gate. The cat, reaching the end of the wall, disappeared into the wood.

For the past 3 years life at Wishing Well Cottage had been 'normal'. The girls, Tansy, Lily, and Violet had started school and were generally behaving as one would expect 6-year-old children to behave. The only 'abnormal' thing about them was their constant good and kind behaviour to each other, everyone, and everything. Intuitively it seemed, they knew to keep their 'abilities' to themselves. Co-incidences were few, and odd occurrences laughed at. Life had been going so well.

Entering the house, they yelled out for Emily, their mother. Finding her in the kitchen they began talking as one, "Catolith is here, Catolith is here."

"Catolith?" repeated Emily.

"Yes, mummy. Catolith is here."

"Who? What are you talking about? Who is … what?"

"Catolith!" they said as one.

"Do you mean… catalyst?" asked Emily, surprised they may know the word.

"Catalyst? What is that?" asked Lily.

"Well, it is something that… initiates… change."

The girls pondered this for a moment, weighing it as a suitable description.

"The Herald!" said Lily with a shoulder shrug. Seeing Emily's lack of comprehension, the girls exchanged glances. Then, apparently deferring to Violet, who frowned slightly, silent consensus was reached.

"What is for tea?" asked Tansy.

"Yes, I'm hungry," said Lily.

"Me, too," added Violet.

Emily looked at her girls, a sinking feeling in the pit of her stomach. "Shepherd's Pie."

Mutterings of approval followed, and the

girls ran out of the kitchen. As the three sets of feet noisily negotiated the stairs Emily reached for the silver pendant hanging from the chain round her neck. Unlike the periapt, the feel of it gave her no sense of comfort. It was nearly 8 years since the periapt had been placed in the cellar, back at the base of the stalactite from which it had been cut. This charm pendant had been given to her by Angelica Wells, the former owner of Wishing Well Cottage, to 'bring her safely home'. Angelica and her two sisters, Ruby, and Myrtle, 100-year-old triplets, had set out to find a bride for their great great nephew Alex, before they died. The periapt had prompted Emily to return to their village, Much Meddling. The winning lottery ticket, given to her by Ruby, had provided her with the means to buy Wishing Well Cottage, after Angelica's death. Finally, Myrtle had ensured that Emily needed to visit the village blacksmith, Alex, whom Emily had subsequently married. Alex, wanting to know that Emily wanted him for himself and not because of some scheme of his great great aunts, had persuaded her not to wear the periapt anymore. Now, she unconsciously sought it out in times of stress: its silky-smooth surface cool to the touch.

As Emily pondered on what the girls had said she busied herself about the kitchen. She mashed the potatoes that had been cooling, adding a nob of butter, and spooned them in dollops onto the meat dish. Taking a fork, she spread out the mash topping and then used the fork tines to make little peaks across its surface. Next, she grated some cheddar and sprinkled it on top. Then she peeled some carrots.

A crashing on the stairs and Tansy appeared. The little girl went through to the outhouse and returned with boots and jacket. Emily called to her and held up a handful of carrots. Tansy beamed and took them, stuffing them into her pockets.

"Don't be too long," said Emily. "Come back when your daddy comes home."

* * *

Tansy skipped and ran, out of their gate, and across the road. Skirting the village pond she waved at the ducks which turned and started swimming in her direction. "Nothing for you today," she yelled and kept going, past The Three Wells pub, along the high street and through the gates of The Ark Aid. The Ark Aid was a collection of businesses occupying outbuildings which were part of Alex's forge yard. Money from here went to support St Peter's Young Disabled Unit, which was situated on the outskirts of Much Meddling.

Tansy continued running but waved at various of the business owners as she passed. Those that noticed waved back or shouted 'Hi, Tansy'. Reaching her father's forge, she went in, grabbed a couple of proven buckets, and filled them from a sack in the corner. Determinedly, she took her haul out of the gate at the back of the forge, staggered across the road and let herself into a field beyond. She was quickly jostled by four eager donkeys as she tipped the bucket contents into a trough. Situated in the corner of the field was on old, unused scout hut with an outside tap. Tansy uncoiled its long mucky hose and dragged it over to an adjacent trough. She left it to fill. As the donkeys tucked in, she stroked their soft fur and carefully inspected them. Their injuries were steadily healing. They trusted Tansy. The little girl had a natural way with them, intuitively knowing how to approach and comfort them. The company of her own donkey, Wonky, had helped them. Together she and Wonky had helped several donkeys to recover and move on to new pastures when suitable places were found for them. On a trip to the Donkey Sanctuary at High Dudgeon, several years before, Tansy had persuaded Alex to help one of the donkeys, which she subsequently named Wonky. The little donkey's hooves were long, and curved, like rockers. Alex, as a farrier, had used his skills to shorten the hooves, allowing the donkey to stand and walk properly. As a result of this encounter Alex had bought a couple of fields at the back of his forge, and the donkey sanctuary was gratefully using it as extra capacity. Alex had bought Wonky for

Tansy. A situation which appeared to suit them both.

* * *

When Alex and Tansy arrived home, Tansy immediately ran upstairs to her sisters and Alex headed into the kitchen. He kissed Emily and then sat heavily onto the sofa, which sat in the corner of the room under the window, and kicked off his boots. "So, six whole weeks of them running around and wanting entertaining. Any ideas what we can do with them?"

Emily rested her hands on the kitchen table and sighed, "Apparently, The 'Catolith' is here." She paused for his response, but he just raised his eyebrows. "All three came running in shouting that the Catolith is here. All I could get out of them before they clammed up was that it is 'The Herald'! They very unsubtly changed the subject and disappeared upstairs as fast they could. They have been deep in eager discussion ever since. So, I take it that you have no idea what they are on about?"

"No. Cat... o... lith, did you say?"

"Yes, that is what it sounded like."

"Cat of stone?" ventured Alex.

"No! Please don't let it involve a cat. We have enough trouble with the ones we have."

The triplets' three kittens were now 3 years old and as independent as their mother Snokettee. Snokettee had arrived on the girls' third birthday and delivered her litter in a laundry basket in the outhouse. The girls had named the kittens, Marigold, Whoops-a-Daisy and Spider, with Lily, Violet and Tansy respectively adopting one each. Over the past three years the cats' personalities had developed and suited each of their adoptive humans. Lily's cat, Marigold, was attentive, loving and mischievous. Tansy's cat, Spider, was adventurous, curious and regularly got itself into trouble and was often covered in mud, cobwebs, spiders and slugs. Violet's cat, Whoops-a-Daisy, was also curious but, in a contemplative, delicate way, whilst being loving and gentle.

With her family tucking into their Shepherd's Pie Emily studied them. Something was different. She couldn't say what, but there was an energy about them, a suppressed excitement. Yes, it was the start of their holiday and school was over for six weeks, but they enjoyed school. No, this was something different. She felt it. Something was coming. Something unsettling.

The doorbell rang and Emily visibly jumped. Alex stared at her but got to his feet and headed for the front door. Emily looked at her girls, but they were happily eating, unconcerned by who, or what, was at the door.

Alex returned with James, the village's vicar, and their great friend and neighbour. Emily breathed a silent sigh of relief.

"Uncle James," chorused the girls, surrounding and bear-hugging him. He tousled each dark brown head in turn and greeted them. Freeing an arm, he held out an envelope to Emily.

"Hi, would you mind giving this to Lesley for me," and went on to explain that Lesley, his housekeeper, had resigned suddenly, needing to go and take care of her sick mother up in Scotland. The envelope contained the money he owed her. She would drop off his spare house keys when she came. He had been expecting to see her himself but had to visit one of his parishioners. Crisis intervention, he explained.

"Yes, certainly," said Emily. "I'll miss her. I liked Lesley. So, no housekeeper. What will you do?"

"You need a wife," chipped in Alex as he put an arm around Emily. "They are much more useful, and don't need paying." As Emily wriggled free and punched him playfully in the midriff, the girls looked on and mimicked her by punching James, who laughed, and winced.

"Right, best get going. Parishioners to minister to. I'll let you lovely people finish your dinner."

CHAPTER TWO

On Saturday morning Louise, Emily's friend, turned up and let herself in. The women had been friends for several years. Lou, and her husband Mike, had moved to Much Meddling shortly after Emily, having bought Ruby Wells' old house, Bode Well Cottage. Their son Nathan was now seven, and a half, as he insisted on telling everyone, especially when Emily's three six-year-olds were present. The four children got on well but, outnumbered, Nathan often felt the need to establish his superiority, and his superior age was the only thing that was indisputable. He was stronger than they were, but not collectively. He was more knowledgeable than they were, but not as intuitive. He was more streetwise than they were, but not as empathic. They rarely deferred to him. Although they made sure to include him when he was present, he knew that they didn't need him, and this irked him.

"I can't stop, I'm on my way to a viewing," said Louise. For the past three years Louise had been working for the Much Meddling estate agency, a job which she thoroughly enjoyed. "I just wanted to show you this," and she pulled a small picture-frame out of her bag and handed it to Emily. "I found it in the attic, wrapped in cloth."

It was heavier than Emily was expecting. She hefted it in her hand, admiring its sturdiness. A glass photograph was framed by deep but faded red velvet and sealed in a guilt-edged metal frame. Studying the image, she had the feeling of déjà vu. Three identical young faces stared back. The resemblance to Lily, Tansy, and Violet was uncanny. She looked up at Lou.

"That type of photography dates from the 1840s. I looked it up. It is a Daguerreotype photo, one of the earliest commercial photographs."

"So," said Emily, "this isn't Angelica, Ruby, and Myrtle, this is another set of Wells triplets."

"I reckon so. I gotta go, but I couldn't wait to show you that."

As Louise let herself out Emily stared at the photograph. The photo was only tiny, but the three young women could be clearly seen. Taking it into the front room, affectionately referred to as Angelica's room, as it still contained all Angelica's equipment for making lotions and herbal brews, Emily hunted round until she found Angelica's magnifying glass. Sitting at the large pine table in the centre of the room she scrutinised the picture. Remarkably she was able to make out tiny details of their faces and clothing. Adjusting the distance of the magnifying glass to the photo she focused-in on something adorning one of the women's dresses. It was a brooch. They all appeared to have similar brooches but only this brooch was fully visible. What Emily saw, amazed, and delighted her. A delicate little fairy rested on a shiny cream stone, which was surrounded by delicate scrolls of filigree work. Emily recognised that fairy. It was one of three now belonging to her girls.

When Alex appeared, she showed the photo to him. He frowned, "So, the fairies were brooches, then rings and then a necklace and then three necklaces." Now, his eyes narrowed, and he held the magnifying glass steady. "I could be wrong, but that looks like calcite to me. The stones on which the fairies are resting, I reckon they are periapts. Look!"

Emily looked again. Even though what she was looking at was tiny she agreed, it appeared to have the same almost translucent shiny surface as her periapt. So, the fairies had been periapts before Angelica, Ruby, and Myrtle had worn them as rings. When Alex had removed the calcite from the back of one of his girls' fairies, he had discovered evidence of soldering. So, when Angelica, Ruby and Myrtle wore them as rings they probably weren't periapts, but attached directly to their respective rings. However, before giving the fairies to the young

Agnes Wells, on a chain, they had had tiny slivers of calcite added, making them into periapts, and Agnes had subsequently made three necklaces out of them and given them to Tansy, Violet, and Lily.

"Right, gotta go. I need to fill up the Range Rover if we are going out this afternoon." He gave her a peck on the cheek, as she continued to stare in fascination at the photo.

As the front door shut, she looked up and waved at him through the window. As he drove off, the wall behind the vehicle became visible. Sitting on it was Snokettee, staring towards the wood. Briefly Snokettee turned and looked Emily in the eye but quickly turned back and continued her sentry duty. The kittens were nowhere in sight, which wasn't unusual as they were usually wherever the girls were. Realising that the house was quiet, she stepped out of Angelica's room and stood at the bottom of the stairs and listened. No, it didn't appear that the girls were up there. It wasn't unheard of for them to be silent, but she didn't really think they were up there and tried to remember when she had last heard them. Checking the outhouse, she saw that their boots were gone, and the back door unlocked. They were either in the garden or out in the woods. It looked like she had a bit of time to herself, and she needed to satisfy her curiosity.

Leaving the house, she turned left and

walked the few yards to the church gates. She went through and followed the gravel path up to the left and round the back of the church until she found the Wells' graves. Working her way along, she studied the dates on the headstones. There were only three from the 1800's with identical birth dates. As she realised that she had found what she was looking for she felt a little thrill of excitement. Having a picture of them made them real people and although she knew it was unlikely that she would be able to identify each young woman she at least now had a set of names for them, Lottie, Millicent, and Clara. Just like Angelica, Myrtle, and Ruby, they had each lived to be 100 years old, dying within days of each other. Emily thought of her girls. Would they live to be 100 too? The thought was amazing, but looking along the row of graves evidence seemed to support that thought. As she headed back to the cottage she wondered what Lottie, Millicent and Clara's lives had been like. Had they been as well respected in the village as Angelica, Myrtle, and Ruby?

* * *

After lunch, Alex drove the family up into the hills and parked by a river, in a wide sweeping valley. There were few trees here, just the odd gnarled hazel, hunkered down beside the water. A well-worn dirt path strewn with pebbles, picked its way amongst the boulders that were scattered amongst tall grasses and bracken. After trekking gently uphill for about twenty minutes Alex led them away from the river and followed a tributary into a side valley. The terrain was steeper here and Emily found that she was getting left behind as Alex trudged ahead and the girls skipped effortlessly into the distance. Alex had brought them here a couple of times before and the girls loved it. They knew where they were going and were keen to get there.

By the time Emily reached a large hole in the hillside the girls and Alex were nowhere to be seen, but they could be heard. She should have remembered to bring her own torch. She stepped inside the cave entrance and waited for her eyes to adjust. It was discernibly cooler in there: damp and earthy. She inhaled slowly and deeply, enjoying the tranquillity and timelessness of the place. A couple of drops of water dripped from the ceiling onto her head. As her vision improved, she ventured further in. It was possible to make out a little of the terrain, beyond the first bend, but not enough for her to continue safely. She knew from previous visits that the cave went into the hillside for a considerable distance before it became unpassable. She shouted to Alex to bring her back a torch. As her voice echoed back at her she realised that the only noise in the cave was now being made by her. As realisation dawned, she waited nervously for the inevitable.

"WooOoo!" "HooOoo!" "WooOoohooh!" The cave was eerily illuminated, as three ghostly faces appeared and bobbed about in the darkness, howling madly. Then, as one, they pounced and started laughing. Emily feigned shock and reprimanded them for scaring her and the girls continued to laugh. Once they all settled down, they set off to continue into the cave. Suddenly there was a booming howl, and up ahead the shadow of a large bear-like creature appeared, making them all jump.

"Alex!" snapped Emily. The 'bear' started laughing and the girls, led by Tansy, surrounded it and, giggling madly, beat it into submission.

Further inside the cave Alex brought them all to a halt so that he could point out some of the features. Shining his torch through a gap in the rock wall he lit up a series of tiny straw-like structures joining the roof of the cavity with the floor. "Can you see those tiny stalactites, starting from the roof, and the stalagmite mounds below, and those drips...that is how they start to form, and how they grow until they make complete columns...all the different stages, illustrated," he said. The girls stared.

"Just like the big one in our cellar," ventured Lily.

"Yes, exactly," said Alex. "It would have started just like that but a lot longer ago."

Having absorbed that bit of information, and keen for something new, Tansy turned away and then Lily. Violet continued to stare, pointing her own torch into the hole. She played it around the scene, tracing the different formations from ceiling to floor, focussing finally on a milky water droplet as it formed and grew and finally dropped, adding to the stalagmite beneath. As the others headed further into the cave, Emily stood behind Violet and put her arms round her shoulders. Crouching slightly, she put her head beside her child's, feeling the soft curly hair against her face, and breathed in the scent of her. "Aren't they pretty?" she said in her daughter's ear.

"Yes, they're just magical," said Violet, and another drip dropped making a tiny, barely perceptible plop.

When they caught up with the others it was because they had reached the end of the passable part of the cave. Here the walls narrowed and the water, which had hardly been noticeable running along the floor, cascaded from a hole above onto huge rocks which had, at some point in the past, fallen from the roof. The water splashed off them wearing smooth grooves in their surfaces.

"How brave are you?" asked Alex. "How dark do you think it would be if we all switched off our torches?"

Tansy instantly switched off hers. Alex switched his off, followed, much to his surprise, by Violet. Emily looked at Lily who looked back at her, uncertain. Emily grinned at Lily and switched off her torch. In the pale light of Lily's torch Violet reached out and serenely took her sister's hand, "It is okay." Reassured, Lily switched off her torch.

"Now," said Alex, "Just listen."

CHAPTER THREE

O n Sunday morning the family trooped over to the church. As they walked up the path Emily noticed that the girls were all focussing on the wall that separated the church yard from their cottage. Emily followed their gaze. There, sitting at the far end near the wood, was a large tortoiseshell cat. Its fur was fabulously coloured, but scruffy looking. Spotted, the cat rose and limped away into the wood, its bent, stumpy tail posing a question. Emily looked at her girls. They said nothing but she knew them well enough to know that they had been pleased by what they saw, and encouraged in some way. As they headed into church Emily wasn't sure what to think. If that was The Catolith, and she was certain that it was, its appearance was a little disconcerting. If The Catolith was a herald, a herald of what!

At the end of the service, they stood outside and chatted to various members of the congregation. Emily's eyes distractedly scanned the wall, but the cat was nowhere to be seen.

Heading home, the family was accosted by Mr Swire, an irascible old gentleman for whom Emily continued to make 'ointment No 23'. Shortly after moving into Wishing Well Cottage, he had let himself in demanding more ointment. He had been one of Angelica's 'patients' and he fully expected Emily to continue as Angelica had. After consulting the local doctors who helped her to make her first batch Emily continued to supply, but under instruction not to take on any new patients. Normally he just passed the time of day, sometimes just doffing his cap. Today, being Sunday, he wore a trilby. He was holding it in front of him, rotating it agitatedly by the rim.

"Summat's up. Av bin seein' cats. Not many, but summat's definitely up! Just thought you should know." With that, he stopped rotating the trilby, gave a gracious nod, and popped it deftly onto his head. A tap and a slight adjustment, then he turned away and set off down the high street, a little fan of elderly women following in his wake.

"What is there about that man?" said Alex, "that he attracts so much female attention. He must be in his 90's now." Staring after Mr Swire, they stood briefly, looking up the high street. Out of the church yard came a couple of women deep in discussion, muttering about the departure of the vicar's housekeeper and the small chance of him finding a replacement, and what did he want with a huge house like that for anyway, when there was just him. Seeing Alex, Emily and the girls watching them, they glowered and turned away, lowering their voices as they went.

"Come on," said Emily. "Let's get some lunch, my parents will be here before we know it."

* * *

They had just finished eating when James appeared.

"Thought I'd just drop by for my keys. I take it Lesley came last night."

"Yes, it is such a shame about her mother. So sad. What have you been up to lately?" said Emily handing over his keys.

"Er… work stuff… and fund raising. That kind of thing. Getting ready for the Crag Race. It won't be long now. I take it that you will all be helping again. Anyway, must go… things to do."

No sooner had he gone than Emily's parents arrived. She got them all mugs of tea, and they settled into the sitting room. Once the initial greetings were complete, enquiries were made about the whereabouts of the three grandchildren who were noticeably absent. Alex went to the bottom of the stairs and shouted up. He then climbed the stairs and had a look in their bedroom. They weren't there. Then he checked the back porch. Their boots were gone. He stuck his head out of the back door and listened, but couldn't hear them.

Back in the sitting room he announced that

the girls appeared to have gone out. He and Emily pondered on when, trying to ascertain how long they had been gone. Unable to work it out he sat down and picked up his mug of tea.

"Aren't you going to go out and look," asked their grandmother, aghast.

"Oh, they will be out in the woods somewhere. They'll be back when they are hungry," said Alex.

"They are only six years old. They shouldn't be out in the woods on their own."

"It is a bit odd," said Emily, "they knew that their granny and granpops were coming," looking pointedly at Alex.

He shrugged and rose. Just then the phone rang. So, he headed into the kitchen to answer it. Emily and her parents could hear him talking but couldn't make out what he was saying but he appeared to be expressing surprise. As she attempted to hear, Emily frowned uneasily at her mother who was showing disapproval at Emily and Alex' lack of parental care. The phone call ended, and Alex returned.

"That was Mike. He was asking if Nathan is here. Apparently, the girls called for him and he went out. A little later he was seen back again but emerging from the garden shed clutching a saw, and an axe! By the time Louise had got outside to challenge him, he had disappeared."

The four adults looked at one another. Then Emily and her parents turned their gaze on Alex.

"What? They'll be building a den," he said, settling back into the Chesterfield.

"With Nathan swinging an axe! He's lethal enough with a teddy bear!" said Emily.

"Okay, okay, I'll go look."

With Alex gone Emily caught up on what her parents had been doing and broke the subject of them baby-sitting for a long weekend, later in the year, so that she and Alex could go away together for their upcoming wedding anniversary.

"We are thinking of going to Paris. We have been wanting to go for ages, and for our anniversary it will be really special."

"Of course, love. I suppose, with the cats, you'd want us to come here."

There was a crash as the backdoor was flung open. Tansy, closely followed by Lily and Violet, ran breathlessly into the sitting room, a scatter of cats at their heels. They threw their arms around their granny and granpops, all talking at once. The cats leapt up on the sofa, joining in the fun. Spider ran along the back behind Mrs Hope and proceeded to knead her shoulder.

"Spider," said Tansy, "Granny doesn't like that." As Mrs Hope sat rigid, eyeing its head suspiciously, the cat continued to pluck at her jumper, half a dead bluebottle entangled in cobweb hanging off its right ear. Spider purred loudly, fully confident of her appeal, totally oblivious to Mrs Hope's disgust. Tansy gathered up Spider and stroked her head, before wiping the hip of her jeans to rid her hand of cobweb, etc. Cuddling the cat, she knelt on the floor. When granny and granpops had freed themselves from girls and cats, and recovered from the onslaught, they proceeded to question the girls as to what they had been doing in the woods.

"Playing," said Tansy, after a slight hesitation.

"Yes, playing," said Violet.

"In the woods," added Lily.

"What was Nathan doing with an axe?" said Emily.

"Chopping," said Tansy.

"Chopping what?" said Emily.

"Wood," said Tansy.

"Why was Nathan chopping wood?"

"Because it was too big."

"Oh, they'll be making a den," said Alex proudly. "Somewhere *secret*..."

The girls all stared at him in alarm.

"They probably have a secret password too. When I was a kid, we built dens in the woods all the time. We had a secret password and a secret knock," he said, rapping Lily, who was nearest, on the head.

"Yes," said Tansy. "A secret den. What is for tea?"

"Yes, I'm hungry."

"Me too."

That evening, after her parents had gone home, Emily phoned Louise and asked her if she knew what Nathan had been using the axe for.

"All I could get out of him was that they had been playing in the woods, but he was excited that they had called for him. I do wish that there were other boys his age in the village. I really must invite some of his school mates over."

"Well, Alex thought they were building a den somewhere. He got halfway to the crag when the girls came running down to meet him. He only had a vague idea of where they had been. He hadn't seen Nathan."

CHAPTER FOUR

The next morning, with the girls somewhere off in the woods again, Emily nipped over to the store for some milk. As she approached the door, she glanced at the notice board in the store window. James hadn't wasted any time advertising for a housekeeper. Displayed prominently was a brightly coloured 'Housekeeper Wanted' notice. The letters were neat and uniform, the words highlighted in different coloured felt-tips. Emily smiled, it looked like Lesley, ever efficient, had written it for him before she left.

Emily collected a carton of milk and headed for the till. A woman, whom Emily took to be in her mid-forties and who, as her father would have said, looked like 'she had had a hard paper-round', was just leaving. As the woman turned away from the counter, the storekeeper turned her attention to Emily, then back at the departing woman with a look of disgust on her face. As the door closed and its chime faded, the storekeeper said conspiratorially, "Looks like she's back."

"Oh?" said Emily.

"Course, you won't know 'er, will ya. Before your time. Trouble, that one. Still, live and let live, I say. Can't be judgemental in a job like this... Just the milk?"

Emily paid and headed home. She wasn't keen on the new storekeeper. She didn't know her well, despite the woman having run the store for over a year, but she was polite to Emily and good at her job. She lived somewhere on the outskirts of the village and didn't appear to have any friends that Emily was aware of. Despite this she was always well informed, or, at least, she always had 'knowledge' that she was eager to impart, strictly in confidence of course.

Back home she cleaned out the cats' dishes and gave Snokettee a stroke. The two sets of triplets, humans and felines, were nowhere to be seen. Snokettee's smooth white fur was always a joy to Emily, sleek and vital: a compact little miracle of life and energy. The kittens' fur was delightful too but soft and fluffy, even though they were now adult cats. Despite this difference all the cats had the same black tails with white tips. Running her hand along Snokettee's back she continued up the cat's tail. Snokettee turned her head so that Emily would scratch under her chin. She obliged and the cat rolled onto her side. Caressing the warm soft fur, Emily pondered on events. What they might be she had no idea, but something was coming. She felt it. As if sensing her concern, Snokettee nuzzled Emily's hand, and then looked her in the eye. Whatever it was, was inevitable. Emily would just have to deal with it.

* * *

Over at the forge Alex wasn't having a good day. A customer had cancelled a set of gates he had already started, and he had just been informed that one of his Ark Aid tenants was moving out. It wasn't that the lack of rent would be an issue, as he and Emily certainly weren't short of a penny or two since their lottery win, but it did mean that he would have to advertise for a new tenant, and that meant paperwork. Alex hated paperwork. He much preferred to work with his hands. Creating 'stuff' was what he enjoyed. Working as a blacksmith and specialist farrier was what defined him and what people knew him for. Being able to donate money to charity, from the rental income in his yard, was a bonus. He also 'got a kick' out of the fact that the buildings in the forge yard were being used, and liked having tenants who were mostly craftspeople, like himself. They were an inspirational bunch, exchanging ideas and combining techniques to produce unique pieces which they sold. Now, the cabinet maker had given notice. This would affect some of the other trades. The stained-glass artist in particular supplied panels for some of his art deco style cabinetry.

As he was at a suitable point to take a break, he decided to go round the other tenants and break the bad news. They may also know of someone new who would like to move in. As he stepped out of the forge, he was surprised to see a little huddle of his tenants deep in conversation. As he approached, they turned to face him. The potter shuffled his bulk and smoothed down his beard, "I was just saying, I had to chase off a tramp this morning when I came to open up. Sleeping in the doorway he was. I sent him packing and he headed off up the high street, but I reckon 'e'll be back."

"Oh," said another, "that will be the one I saw, hanging around up the other end of the high street. Scrawny looking chap."

"Hi," said Alex. "Just thought I would let you know that we are going to be short of a cabinet maker. David has given notice."

The group expressed disappointment as they all liked David.

"So, if you know of anyone looking for a place... and, of course, there will be his flat too..." With that bombshell dropped he left them to it and headed over to What Sup, The Ark Aid coffee shop, and got himself a drink. What Sup had been in the yard for nearly three years now and was a thriving and popular business. Louise had been very proactive and discerning when hunting for tenants for The Ark Aid. When Alex and Emily first decided to open the forge yard as business units, she had had a vision and her job as estate agent had provided her with the means to fulfil it. As well as St Peter's Charity Shop the yard now had the craft workshops she envisioned and a small café, with a sunny awning and little bistro table sets. Speciality teas and coffees were served along with some very delightful pastries and cakes. It wasn't Alex' 'cup of tea' but he did like the coffee. He was also well aware that the shop drew visitors and not only kept them in The Ark Aid for a while each time but brought them back. By the time his drink was ready he had also chosen a large icing topped cherry bun. He quickly ate the bun and then, cup in hand, he decided to nip across the high street to the estate agents and let them know that he needed a new tenant. Louise was delighted and said that she would pop over later to measure up and hopefully take some photos. The sooner the space was re-occupied the better. It didn't look good having one of the businesses closed. However, on a previous occasion when a tenant had left, that window space had been used by the Charity Shop as extra display space. She must speak to them too.

As Alex headed back to the forge he ran into Tansy, on her way back from the donkeys. That is where he assumed she had been, the straw in her hair, seeming to confirm that. She yelled a greeting at him and kept going, disappearing before he had time to comment. She did such a good job with those donkeys. He rarely had to remind her. Now she was home all day she had more or less taken over their care from him. He would like to get her a pony, so that she could ride, but he wanted her to have lessons first. Perhaps he could arrange that over the summer. Fortunately, she hadn't mentioned riding the donkeys, which was good, as he didn't think that was appropriate; they all had sad histories. He felt that even Wonky, who was fully recovered and loved Tansy, shouldn't be ridden. He found it strange that his children were all so different. Neither of the other two showed any interest in the donkeys.

* * *

Emily, keen to know more about the Lottie, Millicent, and Clara triplets decided to go down into Wishing Well Cottage's cellar to have a look through the boxes from Myrtle's old place. Her house, Fare Well Cottage, had been turned into accommodation for relatives of St Peter's Young Disabled Unit clients. Most of the boxes had been looked through, but they had inherited such a lot of documents and photographs from Angelica, Ruby, and Myrtle that it was impossible to digest it all. It was also possible that photos they had assumed were of Angelica, Ruby and Myrtle were actually the previous generation, or, as she was coming to think of them, the 1800s triplets. She found a couple of likely boxes and had a brief look through for photographs. There were a couple, but they were too recent. Looking round the cellar she saw some wooden packing crates with reinforced metal corners, stacked beneath some wall recesses at the cave end. She pulled the first one away from the wall so that it was under a light and looked inside. She pulled out a manilla folder. It contained documents but no photos and wasn't old enough. A quick glance at the rest of the documents and she dismissed the whole contents. As she went to pull over a second crate something shiny caught her eye. In one of the recesses, she found a series of matching, highly polished, wooden boxes. They were of similar design but obviously made at different times. Taking one down she was surprised at how heavy it was. She placed it on the floor and lifted off the lid. Inside was a wooden tray with 36 depressions, each holding a marble. Beneath it lay 2 more trays. 108 marbles in all. Picking one up she held it up to the light and rotated it. This was a marble unlike any she had seen before. It had a black centre, twisted in a spiral, but the marble itself was a translucent amber; it looked like a cat's eye. She studied it for a moment, then turned to put it back in its slot. It slipped from her fingers and bounced noisily cross the stone floor to rest against one of the packing cases. As she bent to pick it up, she noticed photos in the top of the case. Blowing dust off the marble she popped it in her jean's pocket, rubbed her hands together to rid them of the dirt and dragged the case under the light. Yes, this one contained a stack of old photographs. Grabbing an armful, she headed up to Angelica's room, where there was a large table for her to spread them out.

Having cleared the table, she started to lay out her haul, as best she could according to age. Most of the photos were of people but some were scenes. There was one of The Three Wells pub with horse and cart in front, taken before the wall was built with its sign saying, 'Parking at Rear', and another of the church taken from the village green. She kept working her way through the photos, concentrating on those with cardboard backing, which were generally the older ones. Irritatingly few had anything written on the backs. However, she did find one on which someone had written 'Daisy and Charles wedding 16th July 1874'. The bride and groom were surrounded by guests. Looking closely at the faces, Emily recognised one of the 1800s Wells triplets. She didn't know which one, but if she could find records of the wedding with a guest list, then maybe, if only one sister was present, she would know which one was in the photograph. She would ask James to help her search the church records. It shouldn't be too difficult as she had the date. Then she could look online. If she didn't find it there, then the

Library at Barnlees should have copies of old newspapers.

* * *

That night, as they were getting ready for bed, she excitedly told Alex about her research and what she proposed to do. He listened distractedly. However, when she pulled the marble from her pocket, which she had forgotten to return to its box, he showed interest. When she explained that it wasn't the only one and that there could be upwards of 600 marbles, he was amazed.

"Wow, that is a bit different. Someone was a serious collector. That wasn't with Myrtle's things but in our cellar, you say."

"Yes, but they all looked alike. Well, I only looked at the top tray," she said. "I was more interested in the photos."

"Hmm, I wonder what they are worth?"

"You'd sell them?"

"Yes, if it would help the Young Disabled Unit," he said.

"Well, let's see if we can find out what they are worth."

CHAPTER FIVE

T he following morning, Emily woke as Alex got out of bed to go to work. Awake, she got up and put on her dressing gown. Picking up the marble from her bedside cabinet she took it downstairs into the kitchen. She might as well see what she could find out about it on-line, whilst looking for information on weddings in 1874. She collected the wedding photo from Angelica's room and stared at it whilst waiting for the kettle to boil. As she studied the face of her children's ancestor a memory came back to her of her night's dream. She was in an orchard collecting apples, and a church bell was ringing. The kettle boiled and she poured water over a tea bag and gave it a good 'mashing'. Satisfied, she threw the bag in the sink, added milk, and then sat down at the table, laying the photo in front of her.

The church bells were ringing. It wasn't long since they had struck the hour. Four rings. She was sure. Now they were ringing again and continuously. Alarmed she looked in their direction.

Something was wrong. She ran through the trees, branches whipping at her as she went, apples bouncing and scattering from her basket. Over the stile and through the woods, it was the quickest way. More trees, more branches. Leaving the path she dove into the undergrowth, her skirt hitched up, nettles stinging her ankles. She slid and stumbled, crashing into the church wall. Flinging the basket to one side she scrambled over. Dodging gravestones she ran round the side of the church, the bells deafening now, matching the thumping of her heart. Nearing the front of the building she could hear something else, something higher pitched and more strident than the bells – a woman was screaming...

She jumped, as Alex placed his hands on her shoulders, and stared at him. Alex frowned quizzically at her, "Just thought I would kiss my wife goodbye as I head out the door to earn us a crust or two. No need to look so shocked!"

"Sorry, miles away," she said, the memory of her daydream dissipating.

"I could see that," he said and kissed her. "Have fun."

With Alex gone, she looked again at the photo. Some tapping and scrolling later, she brought up some local news articles. After some trial and error, she was able to locate Weddings, and the appropriate year. There were more entries than she had expected, but she soon found what she was looking for. On 16th

July 1874 Daisy Tillotson had married Charles Hardcastle at All Saints Church, Much Meddling. She was pleased, but further searching only gave her links to family tree websites and she couldn't see anything useful without subscribing. She would ask James if he would let her look at the church records, but she would probably need to visit Barnlees Library. Disappointed, that she would have to wait, and feeling oddly anxious, she checked her e-mails and supped her tea. Something was niggling at her, but she didn't know what.

There were footsteps on the stairs, dainty ones. Violet, she knew, was on her way down. The other two would have bounded down, as they crashed their way through the rest of their lives. Violet appeared and floated silently over to her mother. Emily embraced her and felt better. Violet looked her in the eyes and smiled. There was intuition in her look and Emily sighed. How did she know? Her daughter had appeared, to comfort her. All three were intuitive and empathic, but Violet had a greater depth and serenity, and her very presence was calming. Emily hugged her daughter and asked, "So, what are you going to do today?"

Violet withdrew slightly and shrugged her shoulders. There was a crashing on the stairs and Tansy and Lily appeared. Emily removed a cat from the table and gave the girls a bowl of cereal each, then put bread in the toaster. The girls picked up their spoons and tucked in. Whilst handing out glasses of orange juice the front door opened and in strolled Nathan, rucksack over his shoulder.

"Would you like some orange juice with your cereal, Nathan?"

"Yes, please Mrs Wells, and some toast. Two slices."

She gave him orange juice and then toast and watched with irritation as he took the spoon from the jam and used it to take a large strawberry stained scoop out of the margarine tub. Before she could stop him, he had squashed the large dollop of margarine onto his toast and dunked the spoon, now covered in crumbs, back into the jam. Violet looked sympathetically at her mother as she stared at the mess.

Then before she knew it, chairs were scraped back, there was a clatter, the back door slammed, and Emily found that she was alone, in a vacuum of silence. She caught a brief glimpse through the window, as the children clambered over the stile, out of the garden and off into the wood. As she gathered up the breakfast things, she spotted the marble. She put the crockery on the drainer and sat back down at her laptop.

Marbles, she discovered, had a huge online presence. Marbles were big business. All over the world, people collected and traded them. Individual marbles were selling for hundreds of pounds. There were specialist carry and display cases. There were games, specifically for marbles, such as castle shaped marble runs. There were plain glass marbles, and plain stone ones, and marble, marbles. Some had elaborate swirls of colour inside and outside and speckles and glitter and, it seemed, infinite colour combinations. The choice was bewildering. She searched on amber marbles. She found many but none that looked like the one in front of her. So, the collection in the cellar could be worth a fortune...or, nothing at all. She put the marble in her pocket, intent on taking it back to the cellar after she had cleared up from breakfast. She gathered up the plates and moved the fruit bowl back into the centre of the table. A banana, an apple and an orange had gone. It must have been Nathan. The girls might have helped themselves to the banana but wouldn't have voluntarily eaten the other fruit. Did Louise not feed the boy! There was no fruit debris. So, he must have taken it 'to go'. She finished loading the dishwasher, then gave James a quick call. Yes, he would be happy to help her look over the church records. Would afternoon suit?

* * *

James was busy cleaning his front room. He had a meeting with a young couple about their upcoming wedding and the room was still in disarray from the previous day's work. Hopefully he'd find a cleaner soon. He had had one enquiry, but the person was expecting nearly twice what he had paid Lesley and had been very particular about the hours they could offer, which didn't meet his needs. He gave the table a wipe and straightened up a stack of leaflets. Then he plumped the cushions. Standing by the door to inspect his work he decided that he really ought to vacuum, and a squirt of air freshener wouldn't go amiss.

Vacuuming and squirting completed he sat at his desk in the corner and switched on his computer. It took a while to load. He could really do with a new one. To pass the time he went and got himself a mug of tea. Then, computer ready, he set about adding entrants to his list of runners for his Crag Race. The event would start at The Three Wells pub, skirt the village green, head down the high street, up one of the side streets and over a stile, up through the woods, round the crag and back down. Three laps in all. Most of his running mates had entered, including Alex, and to everyone's surprise, Mike, Nathan's father. Nathan had entered the Young Runs event which was one lap of the circuit. This was the events 2nd year and this time he had plans to keep everyone hanging around after the event, in order to entice more money out of them and the spectators. It was all coming together. Just over a week to go.

Young couple seen, lunch eaten, he headed over to the church to meet Emily. As he waited for her to arrive, his attention was drawn by movement, at the end of the wall which separated the church from Wishing Well cottage. A cat had hopped up dragging something large, and hopefully dead, towards the wood. As he watched, revolted, another appeared. It too had baggage, feathered in different shades of grey. Emily arrived and stood by his side following his gaze. She recognised those cats. To confirm her siting, Whoops-A-Daisy hauled herself and her pigeon into view. As Emily and James watched, three identical, white-tipped black counterweights flicked from side to side as the cats hauled their bounty away into the wood. The two humans exchanged looks and turned towards the church.

James unlocked the vestry, and they went in. Emily showed him the two photos and told him what she had found. He was fascinated by the Daguerreotype photo and keen to find out what he could from the church records. From a large cupboard set into the vestry wall he pulled out the most likely tome. Turning the pages back and forth he located the right one. He ran a finger down the left-hand column. Then stopped and pointed to the entry of the wedding of Daisy Tillotson and Charles Hardcastle. Sadly, there was no mention of a Wells in the record, as relative or witness. Other than the bride no other female was mentioned. Emily would have to go to the library, and she wasn't sure when that would be. During the week she was stuck at home looking after the girls and, when Louise was at work, Nathan.

* * *

That evening, during dinner, she couldn't help noticing that there was a hint of tension between the girls. Nothing was said or done that she could 'put her finger on', but it appeared that Lily was irritated by something that Tansy had done and Violet was attempting to keep the peace. As the trio disappeared into the hall Emily heard Tansy say, "She's perfect. You'll see."

Inserting a last mug, Emily set the dishwasher going, grabbed her bag and coat, shouted to Alex, "Goodbye, I'm off to book club," and headed out into the street. It was a lovely evening. The sun streamed through the branches of the trees on the green and reflected off the wakes left by the mallards on the village pond. As she walked past, she smiled at their happy chuckling noises, then positively grinned as she saw several fluffy ducklings zipping amongst rushes at the edge of the water. She stood for a while and watched, happy, until something unsettling intruded on her thoughts. She had a brief glimpse of a wooden structure, superimposed on the scene. She blinked. There was nothing there but, as the image faded from her mind, she felt the echo, as it played her nervous system like a badly tuned harp, of a woman screaming.

At the book club, Cheryl, the host, nudged her in the ribs and asked her if she was alright, pointing out that she had downed her glass of wine, in one gulp. Emily shrugged and sighed. Cheryl crossed the room and, returning with a bottle, topped up her glass. "Anything you want to share?" Cheryl was a nurse at St Peter's Young Disabled Unit and was a good friend. Cheryl had joined the book club at the same time as Emily, but they had grown to know each other better through their joint involvement in fund raising for St Peter's. The unit was now a successful and well renowned home, once again.

"Sorry," said Emily. "Miles away. Just enjoying the wine."

"That isn't the usual way connoisseurs go about it. Should I have provided a spittoon?"

"No, I promise I'll sip this one daintily," and she grinned, swished, sniffed noisily, and took a tiny sip. Rattling it round her mouth and sucking it through her teeth a few times, she swallowed it and smacked her lips, considering the wine. "I am getting… lots of disapproving looks…!"

They discussed the book they had read: a thriller about the disappearance of a young woman, on a Scottish island. Some had disliked it, but most had positively enjoyed it and were keen to read other books by the same author. As the evening progressed conversation inevitably turned to catching up with what everyone had been doing in the two weeks since the last meeting. The start of the summer holidays was the main topic, amongst the three parents present who were bemoaning the hike in the price of holidays during that time, and wondering how they were going to occupy their offspring for six whole weeks. At this someone mentioned the appearance of a tramp in the village. Others joined in, saying that he had been seen round the play area, down by the river, and heading over one of the stiles into the wood. This alarmed the parents. One of the others added that the tramp had been sent packing from The Ark Aid doorway, where he had apparently been sleeping. Emily listened with growing anxiety. Then Cheryl, the voice of reason, spoke up.

"He could be just a homeless person, looking for food and shelter. Walking past an area where kids play and going into the woods doesn't make him a paedophile… after all, we've all done that!"

"You think he's a paedophile?"

"No, I don't. I didn't say that."

"You were thinking it… and you don't have children!"

"No, I don't have children. I am just saying that you can't make assumptions and condemn someone without any evidence."

"As I said, you don't have children…"

"But you don't have to be a parent to care about children's safety."

"You can't possibly know…"

PAULINE POTTERILL

"I just think," said Cheryl, "that it isn't good to go jumping to conclusions…"

"You woolly liberals are all alike. Give everyone the benefit of the doubt…when you should be putting our children first."

To rescue Cheryl, Mags, the other steadying influence in the group, and someone who had lived in Much Meddling all her life, said, "Guess who I saw the other day."

Others, also keen to change the subject, leapt on her question, and Mags continued, "Crystal Winterbottom." They all looked blank, and Mags looked disappointed. "Oh, probably before your time. She and I were at school together. Her mother had a bit of a reputation…" she said, raising her eyebrows. "Oh, well, if you don't know her. Never mind."

With that conversational gambit failing, the group went back to jumping to conclusions.

Emily stayed silent. Her girls were in the woods most of the time now. She must tell Alex. At least Nathan was with them, but then he was only 7…and, of course, a half.

CHAPTER SIX

Having spoken to Alex the evening before, she and Alex gathered the girls round the breakfast table and asked them if they had seen any strangers in the wood.

The girls shook their heads. So, Alex went on to explain about the man seen about the village, and who had been sleeping in The Ark Aid doorway. They remained silent. "We are worried that he may be a bad man," he said, inadvertently looking at Lily. "Some of the men from the village are going to search for him. So, until we know who he is and what he wants, mummy and I don't want you playing in the woods. Okay? You can play in the garden, and the high street, but that is all. I called Uncle Mike and Auntie Louise, so Nathan knows too."

As soon as breakfast was finished, Tansy, Lily, Violet and Nathan rushed out of the front door.

When he left for work, Alex spotted the four of them sitting on one of the benches, under a tree on the green, deep in discussion.

* * *

"If they are going to search the woods," said Lily, "we are going to have to move him."

"But he can hardly walk," said Nathan, "and where can we move him to?"

They thought for a bit.

"How about your garden shed?" said Lily.

"How about yours? You've got more sheds than I have at mine."

"Yes, but mum is in and out of the garden all the time, whereas your parents are out."

"Yes, but dad is in the shed most evenings."

They thought a bit more.

"I know," said Tansy. "The scout hut; it has been empty for years. No-one ever goes in it, and I am there every day looking after the donkeys. It has a kitchen too, and a loo."

So, it was agreed that the scout hut was the answer. The problem was, how? As they pondered on this problem Tansy pointed excitedly over to the other side of the duck pond and the vicarage gate. A petite lady with prominent bosom, blond hair cascading down her shoulders, and long tanned legs, was just closing the gate. Spotting Tansy, who was waving at her, she smiled. Then, glancing at the other children, she did a bit of a double, or treble, take. The triplets were obviously a surprise. She strolled over, placing her feet carefully on the grass to avoid her stiletto heels sinking in. She stood, awkwardly, resting on the balls of her feet.

"Thankyou for encouraging me to apply. I got the job. I didn't think he'd want the likes of me, but he was really nice. I am the new housekeeper. I start tomorrow."

Lily looked her up and down and then held out her hand, "Hello, I'm Lily."

"Hi, Lily. I am Gemma. Pleased to meet you." She took Lily's hand and gently squeezed it. Lily squeezed back, taking in the array of jewelled rings and painted nails, and weighed the worth of the woman that was Gemma.

"Gemma?" said Lily.

"Yes, Gemma."

Lily nodded slightly, glanced at Tansy and gave a reluctant smile. Tansy grinned back, "Told you."

When Gemma left, they returned to the problem at hand and decided to go and have a look at the scout hut.

* * *

James was a happy man. He had a housekeeper again, and she seemed fun. Though slightly 'care-worn' her face lit up when she smiled. She had laughed at his jokes, which was unusual on first meeting. Most people didn't seem to expect a vicar to make jokes. She also hadn't seemed fazed by the hours and the occasional, ad hoc cleaning. He had explained, that on one occasion a parishioner had wanted to see him after church and had spilt coffee and cake over the carpet and sofa, and the room had needed to be ready for an early morning meeting on the Monday. She seemed to think, that under such circumstances, short notice cleaning was perfectly reasonable. She lived at the far end of the village, but it wouldn't take her long on her bike.

He added another couple of entrants to his Crag Race list and then noticed that an e-mail had popped into his mail. He opened it up and did a little dance. Yes, 'Clydesdale' had agreed to perform. So, he had his headline act. This was great news as the rock band had great pulling power, as they liked to say in their advertising posters, and they would help him to get other bands to turn up. After the race, there would be prizes given out, followed by music. The accompanying beer festival would take them into the evening. It would all raise, hopefully, a large amount of money for St Peters YDU. He was so relieved. The bands and beer were a last-minute idea, and he was afraid he had left it too late to organise everything, but it was coming together. He sent a silent prayer of thanks heavenwards and settled down to compose a reply to the band.

* * *

Meanwhile the four children were doing a circuit of the scout hut, trying to find a way in. One of the doors had no external opening mechanism, presumably bolted from the inside, and the other, main door, was locked. They checked all the windows but, despite their aged appearance, they all held firm. Huddled in the hut porch, out of the blazing sun, Nathan suggested going to get his dad's crowbar. Peeved that the girls dismissed this idea, he sulked in a corner. Moments later he turned and called excitedly to Violet. In the corner of the porch, almost hidden from view, was a metal box attached to a concrete post. The box had a small door, and numbered buttons.

Ever since the fete at St Peter's, Nathan had been in awe of Violet's ability to choose 'luckily'. Together they had cleaned up a whole host of prizes on the 'Hook a Duck', raffle and tombola stalls. Now, he had every faith in her ability to choose the right combination. However, Violet looked puzzled. She didn't understand what was wanted. She hadn't seen a key safe before.

"You can do it. You just need to punch in the right numbers to open the door," he said, putting an encouraging arm around her shoulders and giving them a prideful squeeze.

As they gathered round Violet, she put her hand on the box and concentrated. Then, almost casually, she extended her forefinger, and pressed six buttons. There was a satisfying click and the lock mechanism released. She stood back and Nathan opened the tiny door. Inside was a

Yale key.

A triumphant Nathan grabbed it, ran, and plunged it into the door lock and turned it. Then, with a mighty shove, he opened the door. They stepped into the entrance hall. To right and left were doors labelled 'male' and 'female', and ahead, double doors, through which was the main hall. It wasn't huge but it did have a stage. Behind that was a kitchen and some storerooms. Beyond those, Tansy knew, were the external stores, used to stable the donkeys. In one of the windowless storerooms, they flicked the light switch. The ceiling light came on. That was good, there was power. In the kitchen they tried a tap. There was water. Satisfied, they headed back to the entrance. Facing them, in the doorway, was the large tortoiseshell cat. It strolled past them, did a circuit of the hall, crooked tail flicking agitatedly. On completion of the circuit, it rubbed its head against Tansy's ankle and led them all out of the door, question answered, its tail now only mildly curious.

* * *

Emily still felt unsettled, and she didn't know why. The thought of a stranger in the woods was unsettling, but she didn't think it was that. The girls had listened and appeared to be complying with what Alex had said. They had gone out through the front of the cottage, and from an upper window she had seen them by the pond, playing in the dappled sunlight beneath the trees. It really was quite hot out there. She should probably put sun cream on her shopping list. No, there was something else. Having tidied up the kitchen she did a tour of the bedrooms gathering up washing and making beds. She set the washing machine going, washed and refilled the cats' dishes, and then headed into Angelica's room. Here she checked the stock on the shelves. She would need to gather some more rosemary, as her supply of antiseptic gargle was getting low, but that could wait. Right now, she needed to box up candles. Over the years she had become adept at making up her lotions and potions using Angelica's recipe books, but her 'patients' had dwindled over that time. That fact may have been of concern to new 'patients' but she didn't have any. That lack was her choice and the reason for the dwindling numbers, not her negligence. She found that she enjoyed the 'concocting' aspect of her life but didn't have the knowledge or the confidence to take on new 'patients'. Instead, she had started making scented candles. This was something that she loved doing and it fit in nicely amongst the housework and looking after the girls. She got a real sense of achievement out of creating new shapes and the smell was just wonderful. Best of all, they sold well, and the profits went to St Peter's YDU, via a shop in The Ark Aid.

Taking a stack of pre-cut cardboard shapes,

she set about making-up her boxes. When she had completed twenty, she lined each one with shredded, pale peach tissue paper and carefully added six candles to each: six different scents. Then she put on the box lids and stuck on the labels, carefully lining them up with the edges of the boxes. She had been doing this for over two years now and still found satisfaction in stacking up her finished product and admiring the rustic simplicity of the design which gave an attractive sophistication and quality to the product, in a blatant but successful attempt to justify its price tag. At this point, she always inhaled deeply, enjoying the herbal perfume. Later, she would drop them over to the shop, Heaven Scent.

Looking round for the container, which she used to transport her candles to the shop, she was surprised to find it on the floor, under the table, and there was evidence that other items had been moved. Further inspection of the room revealed signs that books had been taken off the shelves and returned. This was disturbing. If others were coming in here, she really must dust! Puzzled, she couldn't think why Alex would be interested in any of this. It must be the girls. Though, why, she couldn't imagine.

Her phone rang. Retrieving it from her pocket, she checked the screen and answered, "Hi Anna, how are you?" Anna was one of the first people Emily had met in Much Meddling. She had been the vicar's housekeeper at the time and was the person looking after Wishing Well Cottage whilst it was for sale. She had given Emily a tour of the house and introduced her to Kevin, Angelica's cat, who Emily had been pleased to accept, along with everything else which went with the property. Over the years the two women had become great friends, despite Anna being several years older than Emily.

"I'm fine. Do you fancy a girl's night out? It has been a while", said Anna. "Lou can make tomorrow evening."

With a get-together arranged, Emily put her phone back in her pocket. As it slid inside, it hit the forgotten marble. Retrieving it, she rolled it in the palm of her hand. It really was unlike any that she had seen online. She held it up and stared at it. As she rotated it, the black twisted strip at its core appeared to wink. Amused, she took it over to the window to look at it in the light. Sitting on the sofa she held it in a strip of sunlight. The black strip had almost disappeared. She rotated it, thinking that she was looking at the black strip side on, but, from every direction the black core was now a thin line forming a central axis in the flecked amber sphere. Tentatively, she moved it out of the shaft of light. The black line thickened fractionally. Slightly unnerved, but not totally sure of what she had seen, she shaded the marble with her other hand. The line thickened some more. Even though it was what she was expecting, having her suspicion confirmed startled her. Emily dropped it. It bounced noisily across the floor and under the large dresser. From the top of the dresser a white furry head peered over the edge. As Emily got down on her hands and knees and looked warily under the cabinet, the cat made a 'perupping' sound and jumped down. Side by side they crouched. Beneath the cabinet was a landscape that would have intrigued any sci-fi novelist: dust, cat fur, cobwebs, crumbs, fly remains, and what looked suspiciously like the desiccated corpse of a mouse, sat amongst fluff balls that levitated slightly as Emily sighed. Snokettee sat back. She obviously had no intention of going under there.

Emily fetched a long-handled brush and swept it under the cabinet. On her second attempt the marble came rolling out. Snokettee pounced on it and sent it skittering round the kitchen. She chased after it, deftly batting it between the legs of the kitchen table and chairs. Whilst Snokettee entertained herself Emily got the vacuum and sucked up the mess, taking a shovel to the rodent remains, the nozzle bore proving to be of inadequate width.

With Snokettee settling herself on the chair by the fireplace, Emily picked up the marble. Had she imagined it? Had the black strip changed with the light? As if on autopilot she took it to the cellar. If the black strip narrowed with the light, what would happen if she took into the darkest place available. Without putting on the light she carried it down the cellar steps. At the bottom with just enough light for her to see by she opened her palm. The marble was now a milky black. The amber had completely disappeared. At the core a tiny light shone. Hand shaking, Emily stepped into the depth of the cellar. The light grew and she found that she could see. What she saw though, wasn't the cellar.

The church bells were ringing. It wasn't long since they had struck the hour. Four rings. She was sure. Now they were ringing again and continuously. Alarmed she looked in their direction. Something was wrong. She ran through the trees, branches whipping at her as she went, apples bouncing and scattering from her basket. Over the stile and through the woods, it was the quickest way. More trees, more branches. Leaving the path she dove into the undergrowth, her skirt hitched up, nettles stinging her ankles. She slid and stumbled, crashing into the church wall. Flinging the basket to one side she scrambled over. Dodging gravestones she ran round the side of the church, the bells deafening now, matching the thumping of her heart. Nearing the front of the building she could hear something else, something higher pitched and more strident than the bells – a woman was screaming...

At the front of the church, on the village green, a crowd had gathered. She elbowed her way through. Grunts and complaints. Swearing and the odd angry punch. She didn't care, she had to see. The woman was frantic now, screaming for help. There were taunts and cheers. Emerging from the throng she stood and stared. A make-shift wooden frame had been constructed which sat on the back of a cart. The cart had been backed into the pond. A long plank extended over the water. On the end was a seat. Tied to the seat, was the woman, just a young girl. Her long dress was ripped, her feet were bare, and her hair was in disarray. Tears streamed down her panicked face as she hiccupped each breath.

She looked on. A man was speaking, addressing the crowd, attempting to whip them up into a frenzy of fear. "No!" she screamed at him, taking in the small group of strangers gathered round him. She had seen them all earlier in the week and knew who they were. These were the witchfinders, going from town to town, village to village, making their fortune and fame by picking on the innocent and exploiting the fear of the ignorant, whist the wiser citizens kept their counsel, sensibly but guiltily protecting themselves with silence. "No," she yelled stepping forward. Hands grabbed at her dress, trying to pull her back from her folly, words of warning hissed in her ear. Ignoring them she pulled herself free and stepped forward.

Startlingly the cellar light blazed. Emily found herself lying on the floor. As she struggled to a sitting position, she found a worried Alex crouched by her side. "Don't move. Stay still. Are you hurt? Did you fall?"

"I, I... No... it was," she looked at her hand. It was empty. She scanned the floor. In a crack between the cellar flags, she saw it, amber now with a thin black pupil. She got to her feet, freeing herself from Alex, and collected the marble. Silently she returned it to its box at the end of the cellar. Alex grilled her for an explanation, but Emily just shook her head. She needed time to process what had just happened. She needed time to recover from what she had just seen. She also desperately needed to know what happened next.

* * *

The children had a plan. Now all they had to do was execute it, but they didn't have much time. Leaving the scout hut, they passed by The Three Wells pub. A small group of elderly men were gathered outside, drinking, and arguing over the best way to sweep search the woods. Some favoured a pincer movement, with teams starting at opposite ends and meeting in the middle. Others favoured starting at one end because, with the numbers they had, they would get better coverage. To the children's relief, someone suggested another round of drinks; this would give them a bit more time.

Entering the woods via Nathan's back garden, so as not to be seen, they quickly trotted through the trees and up towards the base of the crag. The Catolith met them and escorted them the rest of the way. They slid behind a wall of shrubs and crouched as they entered the lean-to that they had constructed against the crag base.

The man smiled weakly and gratefully received the food and drink that Nathan took from his rucksack. As he ate, Lily explained that they needed to move him, and now. The man looked doubtful. She gathered his few belongings and picked up his canvas sack. It was heavy, which was a surprise. With an encouraging couple of head-buts from The Catolith, he roused himself and crawled painfully out of the shelter. Outside, he leant against the rock wall as he got up onto his one good leg. He took the forked branch Nathan had purposefully brought and tucked it under one arm, as a crutch. Taking a deep breath, he took his first painful step and began the long walk down to the village. With the children agitatedly encouraging him he made halting progress. He stopped often, to lean against a tree or sit on a convenient log. Each time Lily, with frequent looks towards the Wishing Well Cottage end of the wood, pleaded with him to move. As the sound of voices reached them, he staggered to his foot and crutch once again. Breathlessly, he forged ahead, until the children, alarmed by the noise he was making persuaded him to slow down. It wasn't far now, and he needed his strength to make it over the wall into Nathan's garden. The voices were getting nearer, gruff and menacing. At the wall, the children pushed and rolled the man over into the garden. With seconds to spare they heaved him into the shed and shut the door.

As a man appeared and leant on the wall Tansy ran to him and brightly asked him what was going on, what was all the noise about? Breathing beer over her he explained that they were hunting.

"Hunting what?" she asked, all innocence.

"Never you mind, but it is best that you stay indoors, where it is safe. You never know what might be lurking in these woods."

With that he set off again, beating the undergrowth viciously with a stick. From somewhere, high up in the woods near the crag, came a triumphant yell. It sounded like the lean-to had been found. Individual thrashings began to merge as the hunters converged on the one spot.

The children listened and waited. Once they were certain that the men were gone, they opened the shed door. The man was sitting on the floor, his tattered clothing draped around him, thin bony limbs clutching at the material in a vain attempt to wrap it round his skinny frame. His face was unshaven and framed by lank long black hair, wisps of which stuck damply to his forehead. He resembled a large, bedraggled bat. He looked broken and exhausted. The next stage of their plan was going to be a struggle, but they had to move him whilst the men were still searching the woods.

CHAPTER SEVEN

Louise was working through her contacts, intent on finding a new tenant for The Ark Aid shop and flat. Finding someone shouldn't be hard, as The Ark Aid held popular and lucrative business units. She scrolled through her waiting list. However, it could be hard finding the right tenant and she needed to find someone quickly. Having empty workshops didn't look good. The new business owner would need to understand the ethos of The Ark Aid and whatever they sold, complement the other businesses. Dave, the current tenant, would move out that weekend. The rent was paid until the end of the month, but she didn't want the unit empty at all, if possible. The Crag Race was less than 2 weeks away and she didn't want to waste any customer time. It was a shame to lose Dave. His furniture was popular with the locals and tourists loved the smaller items he made. She and Mike had been grateful for his expertise when Nathan had put his grandfather's beloved mashie niblick through the casing of their grandfather clock.

Louise had been devastated when she saw the damage, but Dave had removed the damaged pieces and repaired them, expertly matching the different woods of the marquetry detailing. Now she couldn't tell that it had ever been damaged.

* * *

Mr Swire stepped out of the bakery and turned right: a couple of small cardboard boxes clutched in his hand. He was entertaining later in the day and chocolate eclairs and cream buns always provided him with amusement as his guests struggled and failed to consume them daintily. He had a perfectly good set of cake forks, but he wouldn't offer them to his guests. He may not even offer napkins. Well, at 99 fun was hard to come by. Substituting rock cakes for the scones in a cream tea was another of his little amusements.

Intent on placing one foot in front of the other he made his way along the high street, doffing his cap at anyone who passed him. It was a pleasant day, and he probably didn't need the overcoat he was wearing, which he was aware had grown too large for his skinny frame. He was hot, and he should have had a sit down by the pond but that was back in the other direction. He would have to continue to the wall, up by the hairdressers. That was a good spot to rest, and he loved the attention he got from those entering and leaving. The assault of hair dye and hair spray could be a bit overwhelming, even to his diminished senses, but he found it was worth the discomfort. He liked the ladies. He had long since lost the ability to whistle, which was just as well in these politically correct times. Now he could only deliver that type of compliment as a very unsatisfactory hissing spit.

An intermittent high-pitched squeak made him look up. Ahead, and getting nearer, he saw Nathan and the Wells girls dragging and pushing a wooden go-cart with a heap of jumble piled on the back. Darting about behind them, was a melee of cats. As they drew nearer the squeaking increased. They appeared to be struggling.

"Well, hello there, young Nathan," he said. "A lad after me own heart," and winked at him before smiling at the girls and stepping into the road ahead of them. The children stopped.

"A fine bunch o' little ladies you got 'ere for sure. Take care young Nathan, this one," and he pointed at Lily, "will charm you and wind you round 'er little finger, so never believe 'er. This one," pointing at Violet, "will see right through you, so never lie to 'er, and this one," pointing at Tansy and laughing, "will beat the stuffing out of you. So don't ever upset 'er."

"She couldn't beat me," said an indignant Nathan.

"Oh, you've got a lot to learn young Nathan, me lad," laughed Mr Swire. "If you want more jumble, I've got loads. Come round any time and don't forget to bring your charmin' li'le lady friends. What you collectin' for?"

"Donkeys," said Tansy quickly, to the obvious surprise of the others.

Mr Swire smiled and looked the children up and down, "What do donkeys want with jumble?"

"We are going to make jackets to keep them warm," said Lily.

"In winter," added Violet.

"Donkey jackets, eh?" said Mr Swire as Spider rubbed round his ankles. Then, at the sound of voices, he looked up the street. A group of men could be seen heading their way. It seemed that the search of the woods was over. "I guess you lot best be off. Best of luck with your 'jumble', and Tansy..."

"Yes, Mr Swire?"

"I'd a thought you'd a brought your oil can – drawin' all that attention to yoursels." And he tapped the side of his nose.

As the children got the cart moving again, Mr Swire chomped on his dentures and set off towards the rabble. As the children passed the pond and rounded the corner of the pub towards the beer garden they looked back. Mr Swire was standing in the road, arms outstretched, two cardboard boxes dangling on string from his right hand, and a stick in his left hand extending his reach. The children were puzzled. It looked as if Mr Swire was deliberately delaying the hunting party. Did he know, or was he just asking the men what they had found? Pushing hard they continued past the pub, heads down to avoid drawing any conversation from those occupying the odd table. As the tarmac gave way to backstreet cobbles their job became harder and there was an audible groan from their cargo. Lily grabbed at the edge of an old duvet as it slid from the heap, revealing an old boot and ankle, and placed it back onboard. As she did so she noticed that the squeaky wheel was showing signs of splitting. The small, previously solid rubber pram tyre was shredded and about to leave its metal rim which was now warped. It wouldn't last long. She and Tansy pushed harder as Violet helped Nathan to pull. They turned off the cobbles of the backstreet onto the dirt track that led to the scout hut. This was easier and they soon reached the side of the hut, where they were able to park the trolley out of sight.

Nathan quickly opened the main door of the hall and went through and opened the side door, allowing them to move the trolley inside. Exhausted they all collapsed on the floor and watched as the man slowly unfurled and painfully dragged himself off the trolley and leant himself against the wall. As he took several ragged breaths, Lily studied him. He wasn't well and she was worried. Once he had had time to rest from his ordeal, she would see how he was then. For now, she would do her best to make him comfortable. She arranged the bedding on the floor, and he lay down on it, clutching his canvas sack. She covered him over with the duvet. Then, as carefully as she could she removed his boots. He grimaced but offered no objections as she removed the left one. Gently, she examined the discoloured and swollen skin. Thankfully it was intact. She elevated it with a rolled-up blanket, then covered it gently with a soft fleece.

"He needs a bath," said Nathan wrinkling his nose.

"He needs rest and food first," said Lily prompting them all to empty their pockets. This produced a small pile of cold toast, fruit, cake, pie, and bottles of water and juice.

The man roused himself and sat up. He ate the cake and then the pie and took some juice. Then, he settled back down again and shut his eyes. It wasn't long before he was snoring, gently.

* * *

Emily wheeled her box of candles over to The Ark Aid, skirting the pond and passing the pub. A lot of noise was emanating from the beer garden. She couldn't see but she could hear what sounded like a group of elderly men agitatedly discussing something. It was difficult to differentiate the different comments. Probably Richard had put his prices up again. She remembered the uproar last time. The threats to boycott the place, which didn't last long as it was the only pub within walking distance, followed by the threats of temperance which lasted for all of one round. She kept going and soon turned into The Ark Aid. Each time she went in there she felt a 'little buzz' of happiness knowing that she had contributed to all this. She couldn't have believed how well her idea, to move St Peter's Charity Shop in there from the high street, had turned out. Really, she had Louise to thank as it was her vision and hard work that had resulted in what they had today. She loved all the little shops and businesses. Best of all, it made Alex happy too. As she pushed open the door of Heaven Scent she inhaled: cinnamon, tangerine, jasmine all identifiable. After a brief chat with Daniel, who owned the shop, she headed over to What Sup and got herself a coffee. She could never decide what she liked best – the scents in Heaven Scent or the aromas in What Sup. She took her coffee to one of the little courtyard tables, then, as she was staring at them, she succumbed and bought a palmier. Mmmm. Each time she bought one it was with the intention of only eating half, but that never happened. Usually, she sat and sipped and imagined that she was in some Parisian side street, idly watching the world go by. Today it was lovely and sunny and the geraniums in the terracotta pots and hanging baskets outside the charity shop reminded her of a French painting.

If the coffee shop sold liquors, she would have bought one to sit alongside her coffee. She even had a mental image of herself stubbing out a Gauloise, in a non-existent ash tray on the table in front of her, which was alarming as she had never smoked in her life. Still, feeling French occasionally, did no harm and was a small enjoyable pleasure.

CHAPTER EIGHT

With Alex gone and the kids off on some adventure of their own she cleared away the breakfast things and made a mental note to restock the fruit bowl. Snokettee rubbed round her ankles, and she bent down and gave the cat an affectionate stroke. The soft fur was lovely to touch, and she always enjoyed their moments together, especially in winter, sitting cosily by the fire. Every home should have a cat.

Collecting secateurs and a trug from the outhouse, she headed into the garden. Round at the sunny side of the cottage she cut some lavender and rosemary. Finding some borage in flower she cut some of that too. She would put some of the tiny blue flowers in ice cubes. The girls would love that. It was also an easy way to educate them about nature. Why this was important she didn't really know, she just felt that it was. Perhaps, deep down, she felt that this was something that she should have learnt as a child, and she wanted to instil an understanding of nature into her own children. Or did she just know instinctively that it was important for her children, in particular. However, thinking back to the moved items in Angelica's room, it did seem that they may already be teaching themselves. Clutching her trug, she took a stroll round the garden and up through the fruit trees which were showing signs of producing a bumper crop this year. Apples, pears and damsons were all well on their way to a bountiful harvest. Round the edges of the garden, where it bordered the wood, hazel trees and elderflower were in abundance and would yield their own bounty.

At the well, she stopped and put down her trug. Then she removed the wooden lid cover and peered down. Ever since the well had run dry three years ago, she felt the urge to check it whenever she passed. It was fine. She could see light glinting off the water surface. It still wasn't as deep as it should be, but it was gradually getting deeper as the water table filled.

* * *

The vicarage doorbell rang, and James went and answered it. Gemma stood on the doorstep looking very different from the Gemma he had interviewed. Gone were the dressy clothes and high heels. Today she was wearing jeans, trainers, and a white T-shirt, which on anyone else, would have been baggy. Her hair was twirled and piled neatly on top of her head. James welcomed her inside. They danced awkwardly round each other before James managed to close the door. After a little hesitation he invited her through to the kitchen and offered her a cup of tea. She looked a little surprised.

"Oh," said James, "you probably want to get on. Maybe later." He opened a closet and showed her where the cleaning equipment was, mop, bucket, sprays, vacuum, etc. "If you would do the front rooms first, in case I get any surprise visitors, and the cloakroom. Er, I'll leave you to it. If you have any questions just ask."

With that he disappeared into his office and pushed the door to. There was a clattering from the kitchen cupboard as the vacuum was dragged out and a squeak along the corridor as it was wheeled into the front room. There was silence for a while and then the vacuum was switched on, and he could hear her singing. The tune was familiar, but he couldn't quite make out what it was. She had a lovely voice. Intrigued he went out into the corridor. Now he could hear. She was singing 'Edelweiss'. Amused, he stood and listened. Suddenly, the door flew open, and the vacuum was thrust at his feet. Gemma nearly leapt out of her skin and James jumped backwards into the opposite wall. She switched off the machine and stared at a reddening James, embarrassed to be caught listening at the door.

"I, I, er... you have a lovely voice," he

managed to stammer.

"I am sorry, was I disturbing you?"

"No, no. Certainly not. I'll let you get on. Sorry to have interrupted." With that he went back to his study and closed the door. Before long he could hear her happily singing again.

* * *

Louise was excited. She had just had a promising enquiry from a gentleman wanting to view the unit in The Ark Aid. He was a horologist by trade but had branched out into making a variety of mechanical items using old bits of machinery. He had his own workshop but wanted a commercial outlet and The Ark Aid, he said, would be ideal. He had e-mailed her pictures of his creations and Louise was fascinated. Bric-a-brac and candles were all very well, but what he was producing would widen the customer base, no end. What he was selling would interest, not just tourists wanting the odd souvenir but serious collectors of clocks, those interested in mechanics and those wanting unusual and well-made pieces of art for their homes. He would also provide a range of differently priced products, which was always good. Unless he turned out to be an obnoxious idiot then he would fit in well with the other tenants. She just needed to check with Dave, the current tenant, when it was okay to show the man round and arrange a time.

As Gerald, her boss, handed her a mug of tea she looked up and smiled. Over the past few years, she had grown to like him. Her initial view of the man had been coloured by Emily's dislike for him. However, whereas Emily found him intense and creepy, Louise just found his leering awkwardness amusing. The more she got to know him the more she wanted to help him. He was a decent enough human being, and he didn't have a malicious bone in his body. He just had an unfortunate manner which was a shame because he was a good-looking guy. Not good looking in an obvious way but in a solid dependable sort of way. The sort of way that grew on you. She, Gerald, and Tony the third estate agent, had a good time together in the office, always finding something amusing in their day.

She finished typing up the details of a house she had seen the day before and sent it off to the client for approval. She took a sip of her tea and printed off details of her afternoon viewings. Whilst she was stapling them her phone rang. It was Dave, at the Ark Aid, agreeing to her potential client viewing at 5pm. It would mean a long day for her but if she could 'seal the deal' it would be worth it. Hopefully she wouldn't be late meeting Emily and Anna although, if Mike fed Nathan, she could always eat at The Three Wells.

* * *

That evening, leaving Alex to get the

girls to bed, which these days simply meant incarcerating them in their room and hoping they would go to sleep sometime before midnight, she headed over to The Three Wells to meet Lou and Anna. She leant her shoulder against the heavy wooden door, with its stained-glass panels, and pushed. Inside, it was noisy and busier than normal for a Thursday and she was a little surprised. A quick glance round showed her Anna sitting at a table in the far corner waving. She bought herself a drink and went and joined her.

"Hi, how are you? It seems ages," she said as she hitched her chair nearer the table.

"I know. I'm fine," said Anna, "How are you lot?"

"We're good. The girls and Nathan are finding plenty to occupy themselves. What have you and Sasha been up to? How was your holiday?"

"Well, we had a fabulous time in France. Sasha's grandparents are hilarious. They don't speak any English, or won't, and my French is useless, so a lot got lost in translation. I think Sasha was exhausted at the end of it all and for the most part gave up translating. Half the time he just shook his head, raised his hands, and shrugged. I am finding that I am understanding more though, and I live in hope of one day being able to hold a conversation. Sasha takes great pleasure in telling everyone I am effluent in

French. Well, I do know the word merde!"

They chatted for a while and were just wondering where Lou had got to when she burst through the door. She waved, then turned and elbowed her way to the bar. When she finally joined them, she had a full round of drinks and three bags of crisps. She carefully placed the glasses on the table as the crisp packets scattered themselves about, one falling onto the floor.

"Hi, sorry I'm late, but I have good news." She took a sip and ripped open a bag of crisps. "Guess, what?"

The other two stared at her.

"I found a new tenant for The Ark Aid. He doesn't want the flat, so I still need to find someone for that, but we won't have an empty shop."

"Oh, you found a replacement for Dave," said Emily.

"What, Dave is leaving?" said Anna. "Oh, I liked his stuff. Sasha will be disappointed. Where is he going? He isn't packing it in altogether, is he?"

"No, he is moving to larger premises, and he has found an apprentice. So, Sasha can still use him. I can give you his address." Sasha's husband was an architect and over the past three years had used his skills to update and develop St Peter's Young Disabled Unit housed in the old building which was Sycamore Hall. This large stately home was situated on the outskirts of Much Meddling on land that once belonged to the Wells family's ancestors. A certain Cyril Wells had lost it, gambling with his rival Archibald Earnshaw, in the early 1800s. It was only through the recent intervention of Agnes Earnshaw, a Wells ancestor, that the families were now re-united. Sasha had helped turn the St Peter's YDU into a successful enterprise once again.

"So, tell us all about the new person," said Emily.

"Well, his name is Jonathan. He is a horologist."

"Oh," said Emily and Anna in unison, Emily questioningly and Anna with interest.

"He makes and repairs clocks," said Lou. "The best bit is that he makes fabulous time pieces out of old bits of metal and wood. They really are works of art. Some of them are like grandfather clocks without the casing. Those hang on the wall and have their weights and workings on show. They really are incredible. He also makes little mechanical toys out of tin and spare bits from machinery. He should fit in very well with the other shops and will draw a different kind of clientele. I am hoping he is going to come up with a good name – something like Serendipity."

"I like that," said Anna.

"He didn't," said Lou. "When I mentioned it to Mike, he didn't like it either. 'Jon's Junk' was his suggestion. Anyone want another drink?"

Emily took the hint and headed for the bar. Richard spotted her and made a point of moving across and serving her. As he pulled a couple of pints and squirted lemonade into some orange juice, she asked him why it was so busy. He explained that the little posse had grown. The sheriff and his deputies had roped in a few others to hunt for the man in the woods. Apparently, they had found his hide out and were up in arms that the villain had been eating – pigeons. A heap of feathers had been found and bird carcases. They were going to run him out of town. They reckoned he'd be back, so they were setting up wildlife cameras to catch him.

"Pigeons?" said Emily.

"Yes, good luck to him. The more he eats the better as far as I'm concerned. They are a right pain, crapping all over my tables and sunshades. I've had to put notices up to get the customers to stop feeding them."

"Perhaps you should put them on the menu," said Emily as she picked up the drinks and headed back to Anna and Lou.

"So," Anna was saying, "we caught a boat out to a little island on the lake. Sasha spread out the picnic and we spent a lovely afternoon eating, drinking, and swimming, etc."

"etcetera...?" said Emily.

"Very much etcetera," said Anna with a giggle. "We had a fabulous time." With that she switched on her phone and showed them a long string of photos. When Emily and Louise had had their fill of street cafes, shorelines, grinning faces, and scenery, Anna asked Emily what she had been up to.

Emily hesitated. Should she tell them about The Catolith? Then there were the marbles.

"Did you find out anything about the Daguerreotype photo?" said Lou and seeing Anna's surprise went on to explain what it was.

Emily told them about the gravestones in the church yard and the three names Clara, Lottie, and Millicent and the wedding photo she had found, and that she was hoping to go to the library. When she told them about the brooches the three young women were wearing, they were amazed.

"Really," said Lou, "I hadn't spotted the brooches. Those fairies are that old?"

"Right," said Anna, "I'd better be going. Are you and Alex around this weekend, if Sasha and I pop round? We have something we want to ask the pair of you."

"Yes, sure," said Emily.

CHAPTER NINE

The man gratefully took the food from the children. He had slept reasonably well despite the hardness of the floor which was less comfortable than the bed of dried leaves he had been sleeping on in the lean-to. However, he felt more secure here in the little windowless room and there were no ants here to bite and add to his discomfort. The children had left him a torch as he wasn't able to reach the light switch without standing up. They had been thoughtful in other ways too and whilst he ate Lily discreetly took the now full plastic milk bottle, and went and emptied and rinsed it. His foot was still painful and swollen, and the round white nasty tasting little discs the boy had brought, which the children had insisted he swallowed, had done little to help. He wheezed slightly as he breathed, and he knew that wasn't good.

When he finished eating Lily disappeared for a while and somewhere in the distance, he could hear water boiling. When she returned, she had a bowl with steaming liquid in it, and some towels. She made him sit with a couple of towels on his lap to hold the bowl. Then she put another towel over his head and told him to breathe in the steam. At first, he found the enclosed heat distressing but then gradually his breathing eased, and he relaxed and smiled and nodded slightly to himself. As he sat, eyes shut, inhaling the steam, his left foot was uncovered. Gentle hands caressed its surface and took hold of his ankle. Another pair of hands took hold of his foot. Gradually the pain eased slightly. It didn't go completely but it was definitely better than before. He gave his foot a test wiggle and the pain shot back. He winced. Slowly the hands replaced themselves and he lifted the towel so that he could see. Lily and Tansy were looking at him with concern and vague annoyance. He smiled.

Behind them, in the doorway sat The Catolith. The man and the cat looked at one another. Neither made a sound but there was understanding in their look.

* * *

Emily went down to the cellar and pulled out the top box of marbles. She took it to the centre of the cellar where there was a table and removed the lid. She reached for the marble she had previously held, then realised that she didn't know which one it was. The box could have been the other way round. The top tray had 36 depressions, in 6 rows of 6. Her marble had been top left, one row in and one row down. If the box was now the other way round it would be bottom right, 5 rows in and 5 rows down. There was no dust inside the box and so she had no way of knowing which one she had handled. She switched on her torch, switched off the light, pulled up a chair, sat down and took out the marble, one row in and one row down from the top left-hand corner. Then holding it in the palm of her hand she switched off the torch.

Rapidly the darkness was illuminated.

She was on her knees, dappled light flickering on the earth. The smell of damp leaves heavy on the air. Another smell, a smell she could almost taste, overpowering it, cloying and metallic: blood. The boy had collapsed, his limp form supported by the two women at her side, his leg bent and oozing crimson at an alarming rate. He was pale and his breathing shallow. She inspected the rusty metal jaws, clamped round his leg. The brutal device was heavy and designed to be difficult to open. She ran her hands over it, feeling for weaknesses.

"Hurry, Sarah," urged the women.

She looked at the boy's ashen face. Rage surged through her, a deep fiery glow building in her core. It fizzed and grew. She slid her hands to the narrowest part of the uppermost jaw and wrapped her fingers round the cold metal. Rocking back and forth on her knees she channelled the energy mounting inside her, felt its power and focussed it in the palms of her hands. It happened so quickly. The metal transformed, became pliant like lead and then liquid like honey. As her fists closed on themselves, she removed her hands and took hold of what remained of the jaw, and threw it to one side.

"We'll take him back to his mother, you hide that. If any of it is found they'll come looking."

She took a moment to gather herself, recover and settle the energy inside. She watched as Mary and Edith carried the boy away. Then she collected the lumps of metal and lay them to one side. There was blood amongst the leaves. She took a stick, stirred the evidence into the ground and then scattered leaves over the top. She stood back to inspect her work. The smell of blood would draw animals. She glanced round but saw no herbs of use. Then, she sniffed the air. Yes, she was almost certain. Taking a few steps into the undergrowth she sniffed again. It didn't take her long to find it. Taking a handful of leaves, she scooped up the fox stool and took it back to the site of the mantrap. She scattered some more leaves and placed the fox dung on top. Hopefully that would deter any animals for a while. She rocked the tethering stake back and forth until she was able to pull it from the ground. Then, gathering the bits of metal, she wrapped them in the folds of her skirt and clutched the bundle to her. She stood and listened. Certain she was alone, she set off back to the path, checking behind her to ensure she had left no trail. Every now and then she stopped and put down her burden and listened.

Then, reassured she set off again. When she reached the spot she had chosen, the light was starting to fade. She put down the metal and removed her skirt, placing it carefully on a tree stump. She found a forked branch and waded into the water. It was icy cold, and her feet quickly became numb. Using the branch, she agitated the muddy bottom, liquifying it. When the hole was deep enough, she plunged the metal pieces into its depths and placed a couple of large stones on top. Then she scraped the surrounding earth into the hole and watched as the swirling dark mass gradually settled. She stepped out onto a rock and inspected the pool. It was done.

Emily was in darkness. She could see nothing. Disoriented, she blinked. She moved slightly and felt the torch in her hand. She switched it on. She was in the cellar. In her left hand was the marble. She stared at it. She rotated it in the torch beam, a simple amber marble with a black twisted core. Inert like any normal marble.

She sat for a while remembering what she had just witnessed. They had called her Sarah, and the other two women, she knew were her sisters, Mary and Edith. Yes, Sarah, Mary, and Edith. They were triplets, but these were new names. She vaguely remembered an Edith on one of the head stones in the graveyard. She went to stand up, but sat back down. Her legs were shaky, and her hands tingled. When she felt able to stand, she took the marble and put it back in its case. Then she took the case and slid it back in its alcove, this time taking care to note its orientation.

She couldn't wait. She had to see. The light in the kitchen was startlingly bright and she blinked madly as she searched for a pair of sunglasses. Glasses found, she raced out of the front door, into the street, and up the church path. Threading her way through the ancient yew trees that cast dark shadows across her path she rounded the back of the church and headed for the far end of the cemetery. Here she stopped and inspected the headstones. Three small identical white lumps of limestone sat side by side, tiny bits of embedded fossilised shells sparkling in the sunlight. On the first stone she read - Mary Wells born November 1604 – died November 1704. The second stated - Sarah Wells born November 1604 – died December 1704. The third read - Edith Wells - born November 1604 – died December 1704. So, these were the 1600s triplets. Why hadn't she noted their names before! Her mind was in turmoil. So many thoughts rushing through her head. The woman, whose experience she had made witness to with the first marble, was the same one as the second marble. She knew it. She felt it. She was Sarah. She had experienced one of Sarah's memories. Briefly she felt the thrill of the power she had generated and felt awed. Was this the power that her daughter possessed. Was that how Lily, at just three years old, had freed herself from her car seat? Was that how her daughter had saved her own life when a cat's eye had been kicked up by a passing vehicle, passed through the windscreen of their Range Rover, and embedded itself in the back of her seat? Before, she had suspected but not really believed that Lily could have done that. Even having the evidence of the car seat, she hadn't really believed. Now, she had experienced it for herself...

Then she remembered the other memory, of the woman screaming. Who was she? Was it Mary or Edith? Suddenly she was afraid for her sisters. Then she realised that if it was either of them on the ducking stool they had survived and lived to be 100 years old. And, she was Emily, not Sarah.

* * *

James was finishing off his sermon. He had got the general gist of it but was struggling to find an ending that would neatly tie together the rest of what he had said. Something that would succinctly and memorably paraphrase his message. Something that would quietly burst the sanctimonious bubbles of those in his congregation who thought saying amen once a week would grant them life eternal. He had heard them muttering and gossiping and bad mouthing each other and now, he was well aware of the uncharitable and hostile feelings towards the stranger in the village. There was a knock on his office door.

"Come in," he called.

The door opened and Gemma stepped in proffering a mug of coffee. He thanked her. Then asked if she had got herself one. She hadn't, but at his urging she quickly got herself a drink and, when he said he could do with a break, sat down opposite him.

She saw that he was struggling with something and asked him what he was trying to do. He was a little surprised at her interest, but he found himself telling her how difficult he found it trying to get through to his parishioners. He knew that they were all fully aware of the bible's message, but he felt that their attendance was routine without any real meaning for them, and he didn't know what to do about it. He realised that he had been going on at some length and she had been listening patiently, adding the odd encouraging comment. "Anyway, enough of my problems."

She smiled. "You are a good man, vicar. You'll figure it out." With that she stood, took their empty mugs, and went back to her cleaning. Soon he could hear her singing.

* * *

Violet stood in the corner of the small windowless room and watched as her two sisters cleared away the inhalation equipment and did what they could to make the man comfortable. She was puzzled. She couldn't read him. Normally, she got a sense of a person's worth and intentions. Something wasn't right. Yet Lily, much better than her at reading people, seemed at ease with him. The man was looking at her, and reading her, but she had no sense of him. It was unsettling. Normally, she could look at people and they would be completely unaware of the depth of her appraisal, like she was studying them through a one-way mirror. Now, with this man, it was like the mirror was reversed. He could see into her soul, and she didn't like it and she could tell that he knew. She stood tall and looked him in the eye. Then something brushed her ankle. She looked down and Whoops-a-Daisy was leaning against her, back arched and head nuzzling her foot. The cat rolled over and lay on her side at Violet's feet. She knelt, picked up the cat and buried her face in its fur. When she looked again, the man had laid down and his eyes were shut. Her privacy returned.

CHAPTER TEN

E mily drove into Barnlees and parked in a side
street. Checking the parking sign, she hoped
two hours would be enough. The library wasn't
far. She removed the jacket she had on and
draped it over her arm and regretted wearing
jeans. A dress would have been cooler. However,
when she stepped into the air-conditioned
library, she was glad of her choice. Finding a
librarian, she explained that she was looking for
information on Much Meddling in the 1600's and
the 1800's. Did they have any newspaper copies
from back then? They did, but it was mainly on
microfilm. It was gradually being transferred to
computer, but it was a laborious process. She was
led to a small glass room in a corner of the library
and given a quick lesson on how to operate the
microfilm. She found it difficult to manipulate
and fiddly to manoeuvre. Left alone she searched
the shelves for suitable cassettes fitting her time
period and selected a couple from the local
newspaper archives dated 1600-1650.

She took the roll out of its plastic case

and removed the securing tape. She unfurled some of the film, slid the reel onto the holder and then threaded the end of the film round guide bars across the feed plate and onto the opposite spool. She wound it on a little and then pushed the spools backwards so that the film was under the magnifying reader. She turned the dial and spooled the film along until she found the index, adjusting the magnification until it was clear. She didn't know precisely what she was looking for, but she scanned the text hoping for something encouraging. The index seemed to consist, simply, of a list of publishing dates with the first few words of that paper's frontpage headline. The papers were grouped. She picked a random date, then thought better of it and scrolled forward until she found a paper for November 1604, the month that the 1600 triplets were born. She found the announcements section and magnified it. She couldn't see any entries for Wells, or triplets. She returned the magnification to 'normal' and scrolled on to the next paper and repeated the process. Again, nothing. She scrolled on again. Then, she found them. They were there in black and white. Sarah, Edith, and Mary born to Gladys and Joseph Wells 24th November 1604. Why she was so excited Emily didn't really know. The only new information was the parents' names. Now that she had that she didn't know what she was going to do with it, and she realised that she could have probably found that out at the church.

The librarian must have seen her sitting staring at the screen. She appeared at Emily's side and suggested that she might like to try looking online at The Parish Records. These, she explained, were more searchable. She showed Emily how to search by name, by church, by parish, and by event, e.g., birth, wedding etc. She also told her that she could do this at home, for free. Once she had dates for events then she could look up the actual newspaper articles on the microfilm. Emily now quickly found entries for the births of the 1600, 1700, 1800s triplets. Searching further back she thought she had found entries for 1500s triplets, but the details were sketchy, and she could easily be jumping to conclusions. James hadn't been aware of more than 5 generations, her girls being the 5th, and he had the original records and tombstones. She printed off copies of the information she had gathered and went and thanked the librarian.

"If you are interested in the 1600's we have a section of local history, over there," she said, "which I believe includes information on Much Meddling." She walked over to one of the shelves and picked out a couple of books. She flipped to the back pages of the first and ran her finger down the index. "Here," she said, handing it to Emily, before opening the second book.

Emily felt a thrill run through her. There

on the page was a rough sketch of the Much Meddling village pond. Poised over it, on a large wooden frame, was a ducking stool holding a young girl. Emily was about to say, no, it was on the back of a cart, but bit her tongue. Instead, she greedily absorbed the text, turning the page to see what came next. Over the page was another sketch. This one showed another woman standing in front of a crowd of villagers, arms outstretched remonstrating with a group of men. She scanned the article for a date. The scene had apparently taken place in 1622. She did a quick calculation. Sarah would have been 18 years old.

"And, here," said the librarian. "There is probably more, if you look."

Emily nodded distractedly; she couldn't take her eyes off the article she was reading. It seemed that the young woman, who wasn't given a name, had successfully, and at great risk to herself, challenged the witchfinders and gained the support of the villagers to free the girl and oust the witchfinders from the village. It seemed that the witchfinders had subsequently returned with reinforcements, but the men of the village, roused by the oratory of the young woman and her two sisters, had turned them away.

She took the other book and asked if she could borrow them. Then felt foolish as the librarian smiled and said, "it is a library..."

* * *

At just after 2.30 there was a knock at the door and Anna and Sasha were let in. Whilst Emily got them all drinks Alex took Anna and Sasha into the garden and sat them at a table under one of the apple trees. It was nice and shady there, and they had a lovely view of the garden and the well, which sat in the middle of the lawn. It was a nice private part of the garden, out of site of the village green, and not visible to anyone in the church grounds. Also, a group of fruit trees blocked the view of the tombstones in the church grounds, but the top of the church tower was still visible along with the upper part of the stained-glass windows, which Emily liked.

After some initial catching up, they hadn't seen Sasha for a while, and Alex hadn't seen Anna, they got down to what the meeting was all about. Anna looked at Sasha, who, taking his cue from her said, "We were wondering how you would feel about selling Fare Well Cottage." He paused for their reaction, but neither Alex nor Emily spoke, so he continued, "The number of St Peter's relatives using it has dropped, now that there is accommodation at St Peter's and we know that it really isn't making any money, so, we wondered if you would be interested in selling it to us. We really want to move into the village and there isn't anything for sale, that we would want. We have been waiting but there just isn't anything..."

Emily looked at Alex, who just said, "Oh!" and looked back at her. There was an awkward silence.

"Perhaps you would like to think about it," said Anna.

"It is just that... well, we kind of regretted selling Bode Well to Mike and Louise. Not that we would deprive them of it and we love having them so near," said Alex, "but, when we found out how much Wells land and property has been lost over the years we kind of feel that we have a responsibility to hang on to what we have."

"Yes," said Emily, "it might sound silly and greedy, but we have the girls' futures to think of."

"What, you think that they will stay in Much Meddling," said Anna.

Emily and Alex replied as one, "Well, yes."

"Seriously!"

CHAPTER ELEVEN

On their way into church Emily noticed that the girls seemed to be looking around them. This wasn't unusual but it was as if they were looking for something in particular and they seemed to be paying attention to individual conversations as they passed people by. She pricked up her ears. The hot topic this week was James' new housekeeper. It appeared that the village gossip mongers were of the same opinion as the storekeeper, and not as discreet. Listening to what was being said, she was glad that Gemma wasn't there to hear it, and equally, James. She hurried her girls through and pointed them in the direction of their Sunday school class, then found a pew away from the tittle tattlers. She remembered back to when she first came to the village and how unkind these women were to her. It seemed that Gemma was getting the same treatment.

"I wonder what she's done," she whispered to Alex. "I'll ask Mags. She'll know. She's lived here long enough. I just don't believe these women."

Alex gave her a sideways look, "You are just as bad as they are. Just leave it."

She was about to answer back when the organ started up and James appeared. The service began.

This week the sermon was all about treating thy neighbour as thyself, being kind to one another and helping those in need, about not jumping to conclusions and giving the benefit of the doubt. When they stood for the next hymn Emily took the opportunity to glance round at the gossips to see if what James had said had struck home. There was no indication that it had. They were all piously singing their hearts out.

Part way through the service the Sunday School class joined them. Once the children got settled the service continued. It was lovely having the young voices join them. Her three weren't that tuneful but they gave it their all.

James reminded everyone of the Crag Race which would take place the following Saturday. He hoped they would all attend and, if they weren't taking part would support those that were. All money raised would go to St. Peter's Young Disabled Unit. The service ended and they headed out into the sunshine. The girls seemed to make a beeline for the women who had been gossiping. Snokettee and her pride had conveniently appeared beside the women, at the foot of a large cube-shaped yew. The women

looked disdainfully at the three girls and cats. As
Emily drew closer, she could hear them saying,
"it is all very well, givin't benefit o' doubt, when
you don't 'ave kids. If 'e 'ad 'is own, eed talk
differently. I, for one, will be glad if that tramp is
run out o' the village."

So, the message of his sermon had gone
completely over their heads. Emily couldn't keep
her mouth shut, "Well, I do have kids. Young
kids, and I am willing to give him the benefit of
the doubt. Your lads are now in their thirties and,
I am sure, can take care for themselves."

The women backed off on to the grass as
Emily marched past, shepherding the triplets
away. Alex followed behind, raising his eyebrows
at the women in a mock grimace. He was
surprised at Emily. She wasn't usually that
assertive, but he was pleased and amused.

After lunch the family piled into the Range
Rover and headed off into the hills. Alex drove
for about an hour and then turned off onto a dirt
track, passing a sign which stated 'Unsuitable
for Motor Vehicles'. After about half a mile he
stopped. Emily leapt out and opened the gate
which was blocking their way. After Alex drove
through, she closed it and got back into the
vehicle. A little further on he called out, "cattle
grid", and the girls started humming noisily. As
the wheels thrummed their way across the metal
struts the girls humming was rhythmically
interrupted, making an, "uh, uh, uh, uh, uh,"

sound. At the other side they all burst out laughing. Alex stopped and reversed. Then drove over it again. The girls were delighted, and Emily and Alex laughed along with them.

He parked the car under a group of trees and the family set off down the hillside, threading their way through tufts of bracken, walking until they met a river. The water was quite wide at that point, and they set off uphill against the flow. At flatter parts of the terrain small pools had formed with gentle falls of water rolling over smooth rocks. As they climbed higher the ground got steeper and the water cascaded over larger rocks. On the opposite side some sheep bolted off through the bracken, startled by the human intrusion. A little further on Alex stopped and pointed. On the opposite side of the stream was a huge boulder, the size of a double decker bus. It stood alone. Finding the shallowest part of the stream, Alex rearranged a few large stones and then, after a brief search, found a log, which he placed across them as a bridge.

Tansy was first across, followed by Lily and Violet, then Emily and Alex. They walked round the boulder. It was enormous. Alex picked up Tansy and lifted her up so that she could pull herself onto a small ledge that was there, above the overhang of the lower part. Without prompting she climbed out of sight. He pushed Violet and Lily up next. Then he formed a stirrup with his hands for Emily. She shook her head.

"How about I stay down here and take a photo of you all?"

As Alex climbed up, first jumping to grab hold of the ledge then doing a chin up and swinging a leg to get purchase with his heel, she walked away from the boulder and found herself a mound to stand on which gave her the perfect vantage point. She felt a little flutter in her stomach as this man she had married, hauled himself effortlessly up on to the ledge and then clambered up to join their children. She loved watching him move, seeing his muscles ripple under his shirt. She loved everything about him, but most of all she loved the way he interacted with the girls. He obviously adored them and that, simply made her melt inside. She knew she was lucky, so, so lucky, and the knowledge overwhelmed her at times. Soon Alex and the girls were all on top of the boulder beaming at her, Violet held securely on Alex lap, looking slightly nervous, Tansy jumping up and down and waving. She held up her phone and took several shots followed by a short video of Tansy doing a little dance.

Once down from the rock they continued following the stream. After a while the ground rose on either side of them, funnelling them into a tree-lined valley. They heard it before they saw it: the sound of water, drumming through the trees. The canopy cleared and they stepped into a clearing at the foot of a limestone cliff. Water cascaded from on high forming a 3-metre wide, crystal-clear curtain, dropping about 10 metres into a deep green pool. The sides of the waterfall crashed onto rocks that edged the water, forming a mist. Alex sat on a rock and waited, allowing the girls to explore and make their own discoveries. It didn't take them long. All three disappeared behind the waterfall. Emily and Alex waited, expecting the girls to appear on the bank at the other side. No, instead, a couple of rocks flew through the curtain. Then, to muffled yelling and laughter, a hand appeared. There was a shriek followed by more laughter and a disgruntled moan amid even more laughter. Someone had got very wet, it seemed. When they emerged on the other bank Lily and Violet were still laughing. Tansy was shaking a wet arm and sleeve and flinging what she could of the water at the other two. They played for a while, running behind the waterfall, throwing stones in the water and skimming them off the surface, building little dams and making new channels. Alex and Emily joined in, adding refinements and splashing each other, much to the girls' delight.

CHAPTER TWELVE

Mid-morning, when Alex went to get himself a coffee from What Sup he was pleased to see activity at the business unit, vacated by Dave. It looked like his new tenant was moving in. Louise didn't mess about, and he was grateful to her for her enthusiasm. He couldn't wish for a better agent. He bought two coffees and went over to say hello.

The man was in the back madly sweeping amidst a cloud of dust.

"Hi. Just thought I'd say hello. I'm Alex. I own these buildings."

"Oh, nice to meet you. I'm Jonathan, but call me Jon."

Alex held out the coffee, "I thought you might like this. If it isn't your thing, then I'll just have two. If you want sugar, I can go get you some."

"No, that is great. Very welcome."

They chatted for a while, each explaining what they did, with Alex also giving him a brief explanation of what the other business units held. Jon said that he had been waiting for ages for a unit and was delighted to be moving in. He really appreciated having the space to display his knickknackery, as he liked to call it.

"So, have you got a name for your business?"

"I do," he said and went over to a big box by the door. Lifting off the lid he reached inside, pushed a mound of straw to one side and pulled out a wooden sign. Turning it the right way up and facing it towards Alex he said, "What do you think?"

On a beautifully crafted mahogany board six elegant steel letters with tinted, bevelled edges, spelled TEMPUS. Inlaid, at the top left-hand corner and partly sitting behind the T and the E was a quarter cog. It was simple yet elegant.

Alex was impressed. "Did you make that?"

The man nodded.

"Wow, I can't wait to see your clocks."

* * *

James had just received an e-mail from his printers stating that his order for 'numbers' to pin to his competitors vests, was ready to collect, along with his race certificates. Once he had collected those, he just needed the medals, a trophy for the winners and plaques for the second and third places, in both the adult and the children's categories. He had been promised that they would be ready for collection on Tuesday. That was good, he could combine the two pickups as they were both at the same end of Barnlees. All his bands were now confirmed. A friend from his running club was organising the race marshals. Richard was organising the beer festival aspect. Alex was moving the donkeys on the Thursday. The stage would arrive Friday morning and would be built Friday afternoon. He just needed his helpers to clean and prep the Scout Hut toilets. The hall was to be used as a tearoom and, should it be needed, a first aid post. Now all he needed was good weather and the forecast was hopeful. Things were looking good.

When Gemma brought them in a coffee, he explained how it was all coming together and asked her if she would be attending. She didn't think so but offered to help clean the hall on the Friday afternoon. "Really, I thought you would have got enough cleaning, here. I can't pay you for that you know."

"No, I know," she laughed, "but the event is in a good cause. I'd like to help, and it would be good to get to know a few more people."

"I thought you were born here."

"Yes, but I moved away after I left school. I came back, as you know, to look after my mother. She can't get about as easily as she used to. Anyway, best get on." With that she rose, leaving James to continue processing more race applications and to ponder on his opening speech for the music festival.

* * *

The man's ankle was less swollen, but he still wheezed and talking was an effort. Angelica's books hadn't provided any further help. Nathan had got Lily a thermos flask and she had filled that with the inhalation so that the man could breathe from it, when she wasn't there to boil water for him. It wasn't as effective and the steam didn't last long, but it was something, and he seemed pleased with what she had done.

Using a blue plastic bowl from under the sink in the hut kitchen Lily gave the man some warm water and he did what he could to wash. He really needed a bath and a complete change of clothes. The children discussed this, trying to decide if either Alex or Mike would miss any of their clothes. Then they dismissed Alex's collection as being too large for the man, which left Nathan to solve the problem from his father's clothes. He really wasn't happy about that. Just going into his parent's bedroom would get him in trouble. The girls promised it would just be temporary, whilst they washed and dried the man's own clothes, but he felt pressured, and he really didn't like that.

Violet said quietly, "It will be alright, you'll work it out. Your dad won't miss his winter clothes."

Bottom lip prominent, he turned on his heel and stomped out of the room. Keeping its distance, the Catolith trailed behind. As Nathan opened the hut door, he stepped back and held it wide. His bottom lip retreated and formed a grimace. At his feet, a mini funeral procession passed into the hut. Three cats staggered in, each dragging a pigeon. Whoops-A-Daisy, bringing up the rear, struggling to control a still twitching bird. As the cortege passed, the Catolith sat reverently at Nathan's side.

The cats deposited their haul beside the man and headed out again. Lily went to the kitchen and switched on the oven, leaving the man sitting in the middle of an increasing heap of feathers. When the birds were plucked, and the oven heated up Lily placed the birds in the bottom of a baking tray with another upturned tray on top as a lid and put them in the oven.

Nathan had obviously had a think. He reappeared and announced triumphantly, that there were probably clothes at the charity shop. They could get them from there.

The girls looked at him as if he was stupid and exchanged a three-way, 'shall I tell him or will you' look, between them. As Lily and Tansy shrugged in exasperation Violet quietly explained that the charity shop would want money, and they didn't have any. "It is okay. We'll think of something," she said and rested her hand on his arm. He shrugged it off and stormed out again, slamming the door. When the room no longer resembled the inside of a snow globe,

Violet blew a feather off her top lip and plucked others from her T-shirt. "We need to think of another way."

As Tansy left to see to the donkeys, Lily nodded.

"I am going to find Nathan," said Violet.

With no further interactions between the girls imminent, the man lay down and shut his eyes. Left alone with the man Lily sat on the floor and waited for the pigeons to cook. Soon the man was snoring gently. She wondered why he was here. She knew he was here for a reason, the Catolith was proof of that, but she couldn't work out what. She just knew that she needed to make him better. Normally, in someone's presence she understood certain things about them, but with him, it was different. It was like he was hiding himself from her. He was right there in front of her, yet he had no more presence than the sack at his feet. It existed. She could see it. She had felt it. She had held and carried it, yet she had no idea what it contained. She knew Violet was puzzled too. They hadn't discussed it, but she knew. And, as with most things, answers would come, in time.

* * *

Emily was working her way through the housework, busying herself. What she wanted to do was go down to the cellar and pick up another marble. However, since she had obtained the books from the library and seen that what she had witnessed couldn't be explained as a dream and was historical fact, she was uncertain that she wanted to proceed. At first, she had been excited and eager to tell Alex and Louise. Then, when she had the opportunity, she chickened out. She just hadn't been able to find the words. The idea was too ridiculous and yet twice she had had the experiences, the second time 'verifiable' with the library book. The two memories belonged to the same woman, she was convinced. She had observed all of the episode with the mantrap. She, Emily, would have been sick at the sight of the boy's injury but, as Sarah, she had felt completely different. She hadn't felt revolted by the sight of the blood and the bone and the mangled flesh, just outraged. As Sarah, she had been in control and powerful. It was a rush just thinking about it. The memory had ended of its own accord, unlike the one with the ducking stool. Twice that memory had been interrupted. Perhaps she should see that one through to the end, after all, she knew that Sarah had lived through the threats that were there, as had her sisters. She really wanted to know what Sarah had said. Having run out of housework, she checked the time. Alex wouldn't be home for at least a couple of hours and the girls usually stayed out most of the day. She had time.

She pulled out the box and placed it on the cellar table once more, maintaining its orientation. She lifted the lid and took out the marble she knew to be the ducking stool one. She sat down and switched off her torch.

The church bells were ringing. It wasn't long since they had struck the hour. Four rings. She was sure. Now they were ringing again and continuously. Alarmed she looked in their direction. Something was wrong. She ran through the trees, branches whipping at her as she went, apples bouncing and scattering from her basket. Over the stile and through the woods, it was the quickest way. More trees, more branches. Leaving the path she dove into the undergrowth, her skirt hitched up, nettles stinging her ankles. She slid and stumbled, crashing into the church wall. Flinging the basket to one side she scrambled over. Dodging gravestones she ran round the side of the church, the bells deafening now, matching the thumping of her heart. Nearing the front of the building she could hear something else, something higher pitched and more strident than the bells – a woman was screaming...

At the front of the church, on the village green, a crowd had gathered. She elbowed her way through. Grunts and complaints. Swearing and the odd angry punch. She didn't care, she had to see. The woman was frantic now, screaming for help. There were taunts and cheers. Emerging from the throng she stood and stared. A make-shift wooden frame had been constructed which sat on the back of a cart. The cart had been backed into the pond. A long plank extended over the water. On the end was a seat. Tied to the seat, was the woman, just a young girl. Her long dress was ripped, her feet were bare, and her hair was in disarray. Tears streamed down her panicked face as she hiccupped each breath.

She looked on. A man was speaking, addressing the crowd, attempting to whip them up into a frenzy of fear.

"No!" she screamed at him, taking in the small group of strangers gathered around him. She had seen them all earlier in the week and knew who they were. These were the witchfinders, going from town to town, village to village, making their fortune and fame by picking on the innocent and exploiting the fear of the ignorant, whilst the wiser citizens kept their counsel, sensibly but guiltily protecting themselves with silence. "No," she yelled stepping forward. Hands grabbed at her dress, trying to pull her back from her folly, words of warning hissed in her ear. Ignoring them she pulled herself free and stepped forward.

The crowd grew silent as she raised her hand and pointed at the man, "No, that child is not a witch, and you know it. The only evil here is you!" She was glad that she had the pond between herself and the witchfinders. It gave her time. At a hand signal from the ringleader, two of them started to slowly make their way round the water, in a pincer movement. "How many 'so-called' witches have you found and murdered? How many? If they are as powerful as you claim, why do they not free themselves?" The two men were now halfway round the pond, the crowd of villagers backing out of their way. She kept her eyes on the witchfinder. "Why do they allow themselves to be captured and humiliated?"

"Because I am more powerful than they. I know how to contain their magic."

"How many," she repeated. "How many in Barnlees?"

"Twelve," he said smugly.

"See," she said, addressing the crowd. "He won't stop at this girl. He gets paid per witch. What kind of incentive is that to seek the truth? Which of you will be next? Which of your daughters, sisters, wives, mothers will be next. You know her, you know she isn't a witch." She was out of time. The two men grabbed her and dragged her forward. She struggled but, held firmly by each wrist, held taut between the men, she was unable to free herself. Two other men had now joined the first two and she was dragged towards the witchfinder who, at her capture had walked round the pond.

"Perhaps you are a witch," he said. He took hold of her face in his hand and roughly tilted her head back. Then he looked into her eyes. She looked defiantly back. He was strong, and now, she knew he was also heartless, selfish, and greedy. The crowd grew silent as he addressed them, "Yes, I see the signs. We have another witch here."

She stood as tall as she could and, heart pounding glared at him. In as strong a voice as she could muster, she appealed to the crowd, "As I said, he won't stop at just one victim."

Then two other women stepped forward. Two, identical to her. The witchfinder was initially surprised, but then he smiled. "Three witches! Grab them." There was a scuffle, and all three women were dragged in front of him. "Hold them, whilst we deal with this one on the stool."

"Someone stop him. Stop him now or he will murder her. You people are better than this. This village is better than this. We take care of our own." There was an uncomfortable shuffling in the crowd, but no-one moved to protect the girl. The witchfinder sensed he was winning.

"Are there any more witches amongst you?" He looked the crowd over and they all shrank back, looking from him to the girl on the stool to the triplets. It was clear to Sarah, that they were all scared. It was clear too that the crowd were waiting for the triplets to act.

"NO," she yelled, trembling, "YOU have to act, YOU have to do something, YOU have to stand up for yourselves."

"Dunk her!"

"No," screamed Sarah.

Then, as one of the witchfinder's men climbed onto the back of the cart and reached to release the stool, he suddenly fell on his side as the cart moved under him. He rolled off the cart into the pond. As he floundered in the water and splashed his way muddily to the water's edge, the cart continued *out of the water, the horse attached to it straining against the pull of the mud on its wheels.*

"Ha, they have bewitched the horse!"

"No, they haven't," said a deep sonorous voice. "I took the horse and moved the cart. This... stops... now." Out of the crowd, stepped the blacksmith, a giant of a man. He stepped forward and grabbed the witchfinder by the scruff of his neck and threw him in the water. Then he stepped in front of the men holding Sarah and her sisters. "Release them or I'll break your necks." It didn't take long. The hands holding her melted away and Sarah breathed a sigh of relief. As someone freed the girl from the ducking stool, she looked at Edith and Mary. They looked knowingly back.

The scene disappeared and Emily found herself in the dark. She was shaken. The emotions Sarah had gone through she had experienced. Yet Sarah hadn't crumbled. She had been terrified yet she stood her ground in defence of the girl when all the crowd around her had failed to act, and she had risked sacrificing herself in the process, as had Edith and Mary. What was the saying – When good people do nothing, evil prospers.

CHAPTER THIRTEEN

L ily was relieved. The man's breathing was easier, and he seemed a little brighter. His foot was less swollen, and she hoped that in a day or two he would be able to get his boot on again. Whilst the water heated for his inhalation, she cleared away the remains of the pigeons and gave him his breakfast.

Nathan, after his breakfast at Wishing Well Cottage, had gone his own way as soon as they had left the house. Despite Violet's attempt to appease him he was still angry with them. She had wanted to follow him, but Tansy had said to leave him be, he'd get over it. With Tansy off seeing to the donkeys, Violet followed Lily into the scout hut. Now, she stood and stared at the man again, still unable to get anything from him. He smiled back, apparently aware of her discomfort.

When he had finished eating, Lily moved his breakfast things to one side and knelt in front of him. She held out some towels and he took them from her and spread them on his lap, and then she placed the inhalation bowl on top. She covered his head with another towel, and he arranged the ends over the bowl. As he took in the steam, he coughed a couple of times. Lily was pleased. The coughs were less ragged than before. Her inhalations were working.

When he had done, Lily took the bowl to the kitchen to empty the contents, leaving Violet alone with the man. She stood and watched him, and he smiled back. Then he reached behind him and pulled out his canvas sack. He untied the top and rummaged inside, pulling out its contents, one at a time. The first item to emerge was a battered wooden mallet. It was chunky and solid looking, its head rounded, compacted, and well used. The second item was a lump of metal with a flat but sharp end, which was shiny and also appeared to be well used. More, but smaller versions of this were laid out on the floor. Finally, an oblong wooden slab was taken out. This too was well worn, shiny and battered. Having laid them all out, he put them, one by one, back into the sack, which he placed back behind him, just as Lily returned. Was this deliberate? Was he deliberately showing Violet what he had, or just checking his belongings and it was co-incidence that he finished as Lily returned?

"So," said Lily, "is there anything that you need? Anything we can do for you?"

The man shook his head and smiled at the girls. The Catolith did a circuit of the room and followed them out.

* * *

Nathan wasn't happy. He was annoyed with the triplets, and he was annoyed with himself. It wasn't fair. Why were they expecting him to get the clothes? Why couldn't they do it? He wandered round the side of the scout hut. Tansy was busy feeding the donkeys. He watched for a bit, until she looked up and looked about her, as if she was aware she was being watched. He stood perfectly still, hidden by bushes. When she stopped looking in his direction he backed away into the undergrowth and moved round to the side of the hut where he had a view of the front door. Lily and Violet, he knew were in there, doing their 'nursey' bit! They would do it, he knew. They would make the man better. Who was he anyway? Why were they bothering when the whole village, well some of them, were wanting him gone? Nathan needed to do something.

A movement in the bushes, caused him to look. It was Whoops-a-Daisy, and Marigold. Then Spider appeared. Nathan was surprised. The cats were usually where the girls were. He looked about him but, apart from the cats he was alone. He played with the cats for a while and then he got an idea. Yes, there was something he could do. Stealthily, so as not to be seen by the girls, should they come out of the hut, he made his way back to the village and home.

* * *

Jon was constructing some shelving units and trying them in different locations in the shop. It was taking him longer than he expected, chiefly because other Ark Aid tenants kept popping in to say hello. He really wanted to get on, but then willing hands had helped him move things around, which would have been much harder on his own, and he was grateful. He also hoped that he was making friends.

At some point he would get an electrician to put ceiling lights in at strategic points to spotlight his wares, but for now he would use strings of fairy lights. Once he had arranged his shelving units, he set about prepping the side and back wall. Here he intended attaching metal racks from which he could hang his wall clocks. He had specifically chosen the racks to match the brickwork and when he had held them up as a trial, he had been pleased with how they blended in. Now he just had to attach them and ensure that they were secure enough to support his precious clocks.

The counter had been left in situ by the previous tenant and was actually positioned where he wanted it and was wired up for a till and computer, and there was a phone point. Hopefully he could get it all up and running by the weekend. He really wanted to open for

Saturday but ideally Friday so that he could get used to everything, ready for the hoped-for 'rush' on Saturday. Louise had told him all about the Crag Race and the music and beer festival to follow, and was encouraging him to open for that. The rest of the tenants she had said would be opening late to take advantage of it, and he planned to do the same.

He bought himself a coffee and, when he introduced himself to the lady at What Sup, he was given a complimentary cake.

* * *

Emily was busily reading the two books she had obtained from the library and comparing their contents with what she was finding online. She had been a little disappointed when she had realised that the report of the ducking stool incident hadn't tallied with exactly what she had witnessed. When she thought about it, she had realised that although Sarah had made a great speech and her bravery was unquestioned, what she had said hadn't particularly rallied the villagers to her aid. It was the intervention of the blacksmith, that had saved the day. Maybe her words had caused him to act, but Emily didn't think so.

She read the passage from the book again. Maybe it was what Sarah had said later, that had persuaded them. The book did say that the witchfinders had returned and the villagers sent them away. Emily wondered if there was a memory of that.

Further reading led her to information about the Lancashire Witch trials and the subsequent executions on 20th August 1612 at Lancaster Castle. Sarah had stood up to the witchfinders in 1622, only 10 years after the executions. She and the villagers would have been well aware of the risk she was taking. Both men and women had been accused and executed. So, the blacksmith had been taking a risk too. She smiled, certain that Alex would stand up for her if the occasion arose. He would certainly protect his little girls. Was the 1600's blacksmith sticking up for Sarah and her sisters or was he just doing what was right? Did the blacksmith have a liking for one of the triplets? What she had seen of Sarah's sisters, she could see that they were good looking girls. However, he could well have been a relative. Perhaps she needed to do some more research. She really wished she had paid more attention to the blacksmith. She couldn't even remember what he looked like, just that he was very well built, bigger even than Alex.

The doorbell rang and she reluctantly took herself away from her investigations. It was her grocery delivery. She stood back whilst it was stacked in the hall, thanked the driver, and shut the door. Several trips later she had it all in the kitchen and she began sorting it out and putting it away. She stared at the shelf in the larder. She was sure she had more tins of beans than that. She shrugged and continued stacking. Then she went to fill up the fruit bowl. All that was in it was a lemon. She really must have a word with Louise. Nathan couldn't keep helping himself to all her fruit.

When Lily and Violet came home, mid-morning, Emily was busy at her sewing machine sewing triangles.

"What are you doing?" asked Lily.

"I am making bunting for the music festival." She picked up a string that she had finished and showed them. "They will hang on the stage, like this," and she held up a section.

Lily looked at it and said, "Why?"

"Because they will look pretty," said Emily.

Violet took hold of a flag and fingered it. "The material is pretty," she said.

"Where is Tansy?" asked Emily.

"She is with the donkeys," said Lily.

* * *

James was eagerly explaining to Gemma about how the stage would be set up and the order in which the bands would appear. She listened attentively, amused but pleased by his enthusiasm. He then read her his opening speech, keen to know her opinion. She laughed encouragingly at his jokes. He was pleased, glad that she understood them. She even made the odd helpful remark, which he accepted, not as criticism but as a useful addition, and which he thought his audience would appreciate. She had a keen sense of humour, and he was finding, understood timing. It made him smile. As he got on with his work he could hear her singing, the sound moving from room to room, occasionally drowned out by the vacuum.

Gemma was enjoying her new job, and she liked her new boss. He was a curious mix of the spiritual and the practical. She had been uncertain about taking the job, not sure that she would fit in, not sure that she would be welcome. She was a little worried about the cleaning that she had volunteered to do at the scout hut on Friday. She had surprised herself when she had offered her time. It was a spur of the moment thing, wanting to please him. Still, there wouldn't be that many people around and, as she had said, maybe she would make some friends. When she wasn't here her mother took up most of her time and it wasn't easy getting out and mixing.

* * *

Tansy was a little puzzled. Some folded tables had appeared against the side of the donkeys' stables. Someone had been in their field. Did her father know? She counted them. There were 10 of them. She finished feeding the donkeys and cleaned out the stables. Then she topped up the water trough. It took a while to fill as the donkeys were getting through more water than normal and the level was low. Whilst she waited, she stared around the field. It was mostly flat and surrounded by a dry-stone wall. It ran most of the way along the back of the high street properties, beyond her father's forge and The Ark Aid yard. The far end was marked by a row of sycamore trees and the back wall was mostly hidden by hawthorn bushes. In the centre, if you knew where to look, was a five-barred gate leading to a lower field. This second field sloped down to, and was bounded by, a stream that skirted the edge of the village. At the scout hut end of the field a mixture of sycamores and oaks provided shade, for which the donkeys were currently thankful. Having scanned the field her eyes came to rest once again, on the tables. The more she looked at them, the more she felt uneasy. Their presence wasn't good. Once the trough was full, she coiled up the hose and left it hanging over the tap. Then she went for a closer look at the tables. The feeling grew stronger. Their being there didn't bode well.

Donkey duties complete, she let herself into the scout hut, and did a quick tour. She couldn't see anything out of place. It didn't look as if anyone other than the triplets and Nathan had been in there. She went to check on the man. He appeared to be sleeping, but she knew he wasn't. Curious as to why he would pretend she said, "Hello. Good morning."

Slowly he roused himself, but she knew his sleepiness was faked. He was wary of her, which was odd. After all, she was just a little girl. He smiled. She asked him if there was anything he needed. He just shook his head.

"Well," said Tansy, "Lily will be along later." With that she left him.

Outside the hut she was surprised to hear pigeons, not unusual in itself, but lots of them. The noise was coming from round the side of the building. Curious, she headed in their direction. As she grew closer, she could also hear an intermittent twang and what sounded like the thwack of a pebble. This disturbed the birds more and set them to flight, but not for long. Wings flapped and beat, and the birds settled again, their squawks turning to coos. Sneaking through the trees to the clearing, that she knew was in there beyond the scout hut, she saw a flock of pigeons circling and settling on the ground. Scattered in their midst were chunks of bread that looked rather like the sort of bits left on the plates in The Three Wells beer garden. The twang came again, and a pebble hit the ground just missing one of the pigeons. As they soared again, she stepped into the clearing. There, with a catapult in his hands, was Nathan. Furious, she marched towards him. Seeing the look on her face he stepped backwards and lowered the catapult. In one swift movement she snatched it from his hand. Then, she held it by its handle, upside down, and smashed the fork part into the ground. There was a splintering sound, and the catapult broke in two. She stood and thrust the remains at Nathan's chest. Reflexively, he grabbed hold of it. She stood on tiptoe, so that their heights matched, and glared at him, "Don't ever aim at a bird again." Then, stingingly she added, "You might accidentally hit one!"

As she walked away, Nathan rallied and blurted, "It's okay if the cat's kill pigeons for him."

"You... aren't... a cat! He has enough food. What he needs is clothes."

She left him standing glaring after her and set off to the forge to see if her father knew about the tables.

Nathan, even more miserable than he had been before, set off home. He knew he wouldn't be able to get in until one of his parents returned from work, but he didn't know where else to go. He rounded the pub beer garden, scraping the remains of his catapult along the stone wall. None of the few people in the beer garden paid him any attention. He continued along the high street, kicking whatever came in reach of his feet. He had just crossed over the road and was making his way across the village green when he heard a bicycle bell ringing. He stopped and looked round. It was Gemma, leaving the vicarage. She stopped her bike alongside him.

"Hi, Nathan. What have you got there?"

pointing at the broken catapult he was swinging dangerously, by its elastic.

He gathered it up and stuffed it in his pocket, struggling to get all the elastic to stay put.

"Are you alright?"

He said nothing, just stared at his feet.

Gemma bumped her bike up the kerb and leant it against one of the benches on the green. She appraised him. This wasn't the Nathan she was coming to know, and this was the first time she had seen him without the triplets. He was obviously upset, and she didn't think it was purely to do with the catapult which was obviously broken. Leaving her bike, she searched the ground and picked up a branch. She tested it. It wasn't too dry. She snapped off what she didn't want and handed the remains to Nathan.

"If you keep an eye on my bike for me, I'll get some elastic. Whilst I'm gone, peel off the bark, so it is smooth."

As he stared after her she headed into the store. Shortly, she returned with a packet of thick rubber bands. "Wow, you've done a great job of peeling. That looks really good. Nice and smooth. Right let's turn it into a catapult." She took three of the large rubber bands and looped them together. Then she handed them to Nathan and watched as he attached an end to each of the two prongs of wood. Nathan gave it a test stretch. It felt good. If anything, it was stronger than the old one.

"A bit of advice. You need to practice to 'get your eye in'. Make sure that there isn't anything behind your target that could get damaged, or worse, injured. Keep aiming at one thing and adjust your aim and power until you can hit it consistently. Then change the target and distance. That is the way to get good. Practice, practice, practice."

As she got back on her bike, Nathan was skipping down the road, heading for his back garden where he could practice in private. She smiled to herself, pleased that she had been able to help him. He was a good lad. It was a shame that there weren't any boys his own age to play with.

* * *

At the forge, Tansy was impatiently waiting for her father to break off what he was doing and come talk to her. She stood in the doorway, not crossing the invisible line the girls had strict instructions not to cross; they weren't allowed in the workspace. At first, Alex didn't notice her. Then, as he turned to swap one of his tools, he caught sight of her silhouetted in the doorway. He would have nodded and carried on working until a suitable break point, but there was something about her posture that caused him to put down what he was working on.

Tansy was agitated and the feeling had grown. The tables by the scout hut weren't good and she needed to know why. She told him someone must have been in the field and asked him if he knew about it.

"Yes, they are for the music festival..."

Tansy looked puzzled. Then Alex realised that although he and Emily had talked about it, they had talked over and around the children, never directly to them. Tansy clearly had no idea.

"We are going to have to move the donkeys down to the lower field so that they are away from the noise. I am going to need your help. We will move them on Thursday so that the field is empty for Friday when the stage will be built." Alex stopped. Tansy's eyes were wide. "They will be fine down in the lower field. There are trees for them to shelter under and plenty of water. We can move them back on Tuesday, after the stage goes again.

"What are the tables for?"

"Oh, they are for serving tea and cakes in the scout hut. You must have seen the bunting your mum is making to decorate the stage." He turned away and picked up some pliers, "Anyway, we can talk more about it later. I need to get on." He smiled back at Tansy, but the doorway was empty.

CHAPTER FOURTEEN

W hen Nathan didn't appear for lunch Emily became concerned. Normally he would turn up with the triplets, just after midday and, as of the last week or so, keen for something to eat. Unusually, she had to call the girls down from upstairs, and she'd had to go most of the way up, calling for them, before they responded. When she asked them where Nathan was, they didn't know. Lily and Violet expressed puzzlement but Tansy, Emily noticed, offered nothing.

"Tansy, do you know where he is?"

"Probably sulking!"

"Oh?" Emily waited.

"His catapult is broken."

"How come?"

Tansy stared her mother in the face and said, "It wasn't strong enough." Then she added defiantly, "Just like him."

Violet ran from the room, then the front door could be heard opening and closing. Before Emily could react, Tansy and Lily said in unison,

"What's for lunch?"

* * *

Nathan was angry again. After Gemma had left him, he had headed home but before he got there, he had bumped into Mr Swire who had reminded him that he had some jumble. Nathan had been delighted. He could get clothes. Then Mr Swire had insisted that he bring his girl friends with him. Now he was feeling useless again. He couldn't even get jumble without the triplets help. He picked up a chipping from the path and took aim at the clothesline post. He fired. The chipping sailed straight by. He picked up another chipping and aimed again. He hit the post. Stunned, he tried again. The stone sailed straight past, but it wasn't far off. He was just re-loading when his mother appeared.

"There you are. You've got everyone worried. Auntie Emily phoned. I've had to leave work to find you. What are you doing?"

Sulkily he took aim, "This," and fired. He hit the post. "I did it!"

Louise smiled and watched, as he took aim again, his mood a bit brighter. He hit it again.

"I did it again. She told me what to do. It works."

Louise had been about to tell him off, but she didn't. This was obviously an important achievement for him. "Who... is she?"

"Gemma, the vicar's housekeeper. She's really

nice. She said to make sure there is nothing behind that can get damaged. So, you don't need to worry. I am not going to break anything."

Just then, a breathless Violet appeared. "Nathan," she said quietly, "I'm so glad you are alright."

Leaving instructions for Nathan to go with Violet to Wishing Wells and get some lunch, Louise headed back to the estate agents.

With his mother gone he took aim once more. To his astonishment he hit the post again. Violet clapped and Nathan was a happy boy. As the two of them headed to Wishing Wells he asked Violet if she would go with him to Mr Swire's. Hopefully one triplet would do. She said yes.

* * *

After lunch, and with the house to herself again, Emily went down to the cellar. She took out the box of 1600s marbles and opened it. Assuming that they were stored in chronological order she took out the next marble along from 'the ducking stool' one. She sat herself down and switched off her torch. Rapidly light appeared in the darkness, but not much.

She was cold. She was on her side, curled into a ball. Her fingers and most of her feet were numb. She moved slightly. Bedding was pinning her down. She sat up, cast the bedding aside, and reached for her shawl. She wrapped it round her shoulders and felt with her feet for her boots. The air felt icy as she breathed. Something had woken her. She went to the window and tried to peer out. Using a fingernail to pick off a thin sheet of ice that had formed at the edges of the pane, she looked down. There was movement by the well. There were people in the garden. She ran for the stairs and hurried down. Edith was ahead of her, flinging open the back door. Stepping out, an acrid smell assaulted her nostrils. Something was on fire. She looked around. The cottage next door had fierce flames soaring from its thatch. Large blistering pieces of straw fell from the sky, spitting and dying as they hit the snowy ground. She looked up at Wishing Well's roof. Thankfully, a huge blanket of snow covered it, even the area around the chimney stack, which usually melted. Edith thrust a bucket into her hands, and she joined the queue at the well.

With a full bucket she ran as quickly as she could out of Wishing Well Cottage garden. In the street, it seemed the whole village had turned up. A human chain lead from the pond, passing bucket after bucket of water to the cottage next door. She staggered along. Water slopped into her boots. She slowed down and the water settled. It was difficult to see where to put her feet, the glow from the cottage blinding her. She couldn't look away; it was too fantastical and horrifying. She moved along the path, following the person ahead. The bucket was taken from her and an empty one put in her hands. She was being shouted at... to go and get more water. She turned and ran, her right foot squelching in her boot. Two more trips and she found that people were standing back, and just watching: the heat too intense to get near with the water. She watched too. There was a gigantic 'sigh' and the cottage roof caved in. A hot blast. Flames shot from the windows. Blazing debris flew into the air. The crowd scattered as it fell to earth. The fire withdrew, contained by the stone walls of the building, briefly smothered by the fallen roof. A hungry crackle, and it snarled, sucking air through the window holes. Fuelled by the scattered, unburnt thatch, it roared, expelling singeing heat and monstrous power.

There was nothing anyone could now do, but let it burn. She looked around, at last thinking about Jack and Agnes. Where were they? Surely, they couldn't be inside. No, surely not. Over on the green, a small group was gathered: other people hung about on the fringes. Edith and Mary were there. She made her way over. Such relief. In the centre were her neighbours, two shrunken figures, wrapped in blankets.

Emily switched on her torch and found that she was sweating, and her throat was dry. Unsteadily she got to her feet and returned the marble to its slot. She closed the box and put it back in the alcove. So, there had been another cottage next door, in the space where the vicarage now stood, and Wishing Well Cottage had been thatched at one time. She wondered when that had changed and whether it was done because of the fire next door. She had so many questions to which she was unlikely to get answers. She headed for the stairs, torch in hand, and realised that she could still smell and taste the smoke. Was it just a lingering memory or was it in her hair? Back in the kitchen she looked in a mirror. She didn't look any different. As she made herself a cup of tea the smell faded and then she realised that it had gone.

* * *

Nathan and Violet walked down the high street together. Lunch had been a trauma for Nathan, but he got through it, mostly because by the time he and Violet arrived Tansy had eaten. She was playing in the corner of the kitchen, intent on ignoring him, which suited him just fine. Violet had spoken to Lily and so she didn't comment when Violet and Nathan left together.

As they walked up Mr Swire's path, dragging Nathan's go-cart, Violet was amazed by the flowers growing there. The whole path was lined with lavender, which was in flower, and backed by purple bearded iris. The smell was wonderful and the colours magical. Nathan had to hurry her along. When they reached the door, it opened, and Mr Swire beckoned them in.

"So, young Nathan you brought the beautiful Violet with you."

Violet was surprised that he knew which of the triplets she was. Most people, who didn't talk to them on a daily basis, couldn't tell them apart.

"Can I get you a drink and a piece of cake?"

"No thank you, Mr Swire," said Violet.

"Yes, please," said Nathan.

Mr Swire picked up two glasses and poured out some orange juice from a carton. Then he opened a can of lemonade and topped up the two glasses. He picked up one and handed it to Nathan. Then he picked up the other.

"Are you sure you don't want one, Violet?" She shook her head. So, he proceeded to drink it.

"Well, I have a heap of clothes in the front room, for your donkeys," he said with a chuckle. Would your donkeys be wanting some shoes too?"

Nathan and Violet exchanged glances, then gave a hesitant nod. As Mr Swire led the way into the front room Violet was fairly certain that he knew exactly what they wanted the clothes for. If that was so, why was he helping them?

As they loaded three bags of clothes onto Nathan's go-cart Mr Swire said, "I guess the charity shop can make good use of the clothes you don't use. Violet, your great great great aunts would be proud of you lass, and you too young Nathan. And, Nathan, you take very good care of this special little lady."

Violet got hold of the cart handle, but Nathan didn't budge. He stood, looking uncomfortably at Mr Swire, "What about the cake?"

Violet looked aghast.

Mr Swire hid a smile, "You are quite right young sir. I did offer you cake. Wait here." He disappeared into the house. Nathan waited. When Mr Swire returned, he was carrying two pieces of cake. One he handed to Violet, "Cake is always handy, for guests."

* * *

That evening Alex kissed Emily goodbye and headed round to the vicarage for a Crag Race meeting. James was organising his helpers and finalising the details. The room was nearly full when Alex arrived. He chatted to a few people and found himself a seat. Talk of the crag and the woods reminded some, of the previous week's hunt for the tramp. The sweep through the woods had obviously scared him away, as he hadn't been seen since. There was laughter and some approval. Alex kept his thoughts to himself. Another two people arrived, followed by Mike. James started the meeting. He thanked everyone for coming and volunteering to give their time. The event was going to be bigger this year because of the festival, and he hoped they would raise even more money than last time for St Peter's Young Disabled Unit. He split his helpers into those who were taking part in the race and those who weren't. The latter group would help marshal the race. Everyone would be given roles for the music and beer festival and the cake stall.

Members of his running club took charge of the marshals, explaining with the help of a large map of the village and crag where each marshal was to be positioned and what they were expected to do. Various people were put in charge of the car parking team, festival marshals, and the tea and cakes volunteers. Finally, there would be a meeting at The Three Wells on Thursday night for those helping Richard, the publican, with the beer.

The meeting over, Alex and Mike made a quick exit and headed over to The Three Wells. They perched themselves on stools at the bar and were soon sipping contentedly on a pint each.

"So," said Alex, "how much training have you done for the race?"

"Training!" said Mike.

"What, you haven't done any?"

Mike shrugged, "I don't expect to win. So, what is the point?"

"So that you can make it all the way round without injuring yourself, for a start."

Mike plonked his empty glass on the bar and gestured to one of the bar staff that he would like another. "It is just a bit of fun. So long as I'm not beaten by Nathan, I don't care."

Over, at the other end of the room, raucous laughter could be heard. A conversation, which was getting easier to hear because more people were stopping talking to listen, drew their attention. Mr Swire, surrounded by a group of highly pancaked elderly ladies and an almost visible haze of 'Lily of the Valley', was holding forth, drink in hand, and obviously loving the growing attention.

"She was what!" said someone.

"She were t'star turn at Nina Norton's, back in't 70's," said Mr Swire.

"Who's Nina Norton?"

"You not 'erd o' Nina Norton's? You lot know nowt. That place were world famous in these parts. Nina Norton's knocking shop, o'er at Nether Tanning." He paused, a grin on his face. "Grand times could be 'ad there, lads, back in the day. Reight educational." Looking round at his female companions he added, "So I 'eard."

Alex and Mike exchanged glances. "Are we at last learning why he is so popular with the ladies?" said Alex. "Oh, to be a graduate of Nina Norton's Knockin' Shop."

CHAPTER FIFTEEN

L ily was pleased. The man's chest was much better, and his swollen ankle was almost normal size. She gave him breakfast and another inhalation and then explained to him that they were going to have to move him again. First, though, they needed to make him presentable. She disappeared to the kitchen, leaving Tansy and Violet in attendance. Tansy soon got bored and went off to see the donkeys and also to keep an eye out in case anyone should approach the hut. When Lily came back, she was carrying the basin, once again filled with hot water. From a bag she produced a towel, a can of shaving foam, a pair of scissors and a razor blade. Then she pulled out a big mirror and held it up so that he could see himself. He looked, but made no attempt to start shaving. Exasperated, she picked up the scissors and, meeting no resistance, started trimming his beard. Having removed the bulk of his facial hair she handed him the can of shaving foam. He took it and inspected it but didn't appear to know what it was.

"It is for shaving. See..." and she squirted some onto her hands, dunked them in the water and then rubbed them together. The gel foamed massively. She had used far too much. He continued to stare at her and so, her hands covered in dripping dollops of lather, she went ahead and smothered his lower face with it and, in the process, most of his chest. She washed off her hands in the water and attempted to scoop up the excess from his clothes and face. When she had reduced the mess, she held out the razor to him. He still made no move to shave himself, so she started to shave him, dunking the razor in the water to clean off the foam and facial hair.

Violet stood and watched all this. She was both amused and fascinated, both by her sister's boldness and the man's lack of participation. She watched him but she could tell nothing of him. He was completely closed off to her, like looking at a picture not a person. Throughout the shave he kept his eyes on Violet and she stared back. Even as Lily tilted his head from side to side and held up his nose to shave his upper lip, his eyes never left Violet.

Just as Lily was finishing the shave, and wondering how she was going to get the man's hair washed, Nathan appeared. He triumphantly dumped a black plastic bin bag on the floor and then opened the top. Inside was a selection of men's clothes, which he proceeded to hold up one by one for inspection. Violet smiled at him. He had obviously been sorting through what Mr Swire had given, as the collection was much reduced. Nathan wouldn't have been able to carry them all otherwise. She hadn't said anything to the others about the visit to Mr Swire, happy for them to think Nathan had done it on his own. She glanced back at the man, who was looking at Nathan. She felt a connection, briefly, before he returned his gaze to her. He knew. He knew she had helped Nathan but said nothing. Then, it was over, the link broken. He was a 'photograph' again.

Lily was delighted. "Wow, Nathan, this is brilliant. Well done." She rapidly hunted through the collection, sorting and choosing. Soon she had put an outfit together.

"He's bleeding," blurted Nathan, pointing at the man's neck.

Lily looked and froze, her eyes wide. A red trickle was dribbling down from the man's Adam's apple. She grabbed a towel, then looked at it. It was one of her mother's peach towels. She put it down and ran to the kitchen, grabbed a strip of blue paper roll, and returned. As she mopped and dabbed, the man sat impassively. More blood was now oozing from below his left ear.

"Stick some tissue on it," said Nathan. "Dad sticks tissue on when he cuts himself." He knelt and took the blue roll from Lily. He tore off a corner and then two tiny patches. He dabbed the smaller wound and placed a patch on it. A small blob of red appeared, but the tissue stayed put. Then he dabbed and patched the cut on the man's Adam's apple. The patch was rapidly saturated. Nathan added another patch on top. It too became soaked.

"Press it, til the bleeding stops," said Lily.

Nathan pressed. The man coughed, alarmingly. Nathan let go. The neck oozed. Nathan slapped the tissue back in place. After some trial and error, he was able to apply pressure and still allow the man to breathe. "It needs a plaster," said Nathan.

Lily disappeared to the kitchen and returned with a green plastic box with a white cross on it. She opened it and pulled out a plaster. She peeled off the backing and, after Nathan had given the wound another dab, she applied it. They waited. It seemed to be working. Yes.

"Right," she told the man, "You need to wash, all over, and put these on. We'll be back soon to move you somewhere else."

They left him and went out into the hall. "Where are we going to move him to?" asked Violet.

"The cellar," said Lily. "No-one ever goes in there. If we put him down the far end, he won't be seen if someone does."

Violet looked uncertain. Nathan was relieved; it would be nothing to do with him.

* * *

At the vicarage, James was sorting out the items each of his Crag Race volunteers would need in their different roles and placing them in piles on his dining room table and chairs and, not having enough room for it all, the floor. He had heard the kettle and expected that shortly Gemma would appear with a cuppa for them both. It hadn't taken long to establish this routine and he was happy that she too appeared to like the arrangement.

"Oh, there you are. You've been busy," she said surveying the room. "Got time for a break?" She held up two mugs and gestured to his study, there being nowhere to sit in the current room.

He held open the door, which had slowly closed itself, and took one of the mugs off her. Their hands touched briefly, shocking them both. Clutching her mug she led the way to the study, an awkward silence between them.

When they were settled in the study, she cleared her throat and asked him how the preparations were going. They were going well. He was just glad that he didn't have any responsibility for the beer part of the festival, happy to leave all that to Richard and his band of very willing helpers.

"I've been thinking," she said, "and you may have got it sorted, and I just haven't noticed, but have you thought about the clear up, afterwards?

Bin bags and the like, and people to help?"

James hadn't. The previous year, there had just been the race. He now realised that the villagers wouldn't be very happy if Much Meddling was buried in litter, as it was very likely to be. He needed to ensure that any mess was cleared up.

"Would you like me to be in charge of that?" she said.

James could have kissed her. A thought which caused him to turn slightly pink. "Yes, yes, please. Just let me know what you need."

"Okay. I'll have a think. The village green and the field will probably need clearing. So, I will need some volunteers. We can do the green once the race is over and everyone heads round to the festival. Then probably we will need to do the field on Sunday. Lots of bin bags and ideally some of those hand grabbers for picking up litter. I don't know where you'd get those from," she said. "Perhaps we could get some of the children involved. They will probably enjoy using the hand-grabbers if I make a bit of a competition out of it. Right, I'd better get on." She took their mugs and left James to go back to the dining room and continue putting his volunteer packs together.

* * *

As she folded and pinned ribbon along the top of her bunting triangles, Emily was lost in thought. She desperately tried to remember the detail from the memories she had witnessed. Whilst she was experiencing them everything was bright and clear. Now, her recall was shockingly lacking. As Sarah, she paid little heed to her surroundings. Sarah focussed purely on her present events. What to Sarah was familiar and dismissible, to Emily was fascinating but intangible. She wanted to examine the items in Sarah's Wishing Well Cottage, to stand on the village green and look round at the surrounding buildings, look at the people and what they were wearing, but she couldn't. Thinking of the ducking stool memory, parts of which she had witnessed three times, she couldn't visualise any of the detail, her whole attention had been on the events. At the time, she had been Sarah and Sarah was only interested in finding out who was screaming and why. The ducking stool, however, was different. Sarah had looked at that, and in detail, taking in the structure of it, working out what it was and how it operated. From that memory, Emily could have drawn it, and the girl...Emily would never forget her face. That face, that young, terrified face, would haunt her.

"Ow...uh!" Emily examined her left index finger. Blood oozed out of the tip of it. She put down the offending pin and sucked her finger. Then she examined the material and saw that two of the triangles and part of the ribbon had red smudges. Finger in mouth she headed through to the kitchen and found a plaster. Life saved, she returned to her sewing and threw the two offending triangles in the bin. Then, gathering up the bunting she took it to the sink and ran the bloody bit of ribbon under the cold tap. With a bit of work, she managed to rid it of her blood. Using the iron, she got it as dry as she could, decided that she had done with sewing for the moment and went and put the kettle on. Snokettee rubbed round her ankles. Tea made, Emily sat in a chair by the hearth and Snokettee settled on her lap. As she caressed the cat's ears she wondered if Sarah had a cat. She hadn't seen one in the memories, but she felt certain that she would have had. Snokettee began to purr. Wishing Well Cottage, without a cat, just didn't seem right.

* * *

The man was dressed. He was standing but leaning against the wall. The children inspected him. The floral shirt clung to his skinny frame; its material strangely crinkly and the collar unusually pointed. His trousers were strangely wide at the bottom. Still, the different shades of purple and pink in the shirt went well with the deep purple check of the trousers. The girls liked what they saw. Nathan thought he looked a bit like a clown and said so. He had had difficulty finding clothes that didn't look too worn, amongst the collection from Mr Swire and he hadn't thought about putting the items together to form an outfit. Colours hadn't played any part in Nathan's sorting. The man however, seemed quite happy with his appearance. Although, the surreptitious pull at his groin did suggest that he was finding the trousers a bit tight.

Lily thrust a walking stick at him, which she had thought to bring from the collection in the stand by their front door, and encouraged him to follow her through to the kitchen. He hobbled after her. Once there, she turned on the mixer tap over the sink, and held her hand under the water. When she was satisfied with the temperature, she told him to stick his head under it. He was about to do so when she stopped him and turned off the water. She ran out of the room and returned with the scissors. He looked slightly alarmed so she reassured him that she would just cut out the matted bits so he could comb it. Looking dubious, he sat on the chair she indicated, and waited whilst she wrapped a towel round his neck. Then she stood back, scissors held open in the air, and scrutinised his head. His hair was a real mess. Nathan and Violet observed from a distance, looks of disgust on their faces. A number of dreadlocks had formed amongst the ecosystem that was his scalp. She hesitantly picked up the tip of the largest and held it vertical, deciding how much of it to cut off, in order to leave a comb-able amount behind. She stuck the tip of the scissors through part of the lock and snipped. She couldn't cut it all in one go, the scissors weren't big or strong enough. Once cut there was roughly 2-3 inches left. She moved on to the next one, gradually working her way over his head. When all the matted bits were removed, she stood back and looked. Nathan raised an eyebrow and Violet frowned. Next, Lily took a comb and, with a bit of effort, managed to comb through what was left.

"It would be better if you cut off the straggly bits," said Nathan, and Violet nodded.

The man ran his hands through his hair as Lily stood expectantly in front of him, scissors held aloft. One at a time, he looked at each of the children, studying their expressions. Then he nodded. Lily beamed and went to work. As she hacked, Nathan and Violet offered suggestions and encouragement. Occasionally they all stood back and walked round him, various expressions on their faces. Finally, all three were happy.

There was a bang and click from the front of the hall, then Tansy burst in. She stopped short at sight of the man, and said, "What have you done to him?" Then, she collected herself, "We've got to leave, right now. Gather everything. Quick, Nathan, Violet, you check the other room. Lily, clean up that mess. We've got to go out the side door, there are people arriving at the front." She took the man by the arm and hurried him back into the main hall and over to the side door. She pulled back the bolt and pushed the door open.

Outside, the man fell full length. Nathan arrived and hurled bedding and other items out onto the floor then disappeared back inside. Then Violet appeared with the clothing bag and inhalation things. Lily, covered in the man's hair, came out with an armful of towels, threw them down and ran back inside followed by Violet. Tansy hauled the man to his feet and dragged him into the trees out of sight. Then she set about gathering up the items the others had thrown on the ground. The others reappeared clutching the last few items. From the front entrance could be heard half a dozen women's voices and the distinct sound of a key in the lock. Tansy carefully pushed the side door closed and held it to.

"Nathan, hold this. I will go and bolt it from the other side."

"They will see you," said Nathan.

"So, I'll do it when they aren't looking. You two hide everything in the trees."

She set off round the back of the hut so she could approach the women from the donkey field side. She followed them into the hall, saying brightly, "Hello, what are you doing?"

"Oh, hello. Which one are you?"

"I am Tansy," she said, smiling sweetly, "I was just checking on the donkeys. What are you ladies here for?"

"We are here to see what needs doing, ahead of the music festival. We are going to serve tea and cakes in here."

Tansy followed the women through to the kitchen and was a little alarmed to see the odd glint of greasy hair strand sticking out from the gaps in the floorboards. The women, however, were more interested in what was in the cupboards. One was pulling out mugs and teaspoons and muttering that whoever put them away last hadn't done a very good job of cleaning them. Another was dishing out orders and being deliberately ignored by the others. Snubbed, the woman turned to Tansy, "Perhaps you could get a brush and sweep the floor." Tansy was about to tell her that she needed to go back to the donkeys but then realised that she was being given the perfect excuse to get rid of any remaining evidence of the man's stay. She found a broom and a dustpan. It wasn't difficult as she already knew where they were, and swept the kitchen floor, deftly hiding a dreadlock she spotted next to a chair leg. She quickly brushed up the hair and disposed of it in a black bin bag. She then went to the windowless room and swept that. Happy that there was no evidence left of the man's stay she went back into the main hall and, confident that all the women were busy in the kitchen, bolted the side door. There was an audible grunt from Nathan, on the other side, finally relieved of his duty. She put back the brush and dustpan, told the ladies she needed to go, and left through the front door, clutching her bin bag. Round the back of the hut she disposed of its contents in the donkeys' dung heap.

She found the others in the clearing at the side of the scout hut. Lily was explaining how they were going to get the man through the village and into their cellar and giving him instruction. "If anyone stops you, just say 'Where is the bus stop?' When you get there, wait, and one of us will find you when it is safe to take you into the cellar. As Tansy approached, she saw that Lily had scratched a map of the route on the ground. The man was studying it but looking uncertain.

"I don't think he knows what a 'bus stop' is," said Tansy. "Let's wait until the ladies have left the hut then we can take him to the front and point the way to the pond. We can then go play by the pond so that when he gets there we can run off down the alley by our house, so he knows which way to go." She picked up a stick and scratched a big cross at the bus stop on the map. "Sit and wait for us here." He nodded.

It seemed ages but the women finally left and locked up the hut. Tansy went and checked that they had gone and then brought the others and the man round to the front of the hut. She pointed out the way past The Three Wells to the village pond and he nodded. The children then left him there and went to play by the pond, Nathan keeping his distance from Tansy, who scowled at him whenever he looked her way.

As they played a game of 'tig' amongst the trees on the green they started to wonder what was taking the man so long. They were just beginning to think that they would have to revise their plans and go find him, when he appeared, slowly hobbling along, resting heavily on the walking stick. They did their best to ignore him. He passed the row of cottages and started along the front of the vicarage. As he looked up, they ran and skipped their way past the pond to the alleyway by the side of Wishing Well Cottage, letting him see where they had gone.

Part way down the alley they let themselves through the gate into Wishing Well's back garden and played there, waiting to see him go by to the bus stop. He didn't appear. They waited. Five minutes passed. They were puzzled and increasingly alarmed. Finally, they went back to look.

Out in the street, there was no sign of him. Then Nathan spotted Gemma's bicycle leant against the vicarage wall. As he pointed, and they turned their attention to the vicarage, they could hear Gemma's voice. They moved closer and through the hedge could hear her saying, "No, I insist. The vicar won't mind. You can't possibly sit out there for two hours." As they listened, the vicarage front door opened, and Gemma shouted for James. There was a muffled exchange and then the door closed. The children all looked

at one another, horrified. Now what were they
going to do?

CHAPTER SIXTEEN

As she gave the children lunch, Emily was aware of a certain suppressed agitation amongst them. It was as if they were worried about something, but she couldn't imagine what. She knew that something had happened between Nathan and Tansy but now Violet and Lily were behaving oddly too. When she asked them if anything was wrong, they all said 'No', but she didn't believe them. After lunch, with them out of the house she phoned Louise.

"Hi, how are you?" she said. Then, after a bit of small talk she asked, "Is there a problem between Nathan and the girls? They are all behaving oddly."

"Not that I am aware of. He was upset over something the other day but then Violet turned up and everything seemed fine. Why?"

"I don't really know. There seems to be tension between them all, but they deny that anything is wrong. It is just that they are normally all so affable and quickly sort out any differences. I know Tansy broke Nathan's catapult. I was going to get him another, but I haven't got round to it yet."

"Oh, thanks but don't bother. Gemma fixed it for him."

"Gemma? James' new housekeeper?"

"Yes. He seems to have made a friend there. She even gave him instruction on how to shoot it. When he isn't with your lot, he spends most of his time practising. He's quite good now."

After the call, Emily went and looked out of a window at the front of the house. She could see the triplets and Nathan, apparently playing, by the duck pond. From what she could see they looked to be getting on okay. They were deep in discussion about something, but also casting glances at the vicarage. Marigold, Whoops-a-Daisy and Spider could be seen chasing something by the pond. She shook her head and went back to the kitchen.

* * *

The children had been to the bus stop and after some discussion and argument, deferred to Nathan as to what the bus timetable meant. He was adamant that the next bus would be at 1.35pm. That meant afternoon. They weren't convinced. The numbers on the timetable made no sense to them. They would just have to wait and see. Hopefully, Gemma or James would send the man out in time for the bus, and they would get him back. They waited, frequently checking the small clock they had brought with them from the girls' bedroom.

At 1.30 the front door of the vicarage opened and out came James and the man. They watched as the two men slowly made their way along the front of the vicarage and into the alley. It looked like James was taking him to the bus. What if he waited to see him get on?

"Quick," said Tansy, and she set off running towards Wishing Well Cottage gate, cats in tow. The others followed her as she ran swiftly up their drive, round the far side of the cottage to the back garden and along to the near side. Uncle James and the man were just passing the cottage side gate. The man looked and slowed. Tansy kept running and called out, "Uncle James." As James looked, Tansy fell, full length, on the stone path and started crying. James came running, leaving the man in the lane. Atop the wall, the Catolith sat and watched.

As James attended to Tansy, Lily gestured to the man to keep going. Tansy kept crying, holding her knee with her left hand whilst looking alternately at her right wrist and elbow, both of which were starting to ooze. Violet went inside to get their mother. In the distance a bus could be heard, descending the hill. Soon, it could be heard stopping and, after a pause, drawing away again. Tansy stopped crying, and got to her feet, shepherded indoors by Emily. Nathan unobtrusively re-joined the group. James made his excuses, saying he wanted to go and check that the man had got on the bus. The girls exchanged glances. Nathan had returned, so hopefully he had played his part and hidden the man.

Emily bathed Tansy's grazes and covered them with plasters. Her crying had stopped, and she sat there stoically whilst Emily dabbed away with antiseptic. Emily was surprised, it wasn't like Tansy to cry.

James returned. Yes, the man had gone. "Strange chap. Didn't say very much. Strange clothes too, looked like a reject from a 60's comic. Still, shouldn't judge," and he explained to Emily, who hadn't seen the man, that Gemma had found him looking for the bus stop and struggling to walk, and had taken him to the vicarage to wait for the bus.

"Have you kissed her yet?" asked Nathan.

James stared at him.

"Gemma, have you kissed her yet?" he added. "Tansy chose her."

"What?" James frowned and looked at Emily for help, but just turned pink in the process. "No, of course not. Why would you say that?

"Tansy said she'd be perfect, and she is," said Nathan who now looked at Tansy, apparently hoping this praise had pleased her.

"You can't live in that big house all alone," said Tansy, "everyone says so. As daddy said, you need a wife."

"Gemma is perfect," repeated Nathan.

James cleared his throat, and raised his eyebrows, hoping his face wasn't as red as it felt. Unable to meet Emily's eye he turned his attention to Tansy and her knee which was distinctly swollen. "That was a really nasty tumble you took there. Do you think you will be alright for the Crag Race?"

"Yes," she said defiantly.

"Good for you. Right, better get going."

With James gone the children now just had to get rid of their mother so the coast was clear to get the man into the house and down into the cellar.

"Will you show me how to make string flags?" said Violet.

"Bunting?" said Emily, "You want to learn how to make bunting?"

"Yes, please," replied Violet, adding, somewhat forcefully, "Now!"

"Er, well, alright. I do need to get it finished."

With Violet and their mother away making bunting and the sound of the sewing machine handily indicating the location of their mother, Lily went down into the cellar to prepare it whilst Tansy and Nathan, not speaking, went off to get the man.

Within half an hour, they had managed to get the man inside, down the cellar steps and hidden in the far corner, away from the reach of the ceiling lights. They had set up an extension cord and a light, and showed him how to switch it off should he hear the cellar door open. He had bedding and a chair. He smiled approvingly at the children. Finally, he was where he needed to be.

CHAPTER SEVENTEEN

I t was now Thursday morning, and Alex and Tansy went to move the donkeys and prepare their field for the arrival the following day of the festival stage. First, they did a walk round the lower field to check that it was safe and secure. That done, they set about moving the donkeys' troughs. Alex had borrowed a tractor for the occasion, with a small trailer. He backed the tractor as near as he could to the water trough and attached a hook and chain to its far edge. Then he used the tractor to pull the trough over to empty it of water. This done, he was able to pull the trough up planks onto the trailer, again using the tractor. He scooped out as much feed as he could into sacks from the feed trough and dragged that onto the trailer too. Tansy, surrounded by donkeys, followed the tractor across the field, through the gate and into the lower field. Alex dragged the troughs off the trailer, and positioned them, and Tansy started to fill them with feed. The donkeys tucked in. Next, Alex unravelled some hose, attached it to a

PAULINE POTTERILL

small pump and filled the water trough from the river.

Donkeys now moved, Alex looked around. It really was quite beautiful down here and nicely secluded. At some point he would like to put a cabin here, by the river. There was a natural basin, which, if a dam was built in the right place, would fill making a decent sized pool. He knew the farmer who owned the fields opposite. It was unlikely that there would be anything other than cattle in there. Lovely. He watched Tansy for a while. Her movements were a little stiff after her fall and she was favouring her left hand over her right, but otherwise she didn't seem too bothered by her injuries. She was a tough little cookie. He smiled. She stroked one of the donkeys, then bent down running her left hand down its leg. Deftly she lifted the foot, leaning into the animal as she did so. She inspected the hoof and lowered it again. There had been a large wound by the animal's hoof, where it had been tethered, which was now healed. The donkey had long since stopped limping and hair was beginning to grow back but Tansy still checked it. Alex knew that it would be that way until a new home was found and the donkey left.

As he headed to the forge, and Tansy headed home, he realised that he still hadn't done anything about riding lessons for her. Before he knew it, she would be back at school.

* * *

With Violet's help Emily had finished the bunting. She had given Violet a large knitting needle and shown her how to turn the stack of sewn triangles the right way out, so that they could be sewn onto the strip of ribbon from which they would hang. Violet had diligently turned the fiddly fabric shapes, pushing out the points with the big, blunt ended needle. Then she had carefully pinned the edges to facilitate ironing. When the final triangle was attached Emily suggested going over to the scout hut to check that the bunting was long enough.

The others appeared to be out. So, Emily, and an enthusiastic Violet set off for the hut. They spotted Lily and Nathan, playing on the village green and waved at them. When they reached the scout hut, they had a quick word with Tansy who was busy making sure that the donkeys' equipment was safely out of the way of any festival goers. As soon as her mother and Violet went inside Tansy tore over to Wishing Well Cottage. Lily and Nathan were already there, taking food down to the cellar. Tansy went back outside to keep watch. It didn't take them long to do what they needed to do. Thankfully the man no longer needed the inhalation, and his leg was much better than the day before. He was able to stand and walk about the cellar, without the stick. Soon he would be fully fit again. They left him and went back outside to the green and returned to their play. At the edge of the pond, amongst the reeds, Whoops-a-Daisy and Marigold could be seen, stealthily stalking the ducks. In the centre of the pond the mallards had sensibly corralled their ducklings, obviously aware of the threat.

When Emily and Violet returned, Violet ran and joined Lily and Nathan. Emily continued home. As she headed up the drive, a slight movement caught her eye and she looked up at the outhouse roof. There staring back, sat The Catolith. Memories of Kevin, Angelica's cat, who everyone in the village seemed to think was the re-incarnation of Angelica's dead husband, came flooding back. Kevin used to sit up there because he had a great view of the village green and the church grounds. What was the Catolith doing up there?

* * *

Jon was pleased with the progress he had made in Tempus. He had just finished putting up the sign and it looked good. He had already had the odd compliment for it and three enquiries as to when the shop would be open. People had even been peering through the window at him as he arranged his knickknackery. It was a word which he found particularly pleasing, and it wasn't a word one heard much these days. He loved words, especially those that few people knew. He enjoyed seeing the slight shift in their expression as they briefly decided whether to confess that they didn't know what it meant, or chose to pointedly ignore it and pretend that they did. Of course, there were those who genuinely knew, but they were the ones who tended to relish words as much as he did. He had made several new friends that way. It was a little secret code for making friends. Then there were the other people who just thought him strange, but they weren't worth knowing anyway.

As the afternoon wore on, he unpacked more of his knickknacks and placed them on shelves. The more expensive items he placed in easy reach of adults, with the prices showing, but out of the reach of children. He didn't want any breakages. The very expensive items he placed in lockable glass cabinets. Tomorrow he would bring his wall clocks and put those up on display. Yes, he was now confident that he would be able to open Saturday morning, if not Friday afternoon.

* * *

That evening, Mike answered the door of Bode Well Cottage. Anna and Sasha were there. Anna was to stay with Louise whilst Mike and Sasha went to The Three Wells pub for a briefing on their roles in the beer festival. As this would obviously involve some sampling, Anna was going to drive Sasha home afterwards.

Greetings and a quick chat later the two men left the two women to baby-sit Nathan. They set off but didn't get far; Sasha's new car was sitting in Mike's drive. They walked round it, sat in it, discussed it for a while and then their conversation moved on and they realised that they needed to get going if they weren't going to be late. So, they set off down the road to the pub, happily catching up as they went. It didn't take them long to reach the Three Wells. They pushed open the heavy door and stepped inside. Once they had a pint each they were directed through to a back room where the briefing was going to take place. There were eleven volunteers altogether, including Richard. He split the volunteers into two teams, each team to do a shift. The beer tent would be erected just inside the field entrance. It wouldn't then be too far to carry items to and from the pub, and it would catch people on their way into the festival. Plastic glasses would be used, as no bottles were to be allowed in the field. Instructions were given as to the legal requirements for fill levels of the glasses and a reminder to the volunteers that they were representing The Three Wells and to please remain polite no matter how provoking some of the customers may be. There was a grumbling and Richard added, "Have I, or any of my staff, ever been rude to you Charlie Pickles? Even when I've been throwing you into the street?"

Charlie, a red faced, red nosed, middle-aged man with a lop-sided grin, thought about it, then shrugged. "I don't recall," he said, eyes twinkling.

"That wouldn't surprise me at all," said Richard.

There was a brief question and answer session during which Richard repeatedly emphasised that the volunteers were expected to sell more than they drank, the aim being to raise money for St Peter's, not put him out of business. Briefing over, he shepherded them all out into the bar. Hopefully he could get them to spend some money now to offset any loss on the day. As he pulled another pint, he looked round the bar at his clientele. Over in the far corner of the room sat a small group of men, some of whom had been the instigators of the tramp hunting party. Thankfully they seemed to have found something new to entertain them, something which two of them were disagreeing over. Richard kept a watchful eye. He didn't want them coming to blows. This pair he knew could get quite 'heated' in their arguments. It had been a while since there had been a fight in The Three Wells and he wanted to keep it that way. In the other corner a group of young women were giggling and pouting whilst taking 'selfies' on their phones. Sat at the bar, Mike and Sasha were deep in discussion. From what he could overhear it seemed that Sasha was wanting to move into the village but struggling to find somewhere. It wasn't surprising as few people moved out, and rarely ever through choice. Seeing him looking their way Mike gestured for some more drinks. As Richard plonked the two pints on the bar Sasha said, "You don't know of anyone thinking of moving out of the village, do you?"

"Sorry, no. I would have thought that Louise would be the first to know."

"Yes, she's looking but I just thought you might know from the local gossip," said Sasha.

"No, but I'll let you know if I hear anything. Are you looking forward to the race? Are you entering?"

"No," said Sasha, "but I'll certainly be coming to watch. Can't wait to see Mike stagger off up the crag. If he completes one lap, I'll be amazed."

"All for charity. All for charity," said Mike. "I've got shorts and a bloke from work has leant me some trainers. So, I'm all set."

"What, you haven't even got your own trainers. You're going to run a race in borrowed trainers!" said Sasha. "Even I, a man who loves his slippers, knows that you need a decent pair of trainers for running."

"They are a decent pair. He used to run for Barnlees' Harriers. They've even got a compass in the heel."

Richard and Sasha exchanged glances, shaking their heads. As Sasha asked Mike how old his work friend was, in an attempt to ascertain the age of the trainers, Richard excused himself and went back along the bar to serve more customers.

CHAPTER EIGHTEEN

Today was a big day for James, nearly as big as the Crag Race and Festival, as the success of them both depended on today going smoothly. Today was the day the stage and beer tent arrived and hopefully got erected successfully.

As he crammed toast into his mouth the door opened and in came Gemma, earlier than usual. He was surprised but pleased. She was obviously keen to get through her cleaning so she could get over to the scout hut to clean there, and to organise the volunteers James had allocated to her as the post-race and festival clean up party. He offered her tea and toast. Then felt a little silly. She wasn't a guest, she was his cleaner, but he was increasingly feeling that he needed to play host when she was there. He hadn't felt that way with either Anna or Lesley. He had been good friends with them both, but the two women had turned up, done their jobs, and that was that. They had chatted most days, catching up with each other's lives but even though there was no discernible boss/worker division between them, they each had their own roles, distinct but separate. Their relationship was one of mutual respect. He realised that they had been friends as well as colleagues. He also realised that he hadn't had cause to examine these relationships before. That is, before Gemma.

When she accepted the toast, he found he was pleased, pleased that he was able to do something for her. As she tucked a stray crumb into her mouth with her finger, Nathan's question of the day before popped into his head. Had he kissed her yet? This was quickly followed by the idea, and James felt hot under his dog-collar. Another slice popped up from the toaster providing a welcome distraction and he busied himself, his back towards Gemma. Then the doorbell rang.

When he returned to the kitchen, he was carrying a large cardboard box. He placed it on the nearest bit of the table, which happened to be next to Gemma. Gemma glanced at the label, sensing that he was excited by the contents, "Gluten-free wafers?" she said.

"Yes, for Communion. All Saints' Church is all-inclusive now. We've even got alcohol-free wine."

Gemma raised her eyebrows. "I don't suppose you could do cheese. It would go better with the wine and wouldn't be as dry?"

He grinned. "No, but if you have problems with the wafer sticking to your dentures then we now have dipping oil. Anointed, naturally."

"You're kidding!"

"Nope. It can be very distracting, standing at the front, looking at the congregation, half of whom are pulling faces as their tongues ferret amongst their dentures, accompanied by disgusting sucking sounds. Then you see the odd finger surreptitiously inserted to pick the harder bits, whilst they attempt to sing "Rock of Ages.""

Gemma laughed, and he found the sound delightful. When she smiled at him, he felt a warm glow.

Just before 9am they set off to the scout hut. Half a dozen other villagers were there, along with Alex, eagerly awaiting the arrival of the lorry which was bringing the stage. As they approached, Gemma noticed a slight alteration in the stance of two of the men there, and a man, she believed to be the triplets' father, was glancing at them and looking a little uncomfortable.

James introduced them all and she noted that she had been correct, the man was the triplets' father, and his name was Alex. He stepped forward and graciously took her hand, seeming to make a point of welcoming her. She looked him in the eye. He knew, and yet he was giving her the benefit of the doubt, unlike the other two, who were definitely reserved, and smugly amused. With a lump in her throat, she turned to two of the others who James was now introducing. Thankfully, these two appeared oblivious. These two, a man and a woman, were the ones who were to help her clean the scout hut toilets ready for the event. Then, on Saturday, they would organise other volunteers to clear up the green after the Crag Race and, on the Sunday, the field. They seemed a friendly pair.

Alex had opened the field gates and put posts in the ground where the stage was to go. Before long they could hear the sound of a diesel engine as a lorry rumbled through the village. Outside the pub Richard directed the lorry round to the field. James was a little alarmed at the size of it and briefly wondered whether it would fit through the gate. The driver, however, looked confident as he turned the wheel, steering a slight arc to line up the lorry and trailer. Then, after a brief word with Alex, he drove into the field and headed over to the rectangle of posts marking the stage area. Everyone followed, tramping across the dew damp grass. The lorry did a half circle so that it was side on to the rectangle, where it parked. The driver and three others jumped down from the cab and, as they started pulling a tarpaulin off the items on the back of the lorry, the man in charge did a walk around of the proposed stage area, checking the ground. Satisfied, he set about instructing the team of builders. The volunteers, he lined up to form a chain. Soon they were passing items from the lorry to the builders and the stage slowly began to take shape.

At 11am another lorry arrived, and James went over to greet it and pointed it to the area just inside the field gate. This was the marquee for the beer. Richard and a couple of staff from the pub set about helping with the erection, Richard checking the practicalities of its positioning.

Gemma and her two helpers arrived from the scout hut with trays of mugs which they took over to the two groups of construction workers. The hot drinks were gratefully received. As she approached the stage, she became aware that others were now giving her appraising looks. It appeared that word had spread. She looked at James but his demeanor hadn't changed at all. Nobody had told him.

As the morning progressed the stage grew and by lunchtime it looked like a proper stage. Three gantries had been erected across it ready for lights to be attached. Steps led up to each side and screens were being attached to separate the back-stage area. The stage builders suddenly downed tools and announced that it was their lunchtime and climbed back into the lorry cab. James took their cue and, as pre-arranged with Richard, invited everyone, including the men in the lorry, to The Three Wells. They trekked back across the field, collecting those putting up the beer tent, on the way. James made a detour into the scout hut to invite Gemma and her helpers. The helpers however, said that as they had finished what needed doing in the hut, they would go home instead.

At The Three Wells James held open the door for Gemma and escorted her to the bar and bought her a drink. Then they went and sat with Alex, who grabbed a couple of chairs and made room at his table. Alex smiled and asked her how things were coming along in the scout hut. She said that they had finished. She would however, like to put some flowers in the cloakrooms, but she would do that in the morning. James was keen to praise her for volunteering to do the cleaning and went on, and on, about her thinking to organise a clean-up after the race. He also prompted Alex to thank her for offering to clean up the field afterwards, for the donkeys. At the mention of the donkeys, it occurred to Alex that the field may need cleaning up beforehand, for the people.

As the conversation moved on, and the focus shifted away from her, Gemma looked around. Certain people, amongst the volunteers, were casting glances her way. Beyond their group, others were too. Their glances went back and forth, between her and James, she was sure of it. She and James had come in together and it had been noticed. As tears pricked the corners of her eyes, she blinked, summoning anger as a shield. She jumped. James had his hand on her arm.

"Would you like another drink?"

"I'll get these," said Alex, "What would you like? Same again?"

She nodded. As Alex headed off to the bar, a plate of sandwiches was placed on the table by Richard. Others at the table started to help themselves, so she chose a couple and started to eat.

"Here," said James, "have a plate." He was being very attentive. She was both pleased and alarmed. Others were taking note, and disapproving. She didn't need to look around to know. She felt it. In defiance she lifted her head and looked several of them in the eye, taking note.

* * *

Jon was serving another customer. As soon as he had opened Tempus' door at 11am, people had come in. The feedback was all positive and his smaller items were selling well. He had taken two orders for wall clocks and one customer had given him an extra £25 just to buy one of his display clocks so he could have it immediately. Part of him was worried that, if sales continued at the same rate, he wouldn't be able to meet demand. He grabbed a bite to eat between customers and planned what stock he needed to bring over from his workshop.

* * *

Down in the cellar, at Wishing Well Cottage,

the man was spooning cold baked beans out of a tin. The food was odd, but he liked it. It went well with the buttered bread that the children had provided. He scraped the remains of the sauce from the metal sides and licked the last of it off the spoon. Then he took the remains of the bread and did his best to wipe clean the inside of the tin. Having enjoyed that, he ate a couple of biscuits, which he found curiously uniform. Then he ate the apple and sucked the juice out of the little carton they had given him, after a demonstration. Lily had ripped the small tube off the side, bent it, and pushed it through the top of the box. Then she made sucking noises. After initially squeezing juice over himself, he quickly got the hang of it. Once he had eaten, he stood and did a few stretches before pacing up and down, testing his leg. There really wasn't much wrong with it, other than its lack of use over the past few days. It had served its purpose. He was now where he needed to be. Tonight, he could begin.

There was a distant click. The cellar door had been opened. The ceiling lights flicked on. He leapt at the switch of his little lamp, and switched it off. Then, as quietly as he could he sat down, hidden in the dark recess of the far end of the cellar. Footsteps began a descent. They scraped and clicked, carefully and heavily, too heavy for a child. He shrank into the corner.

The person had reached the bottom of the

stairs and was getting closer. He held his breath. He couldn't see, but he was almost certain that the person was female. When she let out a sigh, he was sure. There was a scrape and a jolt of the little table which sat in the centre of the cellar. Something was laid on the table. Then, she was heading his way. He froze, eyes tight shut, wrapped in the darkness of the shadows. She nudged one of the packing cases to one side and took something from the wall recess about an arm's length away from him. Then she was retreating. She took the object, and he heard her set it on the table. Oddly, she left it there and headed for the stairs. As she climbed the stairs, he hitched himself up, curious to see what she had put on the table. It was one of the wooden boxes from the wall recess. As he looked, he was plunged into darkness. She had switched off the light, but it sounded like she was coming back down. Puzzled and uncertain he peered round the side of the packing case. A faint glow of light was dancing down the steps ahead of her. When she reached the bottom, the light danced crazily about the cellar until it was placed on the table, blinding him. If she looked his way, she would surely see him. If he moved, she would surely hear him. She fumbled with the box. Then the light went out. Then he heard footsteps: heavy metal tipped ones, running. As his eyes slowly adjusted to the dark, he became aware of a glow overhead and grey shapes moving dizzily by.

She ran, clutching her bundle. It was dark already. She had wanted to come sooner, but it had taken her longer than she thought. She kept to the middle of the road, away from the shadows. It wasn't far but it was wise to be wary. She skipped across a puddle: the moon's reflected glow bouncing off its surface. Ahead she could hear voices, laughing and shouting, raucous and drunk. The dark doorway loomed ahead. Unable to see anything within its confines she stepped forward, heart thumping, and put her shoulder against the familiar heavy door and pushed. Inside faint glows eerily lit groups of faces. Some turned to stare: some friendly, some leering. As she fought her way towards the bar, hands reached out and grabbed at her. She clutched her bundle tighter and used her hips and shoulders to fend them off. Rough hands encircled her from behind and pulled her backwards. She sat heavily on a lap, a prominent lump at its centre. The sickly smell of stale ale enveloped her and she held her breath as teeth raked her neck. A clammy hand fought its way inside her cloak and clutched her left breast. She yelled but no one came to her aid. Those standing round stood back to watch the show, laughing and jeering. His right hand was now on her thigh, travelling up inside her skirt. She flailed her legs trying to kick him in the shins, but this only displaced her clogs. His hand was now exploring her groin. Furious she threw back her head, hitting him in the face. His hands flew up to his nose. Freed, she elbowed him in the ribs and stood. Then she turned and knelt heavily on his crotch. The crowd cheered and parted as she stepped away from the man, now lying curled up on the floor.

Behind the bar she took a stub of candle from a tin box on the wall and placed it in a tin candle holder. Then, taking a spill, lit it from the oil lamp on the end of the bar and transferred the flame to the candle. The noise of the bar receded as she went through a door and along a passage to the stairs. With her crumpled bundle tucked under one arm she held the candle aloft, climbing slowly as the candle guttered, observing the flame to ensure it stayed lit. At the top of the stairs, she turned towards the back of the property and called out.

"Edith, are you there?"

A reply could be heard from the room at the end. She entered. Edith was sitting in a chair by the fire looking worried. Sarah smiled, "I'm sorry it is so late but I wanted to give you this, before tomorrow." She handed the bundle to her sister and sat herself down in a chair opposite. Perched on the edge of the seat she waited eagerly whilst Edith unfolded the crisp white sheet in which her gift was wrapped.

As Edith folded back the last flap she gasped. Briefly she studied the contents. Inside was a heap of cream material, the uppermost part intricately sewn. She ran her fingers over the smocking, caressing it. Then she carefully took hold and lifted it up. Standing, she let the bundle unfurl. Then she turned it and held it against herself and did a twirl.

"It is for your wedding night. So, I had to give it you now."

Sitting again and examining the nightgown Edith looked at it in amazement. "This front panel, the smocking, it's silk. Where on earth did you get the money?"

"It looks like silk, but it is ribbon." Sarah grinned, "Lots of strips of silk ribbon, sewn side by side to form a vertical panel for me to do the smocking on. Mrs Blackledge saved up the ends of rolls for me, in exchange for eggs and honey and hazel nuts, and I don't remember what else."

"It must have taken you weeks to do all this. Oh, Sarah. It is beautiful." She put the gown to one side and stood, opening her arms to her sister. "Thank you, Sarah."

Emily wiped a tear from her eye, Sarah's delight her own. She sat a moment, then shuddered and quickly switched on the torch. She placed the marble back in its slot, shut the lid and quickly replaced the box in its alcove. She wanted to get out of the cellar: the dark cellar. She could still feel the man's hands on her body, roughly probing her, uncaring, demanding. She resaw the looks on the faces of those in the pub. No-one had had any intention of helping her. To them her distress was entertainment. There had been women in the pub, but they had been laughing along with the men. Sarah, she realised had fought her way out of the situation, as if it was a normal occurrence. Sarah had been mad, not frightened. She hadn't even mentioned it to her sister. Shocked, Emily realised that this was probably life back then. Women didn't have any rights. Their only recourse was self-preservation.

In the kitchen she put the kettle on and stared into space until it boiled. The whole incident had been deeply disturbing, but there was something else. Throughout the whole memory she had had the strange feeling that she was being watched, but that made no sense. Apart from in the bar, Sarah had been alone, until she was with Edith. Then it was just the two of them. The more Emily thought about it all, though, the more the feeling grew. She had felt it in the cellar, too, after the memory. The other memories hadn't been like that. They had all been frightening and disturbing in their own way but this last memory, which she believed was essentially a happy memory for Sarah, felt different. As Sarah, she had had no sense of being watched, but she, Emily, had felt it.

* * *

Rousing his troops, James shepherded everyone out of the pub. At the door, he paused, again holding it open for Gemma. A slight breeze from outside carried her perfume, and on impulse he gently took her arm as they stepped into the street.

"Gemma, on Sunday, after the festival is over,

would you like to come for Sunday lunch with me?" Amazed that he had actually said it, he stood, holding his breath.

She looked a little surprised. Briefly, he thought that she was going to say no, but then the corners of her mouth turned up, and kept going until the grin reached her eyes. She nodded. Together, they headed back to the field.

By mid-afternoon the beer tent was up, and a row of tables set up inside. Richard attached labels to them identifying what was to go where. In the back corner he placed an easel with a board, which held a plan, showing the layout of the tent, and a rota for the volunteers. By 4.30pm the stage was complete and ready for the lighting to be attached and tested the following morning. The canvas sides were secured and did what they were meant to do, which was screen the backstage area from the audience and give the acts somewhere to get ready and wait their turn. A double layer of net fencing was erected to mark out and protect the lighting and speaker cables which would be fed from the generators to the stage. As the men packed up to leave for the day, James stood back and looked at it all. It was going okay. It would be alright. There was nothing further he could do this evening. He looked around, instinctively looking for Gemma. The Scout Hut was silent and sealed and when he reached the vicarage gate there was disappointment where her bicycle had been.

* * *

"Louise has done it," said Alex, almost before the back door was shut.

"Done what?" asked Emily.

"Found a tenant for the flat. Apparently, she's a writer."

"Oh, what does she write?"

"I don't know, books I suppose."

"Didn't you ask?"

"No. What is for dinner?"

Emily stood, with her hands on her hips.

"Louise seemed quite excited; thought you might have heard of her – Pauline something."

Emily reached for her phone and, at the sound of three sets of feet bouncing down the stairs, disappeared off to the living room leaving Alex to be enveloped by his daughters.

Later, as Alex stacked the dishwasher, Emily was unusually quiet. "Everything alright?"

"Huh?"

"Ever since you spoke to Lou you've been in a world of your own."

"Just thinking."

"So, do you know this Pauline, whatever-she's-called?"

"Potterill. No, but I don't know any authors. I don't think I've ever met one before. The book club will be thrilled. She writes romantic comedy. I've always wanted to do that."

"Since when? You've never said anything

before."

"Lou and Mike and I used to mess about writing what we called Pills and Swoon. We never wrote any of it down, but it was fun. Anyway, one day, when I have the time."

* * *

Alex put the bolt on the back door and shut the kitchen door, checking the front door as he passed it. Then the stairs creaked noisily, and the downstairs lights went out. Snokettee crouched by the cellar door and meowed quietly. The man laid out his tools and set to work.

CHAPTER NINETEEN

J ames pulled on a T-shirt and searched the
floor for his undies. Inserting one leg, he did
a little hop around the room before collapsing
on the edge of the bed and wiping his eyes. Able
to focus he completed the task and pulled back
the curtains which were noticeably warm. He
beamed at the sun. Today was the day.

He hummed as bacon sizzled and, as he
dithered over the choice of ketchup or brown
sauce, the toaster popped. He smothered butter
and then the brown sauce on his toast, piled
on rashers of bacon, and sandwiched his little
piece of heaven with another slice of toast.
"Mmmmmmmmmmm."

Wiping crumbs from his face he poured
himself a mug of tea and headed to his study. Tea
always tasted so good after a bacon 'sarnie'. The
first thing on his check list was to check his e-
mails; he didn't want any last-minute surprises.
He could lose one or two volunteers, but some
were key. There were a few e-mails, which he
quickly worked his way through. Mrs Arkwright

was really sorry, but she had forgotten to buy chocolate buttons for her chocolate button cake, and did he think it would be okay if she just put a note apologising for the lack of buttons beside her chocolate button cake? Mr Green wanted to know if it would be okay to officiate in his wellingtons as it may be muddy by the second stile on the way up to the crag, only he wasn't sure they went with his bow tie and as he was representing the vicar's charity he didn't want to 'let the side down'. James restrained himself and simply replied 'yes, that would be fine' to both.

To the dying chimes of his bell, James opened the front door. On the step was Gemma. A little surprised, he stepped back and let her in. "Why did you ring?"

"Well, it isn't a workday. I didn't like to just walk in when you weren't expecting me."

"Oh, okay." He found he was both pleased and strangely disappointed. "Would you like a cup of tea or something?"

"Only if you are having one. It is a busy day." As she smiled her eyes crinkled at the corners and seemed brighter than normal. She had a lovely smile and she suddenly looked a lot younger. He saw the girl in her, swallowed and looked away, busying himself with the tea pot.

* * *

Over at The Ark Aid Jonathan was busy inspecting his knickknackery. Various adjustments were made after each angle of inspection. He smiled to himself. Most would have thought these minor changes otiose, he thought. Finally satisfied, he checked the amount of change in his till. He was ready. For the fifth time he straightened a pile of business cards then did another pace of the shop, pausing to peer through a tick tock of clocks for a view of What Sup. He would just have to make himself a drink. He turned away, then quickly swivelled back; there was a figure at one of the tables. He moved to one side for a better view. The figure wasn't at the table, but on it and staring directly at him.

* * *

By mid-morning James had dispersed his volunteers to their various tasks. Eleven o'clock was fast approaching. Numbered children milled about as parents fussed with bottles and tubes of sunscreen. Tears fell as a father frantically rethreaded a shoelace and ceased promptly at completion. James spotted Tansy, dark brown curls tied back for once, earnestly working through a warm-up routine. He smiled with amusement. He recognised that routine; she had obviously been watching him. Then, almost hidden by one of the green's oak trees, he saw Nathan, copying her every move. Tansy raised her right knee and took hold of her heel. James frowned; he had never done that. Then she raised her leg above her head and stood there, like a smug stork. James had never ever done that, but if he had, he would definitely have been very smug about it. In the shadows of the trees, Nathan fell over.

As the church bells began to strike eleven the Young Runs Race began. Bony little elbows flying, they jostled their way around the green and tore off down the high street, bulbous trainers slapping on the tarmac. Like a spillage of Smarties, fluorescent tops wove and bobbed. Parents yelled encouragement, some of them running alongside. Ahead, the front runners disappeared down a side street towards the first stile. There was a howl and fevered activity as spectators leapt to the aid of a prone competitor. James looked around but one of his First Aiders was already running, bright green backpack bouncing awkwardly. James sent a prayer skywards; hopefully it wasn't anything serious. Then felt guilty as he acknowledged that his first thought was concern for the smooth running and completion of the day. Obviously, he was concerned for the child, but there was a lot riding on the event.

By the stile Mr Swire was cheering, "Don't let that Tansy beat you young Nathan. Pump those skinny legs o' yours. Guwon!" As Nathan disappeared up into the wood, Tansy scrambled over the stile. "Keep going my lovely lady, give that Nathan a run for 'is money."

Between lungful's she blurted, "Will you sponsor me, Mr Swire?" and gave him her best 'cutesy' smile. "Please."

He grinned back and yelled after her, "I'll give you a tenner if you can beat young Nathan." As the middle of the pack started to bunch up and fight for their turn to climb over the stile he stood back and watched as the woman from the bakery attempted to keep order, her orange marshal's vest bustling its way into the melee with lots of, "Don't do that. Stop it. Please behave. That isn't nice. Ouch, you little shit."

Chuckling to himself he set off back to the high street to position himself at the finish line. Behind him, the orange vest sank into the quicksand of children.

* * *

At the top of the crag the front runners were rounding the cairn. Nathan pounded onwards: hair plastered to his head. He stole a quick glance backwards. He could see Tansy, teeth gritted, doggedly rasping in air, determined to close the gap between them, despite the sticky dressing flapping on her knee. Crumbled limestone chippings moving under his trainers he stumbled round the cairn and with relief started the long series of zigzags back to the wood. Now, at each turn, he could see her. Legs flying, he scanned the path, eyes flitting from stone to stone, foot placement to foot placement. Before diving into the trees, he took one last glance. Was she nearer or not? As stone turned to soil the going was easier, less jolting and slipping. The less obvious tree roots, however, made the going just as treacherous. Concentrating hard, he passed another marshal and a noisy cheering group of villagers. "Go, Nathan." At the last stile, he hopped from foot to foot, as five older boys climbed over. Not far behind he heard, "Go, Little Wells, go." Impatiently he waited his turn, then threw himself over, Tansy on his heels. He tore down the street and into the high street, his longer legs giving him the advantage. Tansy, having studied James, ran more efficiently. As they approached the finish line, he sensed she was gaining on him. His parents were there, yelling him on. Mr Swire was there, "Run Young Nathan. Run." The villagers were cheering. The line was in sight. He was nearly there, but he couldn't help himself. He had to know. He glanced over his shoulder. His right trainer caught his left trainer and, in front of the whole village, he fell, full length. Amongst a blur of faces his eyes met Tansy's, crouched in front of him, concern on her face. Fending off his helpers he staggered to his feet and limped towards the finish line. Blood dripping from both knees, he wiped his eyes, determined not to cry. He staggered, and to his utter consternation Tansy took his arm and helped him over the line.

* * *

Emily was enjoying herself. She beamed and poured another three cups of tea, then turned and refilled the milk jug. Her lemon drizzle cake was going well; she wished she had made two. A brief lull in the thirsty and she took a moment to admire the hall. It all looked so magical. The bunting, the pink and white gingham tablecloths, the bunches of pansies sitting in beribboned jam jars casting specks of dappled sunlight, created a perfect picture of pastel prettiness. More people, balancing cake and napkins moved in front of her.

"Two coffees, milk no sugar."

"Help yourself to milk. No, please," gesticulating, "pay at the end."

"Yes, it is a lovely day. Great to see you."

She poured more drinks.

"Sophie. Hello, how are you? I haven't seen you for ages."

"I'm good. How are you and Alex and the girls?"

"Great." The two women, despite getting off to a bad start, had become good friends whilst helping to save St Peter's Young Disabled Unit. Sophie had married Simon; the son of the disabled unit's owner and Simon's son Trevor was at school with the triplets. "And, hello little Eliza, how are you?" Emily walked round the table and crouched by Sophie's wheelchair, smiling at the child on Sophie's lap. Tickling the child's cheek she asked, "How old is she now?"

"18 months."

"You're such a little cutie, aren't you little one. Are Simon and Trevor with you?"

"Yes, they've just gone to see how Nathan is."

"Huh?"

"Yes, it was such a shame. He tripped, yards from the line. Tansy stopped, bless her, and helped him over."

"Is he okay?"

A man in a Hawaiian shirt rested a hand on the back of Sophie's wheelchair. Sophie whipped round and Emily stared. "Excuse me," he said, "me cake's getting cold."

As Sophie glowered at the man Emily apologised, "Sorry, yes. What can I get you?" As she poured him a drink she said to Sophie, "Find a table and I'll bring your drinks over. Nathan is okay I hope." Sophie nodded and pushed herself rapidly over to the only free table, knocking a chair to one side so she could park.

* * *

Violet stood wide eyed as the first aid lady picked grit out of Nathan's knees and hands and his right elbow. Louise stood back and let the lady work, knowing full well that Nathan wouldn't be as compliant if she cleaned him up. The woman, as well as being more efficient was also more sympathetic than she would have been, telling him what a brave little soldier he was. Louise knew that wouldn't be the case if it was just her, and no triplet present. Outside the door she could hear Mike chatting to Simon, and Trevor kicking the skirting board.

"His mouth is bleeding," blurted Violet who had been earnestly studying Nathan's face and unconsciously mimicking every wince.

"Oh dear," said the lady, "looks like you've bitten your lip too, love. Let me see." Nathan stuck out his bottom lip. "Ooh, that looks sore. Don't worry, duck, that will heal up quickly." Applying the last plaster she smiled, "A nice cold drink will help stop your lip bleeding and I think you deserve a huge slice of cake for being so brave." Then she held out a sticker to Violet, "Perhaps you would like to present him with this. I think he deserves it, don't you."

Outside the room Nathan ripped off the sticker and threw it on the floor. As he headed, stiff legged, towards the cakes, Violet quietly retrieved the sticker and carefully straightened it out.

* * *

His voice crackling over the crowd James announced the winners. A friend from his running club presented the medals to gleeful recipients standing atop a makeshift podium. "And, in the under 8's category, in joint third place we have Tansy Wells and Nathan Parker."

There was a round of applause and Tansy hopped up onto the platform. After an exchange with James, he announced, "We will have to present Nathan's medal to him later." He announced the second and first place medalists and photos were taken. "Okay, that concludes The Young Runs presentation. Well done everyone. Just a reminder, the adult race starts at 1pm. Competitors please be on the start line by 12.50. Thankyou. Refreshments are available, that way. Just follow the signs."

He breathed a sigh of relief and made his way to the scout hut, amid pats on the back and words of congratulation. He spotted Gemma, black bin bags over her arm, deftly locking another bag into place. "How is it going?" he asked.

"Gosh, I never thought there would be this much rubbish, and it is only early." She tied the top of a bag and headed off round the side of the hut.

He stepped through the door and into the noise, breathing in the rich aroma of coffee and the more delicate scent of icing sugar. A mug was placed in his right hand and a plate with a selection of sticky items in his left. "No, no vicar, you aren't paying. Get away with ya." Swept up in an enthusiastic crowd of well wishers he found himself in the middle of the room. Nodding politely, he sipped his coffee. Cup in one hand plate occupying the other he glanced longingly at the coffee cake he was unable to pick up. He really wanted to sit down but his followers seemed oblivious to his predicament. Finally, balancing his plate on top of his mug, he sank his teeth into the moist cake and savoured the icing. Then he started on the rest of the cakes, knowing full well that it would be 'noticed' if he abandoned someone's creation. Feeling slightly sick, he glanced at his watch and announced that he needed, "to get back for the afternoon's race", and possibly throw up. On his way out he detoured by Sophie's table which now included Simon, Trevor, Louise and Nathan.

"Oh, Nathan, you have been 'in the wars'. So sorry. However, you got joint third prize in the under 8's. Well done. I'll give it to you later. Tansy has got hers. Must go." He nodded to the rest of them.

All Saints' Church Bell struck one and the Crag Race began. Off they went, all 98 of them. James watched enviously as the back runners disappeared from view and prayed that they would be spread out enough not to have too much bunching at the stile. He had deliberately routed the adult race via the furthest stile out of the village. With the competitors gone most of the crowd wandered off to the beer tent but a few diehards milled about. In an upstairs room of The Three Wells, a look-out was poised, his binoculars trained on the cairn at the top of the crag. At the 16-minute point he started his commentary.

"Yes, we have our first runner. It looks like one of the Barnlees' Harriers. Yes, number 12, George Barnes, closely followed by number 26, Pete Smith, also of Barnlees' Harriers. George has rounded the cairn and is on the downward leg. On their heels is 22, Sam Greenfield and 16, Heather Blackridge, 23, 34. Oh, they are coming thick and fast now I see Alex Wells and Tom Mills, number 45, I think that is Shirley Crabtree, yes, Shirley Crabtree, Number 62, 61. Oh, and there is a surprise. I think I see, yes, Mike Parker. Well, I never. Next is 58 and 47."

James laughed, an open-mouthed Louise was staring up at the pub window, aghast that anyone should be mocking Mike's athletic prowess. "Oy," she shouted, "belittling him is my job."

* * *

The Catolith sat motionless and silent on top of Wishing Well Cottage outhouse, scrutinising the assertion of humans on the village green. In the cellar Lily gave the man some sandwiches, a banana and a handful of biscuits. He took them gratefully and watched as Snokettee and Marigold rubbed round Lily's ankles. At his side, lay a worn grey cloth: several different sized lumps hidden underneath. Lily glanced at it but said nothing. He saw her look and acknowledged her discretion. She wouldn't ask and he wouldn't tell.

* * *

"Oh, Nathan. What happened to you?" Gemma stood, hands on hips, clutching yet another bin bag. "I hear you came third. That is marvellous. Well done."

Nathan stood, resting on his right leg; his left slightly swollen. He licked his lip, the bitten part enhanced by a pout, "Joint third."

"Yes, but I hear you would have easily beaten her. It was just bad luck. That is sport. Besides, I'll bet she can't use a catapult like you. Now that really is a skill. Right. I'd better get on," and she let Nathan by on his way to the gents. Singing happily to herself she carried a collection of rubbish round the side of the hut. Letting the big plastic lid of the council bin fall, she was surprised to have Nathan hold out a bag. "The gent's needs a fresh one," he said, "this is full. I'll take it for you."

"Thank you Nathan. That is so kind, and you with all those injuries too." She handed him a bag and he practically skipped back towards the gents.

* * *

A ripple of noise travelled up the high street followed by a tsunami as the first runner came into view. The crowd clapped and cheered and increased as people spilled out of The Three

Wells and ran round from the beer tent. George Barnes was still in the lead at the start of the second circuit and waved regally as he rounded the pond and headed back towards the crag. After the first few competitors had passed, the crowd thinned again, leaving mainly those cheering individual competitors. Emily, having finished her stint in the scout hut, joined Louise and shouted encouragement at Alex as he ran past, and a red-faced Mike when he eventually appeared.

Once the front runners had completed their second circuit, barriers were erected as a run off lane for the finishers; a wide red ribbon stretched across the entrance. Overhead hung a banner stating 'Finish Line'. Weary stragglers hobbled past eyeing the exit enviously and a few walked off the circuit at this point, conceding defeat. A dogged few alternated between running and walking, determined to do the whole course.

From the pub window, the commentary continued. At the cairn George had fallen behind and Pete Smith was in the lead with Sam Greenfield hot on his heels. Sam stumbled on the descent and Pete increased his lead. Shirley Crabtree was next, then Heather Blackridge. Both appeared to be closing the gap, lighter and more agile on the descent. As the leaders disappeared from view, those rounding the cairn came in clumps and lone individuals. There would be a long gap and then more would appear. Many were now walking but once round the cairn set off running again.

A screaming cheer was heard as the leader appeared over the stile, quickly followed by three more runners. The noise grew louder and louder. Pete it appeared was the favourite. As he turned into the high street the crowd returned to the pavement to allow passage. George and Pete were now neck and neck, Heather and Shirley fighting it out for 3rd place. Emily clamped her hands over her ears, and joined in the cheering. She didn't know the runners and wasn't certain which was Pete and which was George so she shouted "Come on 26".

Louise grinned at her and nudged her in the ribs. Then yelled, "Move those fabulous legs you great hunk."

Number 26 crossed the line first and Pete Smith was announced the winner. As Emily jumped up and down madly clapping her hands, Louise nudged her in the ribs again. She was shouting something but Emily couldn't hear. Now Louise was pointing. Alex came sprinting past, overtaking a couple of runners who had eased-up with the finish in sight, and crossed the line in 10th position. Emily fought her way to the finish area, leaving Louise to her lonely vigil.

At the finish line officials were encouraging competitors to keep moving as a steady stream of dripping finishers flooded the finish area. Emily spotted Alex in their midst, but nose wrinkling decided against wading in. He eventually heard her and headed her way.

"Well done. I can't believe you came 10th. Amazing. Even better than last year. I love you."

"And next year I plan on being even better. Aren't the girls with you?"

"No. Er, Violet was with Nathan, and last time I saw Tansy and Lily they were in the scout hut basking in old lady adoration!"

"Well, I'm going home to cool down, shower and change. Then I am heading over to the beer tent."

"Aren't you waiting for Mike to finish?"

"You are kidding. Last time I saw him he was trying to force his way over the stile against the flow of those on their way down. He'll be ages yet."

As he turned and headed to the cottage, clutching his finishers' goody bag, Emily smiled; the bag looked so incongruous against his huge frame. Shoulders visible above the crowd he rippled his way through, amiably greeting and chatting as he went, so confident and comfortable. She envied that in him and loved him for it. Her heart swelled.

CHAPTER TWENTY

J ames headed over to the scout hut praying that there would be some cake left. What he really wanted was a cheese and ham baguette from the pub, but he doubted he would get near the bar. He nearly made it to the scout hut. He could see Gemma through the doors still busy with binbags and wielding a hand-grabber.

"James, James, over here." He took a deep breath, put a smile on his face and went to join the substantive group, gathered round a table at the side of the hut, who appeared to want him to settle an argument.

"You're not seeing that woman are you, vicar?" The man swayed slightly. James frowned.

"Aye vicar," said another, "not the sort a good man like you should be associating with." The man hiccupped and nudged his companion in the ribs, slopping amber liquid onto the grass.

"What?" said James. "Who?"

"That cleaner, o' yours."

The group sniggered. "Scrubber, more like."

"Gemma?"

"Gemma! Is that what she's calling hersel'," scoffed the man. "She were christened Crystal. Crystal Winterbottom."

"No, her name is Gemma Modoran," said James.

"Is that what she told ya? No. She were christened Crystal Winterbottom in that church o' yours." There were several nods and sniggers.

"Aye, a wrong un that one. I'm surprised at you vicar. You really don't wanna be seein' 'er."

"I'm not 'seeing' anyone," said James, spreading his hands in an over-elaborate gesture.

"Chequered history, that one."

"Aye, she's a reight slapper."

There was a small commotion and out of the crowd stepped Nathan, red faced, "Any man should be pleased to have her."

Everyone looked at Nathan, 7 years old and, of course, a half. Nathan glowered back, appraising his now silent audience. In the background the world carried on; raucous laughter could be heard, interspersed with chords being strummed as bands tuned their instruments. Donkeys brayed down by the stream, and a bus rumbled by on Much Meddling's outskirts. There was a chuckle. Nathan didn't like being laughed at and an explanation was obviously needed. With conviction and enthusiasm, he supplied it, "She's a real goer."

"Nathan," shrieked Louise, normally quite

casual in her parenting, "Where on earth did you hear that?"

Nathan thought, then searched the crowd. Finding what he was looking for he pointed, "Daddy."

Attention now shifted to a rapidly reddening Mike who sat spluttering in their midst. The crowd parted, stepping aside to accommodate his embarrassment and take a good look at him.

"Mike," shrieked Louise, usually quite trusting in her marriage, unable to comprehend why any man should possibly want anyone other than her, "How would you know?"

This turned out to be exactly the question everyone wanted answering. All eyes reverted gleefully to Mike.

"I, I was just repeating what they said, at the pub the other night, because," he added lamely, "I thought it was amusing. I've never met the woman."

There was a collective groan. Then someone looked up, and they all turned. Peering white-faced through one of the scout hut windows, was Gemma. As they looked, she turned and fled. James stood rooted to the spot. Nathan set off running to the front of the hut.

James was stunned. Why would she lie to him. Then, more rationally, he thought that maybe she just didn't like the name Crystal, but then why change her surname, unless, and his heart sank, she was married. He needed to speak to her.

Unable to find her and with time rapidly approaching 2.30pm, he headed to the finish line for the medal presentation. He announced the winners and placed medals over peoples' heads, not really conscious of what he was doing. If she was married...

The ceremony took longer than he had anticipated. Photos were wanted, quotes demanded. Turn and smile. Shake hands with the winner. Present the medal again. This way. Smile. When it was finally over and he was free, he checked his watch. It was nearly 3pm. Forcing his way through the beer tent queue, he jogged round the side of the donkey field, through one of the barriers to the back-stage area and up the make-shift steps. Someone handed him a microphone and he stepped out onto the stage. Wow, so many people. He was used to addressing an audience, but nothing like this. So many faces, all looking expectantly in his direction, some holding their pints aloft. Some already swaying, holding their phones aloft, despite the lack of music.

Hoping that his breathing would settle soon he strolled to the front of the stage. There was a cheer.

"Hello everybody. Welcome to Much Meddling Music and Beer Festival. Are you having a good time?"

"Yes."

"I can't hear you. I said, are you having a good time?"

"YES!"

"Right. Thank you all for coming. Let's get this show started. Please give a big welcome to our first band – Granite." As he backed away clapping, the group ran on to the stage and picked up their instruments. Soon the whole stage was vibrating, and the crowd were happily nodding to the beat.

* * *

When Louise bumped into Emily, she couldn't wait to tell her what had happened.

"No," said Emily. "Really? Her name is Crystal! Not surprised she changed it. How is James? Do you really think he's interested in her?"

"Judging by his reaction, I'd say so."

"And you say Gemma, saw?"

"Yes, she looked absolutely mortified before she ran off. Nathan hasn't been able to find her."

"Has Mike recovered?"

"From the race or his embarrassment?"

Emily grinned, "Isn't that one and the same? Did I hear right? He came 85th."

"Yes, but he did manage to break into a trot to cross the finish line, on route to the beer tent. He nearly made it. When I found him, he was sitting backwards on one of those A-frame bench tables, couldn't get his legs over the seat. Some kind soul had got him a beer. When the crowd thins I may need to go get the car."

* * *

The sun scrolled across the sky and Much Meddling rocked to the sound of various local bands. The ground around the beer tent grew soggy and plastic glasses got squashed and churned underfoot. Arms got linked, and friendships strengthened. Voices grew hoarse and ears rang. As shadows grew, the stage lights grew proportionately brighter and James got back up on stage to announce the final act.

"Right, you lovely people. Thank you all so much for coming and supporting this event. We couldn't have done it without you, and these fabulous bands who are giving their time for freeee... A big round of applause for them all..." The crowd leapt up and down shouting and clapping. When they began to settle James continued. "So far, we have raised an incredible £6,000 for St Peter's Young Disabled Unit. Thank you, thank you, thank you. Right, do we have a treat in store for you now. Yes, the band you have all been waiting for... the one and only... Clydesdaaaaale!" The field erupted with cheering and clapping, and four young men jogged onto the stage. Multicoloured lights swept the crowd. A guitar wailed a chord and the drums started to pound. The spotlight swung to the side of the stage and the lead singer leapt into its glare.

James threw him the microphone, which he caught and held aloft, punching his fist in the air with the beat, rousing the crowd. As James retreated, hands over his ears, the singer tossed his hair and belted out, "Grab me, hold on tight. It's gonna beeee, wild tonight."

CHAPTER TWENTY ONE

Opening her eyes, Emily glanced at her bedside table. It was 8.34am. Glancing the other way she groaned. Alex was sprawled on his back, mouth open, cocooned in an invisible haze of old hops. He snorted slightly. As she sat up he rolled on his side and reached out a hand, sliding it up her leg. No, No, No, No, Noooo... Slipping out of bed she shrugged on a robe and headed for the door. Looking back, she sighed. He now lay on his side, drooling slightly; she feared for her linen.

It was another lovely day. Clutching her cuppa she sat herself in a corner of the garden. For a while she watched a ladybird, basking on a leaf. When it flew off she followed its flight, until it disappeared into a buddleia. Glancing round she realised that she really ought to do some dead-heading; brown roses were only attractive when dried. She took another sip, enjoying a little peace. She smiled. The school holidays were already half over. As if summoned by her thoughts, the back door clicked, and out shot

Spider along with Tansy, barefoot and tousled, eager for the day. Emily sighed.

"Hi, love. Go get dressed and I'll get you some breakfast."

As Tansy turned, bronze flashed at the end of some bright red ribbon. The little girl was wearing her medal over her pyjamas.

"Are the others up yet?"

"Don't know."

"Tell them breakfast will be ready shortly. Then we need to go help with the clear up: make sure your donkey field is okay."

* * *

As they left the house Violet asked, "Is Daddy not coming?"

"No, love, he'll be joining us later."

"Were they serving skinfuls last night?" asked Tansy.

Emily looked at her daughter, "Pardon?"

"They are bad, He should have stuck to beer," said Tansy as the others nodded sagely.

A little group was gathered round the scout hut, clutching bags and hand-grabbers, waiting. As no-one was doing anything Emily suggested they form a chain and walk across the field picking up litter as they went. There was no sign of James or Gemma, but there was lots of muttered speculation.

Emily stepped forward, scanning the ground. Picking at a split plastic beer mug she pulled, but then had to use her foot to loosen it from the mud. At her side, an increasingly furious Tansy was rapidly filling her plastic bag. Emily watched as her little girl trudged off towards the rubbish heap and flung her bag on top. Then she started yelling at someone and James came into view, dodging to one side as a hand-grabber flew past his ear. Unarmed now, Tansy stood, hands on hips glowering at James who, by his stance was apologising profusely.

Emily started towards James, who was now watching Tansy running off homewards.

"I am so sorry," said Emily. "She could have done you some real damage with that. Are you alright?"

"Yes, I'm fine."

"Of course," said Lily who had just joined them, with Violet at her side. "If she had wanted to hit him, she would have."

"Yes," said Violet. "She wouldn't have missed."

"She is upset at the state of the field," said Emily. James looked. The entire field was churned up and there was hardly an area in which things weren't glinting. The only relatively clear path was where the litter pickers had gone, and it was plain that at least a second pass would be needed.

"Is Gemma here?" he asked.

"No."

"I'm sorry I'm late but I have been trying to

contact her. I guess you heard about yesterday. I haven't seen her since. I'm getting quite worried."

"Girls, you go and join the other litter pickers and Uncle James and I will follow on, picking up what they have missed." As the girls ran off, disappointed, Emily continued, "So, talk to me…"

"Oh, Emily. I just don't know what to think. Am I being stupid?"

"For caring for someone?"

"I was starting to think that, well…"

"Well, what?"

"She lied to me."

"Well, it does seem odd," said Emily, "but people change their names for all sorts of reasons."

"Yes, usually because they have 'a history'; something they are trying to hide. I remember when I was in the Fire Service, we had this arsonist. It took the Police ages to track him down: changed his name a couple of times."

"You need to talk to her. Straighten things out."

"I guess you are right. Right now, I need to go change into my dog collar, ready to stand in the dock and face the sanctimonious of Much Meddling."

"Yes, I'd better drag my lot back. Wouldn't want to miss the show."

* * *

On the way out of the church Emily felt a hand on her arm. Looking primly at her was one of the ladies of the village, "I see Alex isn't with you today. I hope he is alright. Not like him to miss church."

"He is just a little under the weather. That is all." said Emily.

"That would be the skinfuls," added Violet.

Emily ushered her brood away, but the woman followed. "I hear the vicar's cleaner has been lying about herself. I'd keep my kids away from her if I were you, after what she's done."

"Thank you but I don't want to hear your gossip." Emily was stunned that she had been so bold.

"No," said Tansy, "she can get it from Auntie Louise."

Back at the cottage, they found that Alex had arisen. He sat at the kitchen table, a large cafetiere at his side and some uneaten toast.

"Well, I'm going to get us some lunch," said Emily. "I take it you don't want any, Alex."

"No thanks. I'm going back to bed."

"But Daddy, the field," said Tansy.

"I know love. Later."

* * *

James was worried. He still hadn't been able to contact Gemma. After church he had gone straight to the end of the village to her address: a three-storey terraced house which was split into six flats. He rang the bell for 12d but no-one answered. She either wasn't there or wasn't answering. He pressed 12e and a woman answered. He explained that he was looking for the lady in flat 12d but couldn't get an answer. The woman now sounded suspicious and asked him what he wanted. He just wanted to talk to her. After a little further persuasion, and mentioning that he was the vicar, the voice informed him that there wasn't a woman living in 12d, just a single man. Puzzled, James persisted, saying her name was Gemma, or maybe Crystal.

"Look luv. You've got the wrong address. There is no woman living at 12d or, any Gemma or Crystal in the other flats."

Slowly James turned away. Why would Gemma lie? Why would she do that? He was starting to think that she cared for him, and he believed that he cared about her.

Crack! Stopped dead in his tracks, he staggered backwards and let out a stream of expletives. Then stood, head in hands trying to calm his breathing whilst waiting for the pain in his skull to subside. He sent prayers for forgiveness skywards whilst simultaneously aiming malicious thoughts of vandalism at a lamp post. Feeling even sorrier for himself than he did before, he headed home in search of a mirror.

* * *

"What happened to you?" asked Emily. "I thought Tansy had missed."

"She did. This was a lamppost."

"Ooh, that looks nasty. You've got a right lump. Are you sure you should be doing this? We can manage without you."

"No, I'm fine. Got to show willing. I see Tansy is back on task." At the other side of the field the triplets were busy running round chasing litter, some of which was air-borne.

"Yes, she wants to be able to move the donkeys back as soon as possible. I just wish Alex would join us. She feels he is letting her down."

"Do you think she will forgive us? Angry Tansy is a scary thing. I swear she grew by a foot when she was yelling at me. I've never seen her mad before. She is always so calm and friendly."

As the afternoon wore on more helpers arrived and the field started to look better. Alex eventually turned up, looking sheepish and delicate, the latter an incongruous state for his huge frame.

At 5pm a bell sounded, summoning all the helpers to the beer tent. Pie, peas, chips and a pint were served, plus water for the still delicate. James thanked all the helpers who had cleared the village green, and Alex added his thanks, to those who had cleared the field. There would no doubt be a bit more to do when the stage and

PAULINE POTTERILL

beer tent came down but he was confident that
the field would be back to normal soon. Tansy
chomped on her chips.

CHAPTER TWENTY TWO

H aving dried and put away the dishes, squirted some air-freshener and swept the floor, James made another trip to his landing window. Still no sign of her. He checked his phone. Then he ran back downstairs. No light blinking on his answerphone. She was 5 minutes late. Then 10 minutes. Then 45 minutes. He had hoped that maybe, just maybe she would turn up for work. Finally, he acknowledged that she wasn't coming. He went into his office and checked his e-mails but he just couldn't concentrate. Soon he would need to go over to the field to meet the teams who would dismantle the stage and beer tent, but she might turn up whilst he was out. Logically that didn't matter as she had a key and would be coming to clean, but he desperately wanted to see her, to talk. He had so many questions, and despicably he felt, fears.

He left a note on the kitchen table and reluctantly headed off to the field. Eyes darting from person to person, checking every female, his disappointment grew. Then, in the distance, he saw someone on a bicycle heading his way. His heart skipped a beat, but it wasn't Gemma. When he reached the field, although there was no reason for her to be, she wasn't there either.

The morning dragged. People posed questions, chatted aimlessly, commented on the lump on his forehead. Offered sympathy. Some insisted on telling him home remedies for getting it to go down quicker, but he wasn't interested. Annoyingly some asked if he was alright. He wanted to explain, but that wouldn't do; he was the vicar, and it was his role to support others. Besides, he didn't want their judgement. No one, but little Nathan, had a good word for Gemma.

By lunch time the beer tent was down and loaded on a lorry and the stage had been dismantled. Richard, once more, provided sandwiches and chips. Tansy, at least, seemed a little happier. She had taken it upon herself to organise the litter pickers. There weren't that many now, as it was a weekday. Her team was slow but thorough, which pleased her, and she had promised to show them the donkeys when they were done. Enterprising, thought James.

* * *

Louise stared out of the estate agents' window. A familiar figure strolled by towing a trolley, in the company of a much taller familiar figure. The pair were deep in conversation. Then they turned into The Ark Aid.

"Isn't that Nathan with Mr Swire?" asked Gerald.

"Yes, and I have no idea why," replied Louise. "I thought he was with the triplets. Do you mind if I nip out. I need to go over anyway and talk to Alex about a moving-in date for the flat tenant."

There was no immediate sign of Nathan, or Mr Swire, but the trolley was parked outside St Peter's Charity Shop, piled high with all sorts of items. Then Nathan appeared and hefted a large leather suitcase off the trolley, stopping mid lift as he saw his mother. She was just about to speak when Mr Swire appeared.

"Oh, hello. He is a grand lad your Nathan, very helpful. I couldn't 'ave managed all this, without 'im and 'is trolley. I'll be givin' 'im a bit o' pocket money, don't you worry."

Nathan grinned. "We fixed the wheel. He showed me what to do."

"Well, it wasn't much good as it was, lad. Any road, another couple o' trips should do it."

Louise felt she ought to comment. She felt uncomfortable about the situation but couldn't think of any suitable objection. Instead she went to see Alex and let him know that the flat would be let from Thursday. Then, because she wanted a 'nosy', stepped into Tempus to see how Jonathan was getting on settling into his new premises. Jonathan was pleased to see her and enthusiastic about his weekend sales and pleased that she had encouraged him to move in, in time for the Crag Race. The door chimed and Jonathan gave his attention to a customer, leaving Louise to wander, immersing herself in the rhythm of the different mechanical sounds which changed in different parts of the shop: from the delicate tick tocks of the small timepieces to the sonorous notes of the grandfathers. In one of the windows a 2ft high Ferris wheel cranked its way round: tiny people sitting in tiny, beautifully painted seats with expressions of pure delight on their tiny faces. Beside it a carousel turned, miniature horses rising up and down with ruddy faced children on their backs. Next to that stood a Fairground Steam organ, little valves moving up and down, a mechanical tune playing merrily. She watched, fascinated, inspecting every piece, until Jonathan appeared at her shoulder.

"What do you think?"

"They are absolutely brilliant! Did you really make all these?"

He nodded.

"Well, I have to say that they are very impressive. I must bring my husband here. I'd love to show him your wall clocks. I would really like one for the living room."

* * *

Emily was getting a little irritated. Usually eager to play outside, the triplets were showing no sign of leaving the house again. Having finished the litter picking and then watched as the last of the stage was packed away, they had all returned home. Emily had been looking forward to another trip to the cellar and another of Sarah's memories. She desperately wanted to share her discovery with someone, especially Alex, but every time they were alone together, and she had the opportunity, something stopped her. She either couldn't find the words, or it felt wrong to share. They were someone's private memories and it felt like a betrayal to share them. Yet, she had no qualms about prying herself; it was as if she was meant to know. She knew that there were other trays and that it was likely that they contained memories of other Wells' triplets, but for now she was not inclined to experience them. It was Sarah who was holding her interest; she felt that she was getting to know and understand her and was also developing a huge admiration for her. Then, as she mentally revisited the memories and thought of the last one, she again had the unnerving feeling that she had been watched: she Emily, not Sarah.

When they sat down for their evening meal Alex was looking pleased with himself and kept glancing at Tansy. He scraped the remains of custard from his dish and sucked his spoon clean. Placing it noisily in the bowl he cleared his throat.

"How would you girls like to have riding

lessons?"

Three identical faces stared back, with three different expressions. Violet looked horrified, and Lily looked indifferent. Tansy looked delighted but then frowned, "not to ride the donkeys; it wouldn't be fair."

"No, if you learn to ride I will get you a pony." Looking at the others he added, "if you would like that."

"Alex," said Emily, "you should have talked to me about this. I'm not sure, if it is a good idea. They might get hurt."

"They will be fine."

Violet shook her head and Lily again looked indifferent.

"Only if you want," said Alex.

"Yes, please," said Tansy and threw her arms around him.

CHAPTER TWENTY THREE

Bright light bounced off the sloping roof of the well as Emily looked out of the kitchen window. Working her way along the line of arms and legs with sunscreen, ensuring that bits of skin weren't missed, she found herself longing for an overcast sky.

"Morning Mrs Wells."

"Oh, hello Nathan, you're early. Take a seat. What would you like for breakfast?"

"Cereal and toast, please. Four slices."

"Four slices?"

"Yes, please. And a banana."

Splashing milk over some cornflakes she studied him. Something was different: less slouch, more eye contact. There was a crashing on the stairs and Tansy appeared, medal hanging from her neck. She hesitated, then sat opposite Nathan. When Emily placed a bowl in front of her daughter, she noted that the medal was now hidden inside her dressing gown.

With the arrival of Lily and Violet the noise level increased, and all four children were soon chatting happily. Whatever had happened between them all, appeared to have been forgotten. Mentally noting to buy more bread she planned the rest of her day. As soon as the kids went out, she would clear away the breakfast, put on the washing machine and then, when she was sure they were happily amusing themselves outside, go down into the cellar.

"Do you have any of those cereal bars with nuts, Mrs Wells?"

"Probably. Haven't you had enough?"

"Roughage and protein are important."

"But you have already had cereal, and a banana, and 4 slices of toast."

"Yes, I'm a long streak 'o nothin' and I need fattening up."

Eyebrows raised, Emily went into the pantry. There was whispering and then Lily shouted out that she would like one too. Then Tansy and Violet joined in with the request. There was more whispering, which ceased abruptly on her return. She placed the packet on the table and started clearing the crockery and stacking the dishwasher. As she re-arranged items in the fridge to make room for the milk and margarine, there was a scuffling. Behind her chairs scraped and there was a groan from the sofa as Nathan threw himself into its depths. She closed the tops of the cereal box, struggling to fold the inner bag, which was now split. The cereal bar packet, she placed in the recycling. Overhead, there was a shout, "Mum...mee, can you help meee..."

Violet was searching through her drawers. "I can't find my yellow jumper."

Puzzled, Emily surveyed the room. Drawers were open and clothes scattered about the floor and all over the bed. Violet, the calmest and tidiest of her three children was flinging her belongs about in a frenzy.

"Your yellow jumper? Isn't it a bit warm, at the moment, for that one?"

"I like it."

"It is a winter jumper. It is in a box in the attic."

"But I like it."

"Well, I am not getting it out now. You will have to do with what you have got. Put this lot back."

Violet scooped up an armful from the bed and stared at her chest of drawers. Then she returned her armful to the bed and picked up a t-shirt and started to fold it. Emily watched and at the third attempt she shook her head and reluctantly joined in. "Couldn't you have looked without taking everything out?"

There was a shout, "Violet, we're going out."

Violet looked expectantly at her mother. "Oh, go on. I'll finish this," said Emily.

The front door slammed and the house appeared to sigh. Emily ran to a front window and watched as the triplets and Nathan strolled across the green and into The Ark Aid.

Satisfied they were gone for a while, she headed down to the cellar. Eager and unable to decide, she chose a marble at random. She got herself settled, switched off her torch, opened her hand and took a deep breath. There was a brief, but distinct smell of bananas, then she found herself swaying and blinking...

Chilled but exhilarated, her limbs at odds with her body, she threw her head back and pushed off from the bank. Screwing her eyes against the glare she twisted onto her front then dove beneath the surface. She scanned the rocky riverbed, picking and searching in the crystal clear water. Feeling, turning the pebbles, discarding. Lungs bursting, she shoved for the surface. Gasping, she pushed her hair from her face and wiped her eyes, blinded by the surface glare. Inhaling another lungful of air, she swam back down. Hands methodically sorting she inspected a lump of quart and took it to the surface. Adding it to her collection on the bank she again dove into the cold depths. Swimming upstream she followed the centre of the flow and dove deeper. Here a natural bowl held a constantly churning collection of pebbles. Fighting against the current she sorted through the stones. Tiring, she headed for the surface. A brief rest, then down again. It was getting harder, and her wrists were starting to ache. Her feet were already numb. Back up. Then, through the refracted water she saw what she was looking for. A few frantic kicks got her back down in position and she scrabbled at the riverbed, fingers clutching at her find. Grasping it firmly she took it to the surface and lay, floating on her back until her breathing was back under control. Otter-like she floated, inspecting her find. It was a good size, beautifully smooth and with a worm-sized hole through its centre. As she held it in the sunlight the top of it started to turn from dark grey to a creamy blue. She swam to the bank and added her stone to her collection. Listening, and being satisfied she was alone, she dragged herself up onto the grass and sat in the sun, rubbing some warmth back into her bare body.

Emily shivered. Finding herself in the dark she slapped her hand about the table until it found the torch. Before she could take hold it started to roll. She grabbed and it shot out of reach, onto the floor. She froze, listening to it bounce and roll. Pushing back her chair she crouched. Reaching out on the cold dusty floor she started a sweep-search, tentative at first, then more frantic as her search area grew. In the vastness of the surrounding void paranoia lurked. She was certain she could hear breathing. Then, amongst the grit and grime she touched rubber, knocking it out of reach. A couple of tentative pats and her hand rested on the torch. Grasping it she sought out its rubber covered button and pressed. Then she pressed it again. She shook it. It rattled as the batteries slid about inside. Suddenly, it seemed an awfully long way to the top of the stairs. Unnerved, she ran her hands over the torch, inspecting it, desperate to see. Feeling a gap between the main body and the end, she screwed it back together and pressed the button again. There was light: just a thin beam, but there was comfort in its weak glow. Getting back to her feet, she headed for the stairs, eager to get out of the cellar, eager to reclaim her privacy. It had been very distinct. She had been watched. She Emily, and not Sarah. She felt naked. She had been naked, and someone had been watching, but Sarah, she was certain, had no knowledge of that.

She put on the kettle and threw a teabag in a mug, then stuffed it back in the caddy and reached for coffee. Again, she shuddered. She needed to distract herself. Taking her mug and her book club book into the garden she tried to concentrate. She was only a third of the way through it and the next meeting was that evening. Perhaps she could skim read it, at least get the gist of it. She opened the book at chapter 12 and read the first page. When she turned to the next, she realised that the preceding events were a complete blank. She tried again but her thoughts kept straying to a creamy blue hag stone. Hag Stone! Sarah had found a Hag Stone. That is what she had been searching for in the river. Emily dropped her book on the floor and headed for her laptop. Rapping her nails on the worktop until it fired-up she then tapped and scrolled.

Hag Stone – there was so much information. She looked at article after article. It seemed that they were naturally occurring stones containing holes created by water and were considered to have the power to ward off evil. They were hung in barns to protect cattle and round necks to protect people. It was possible to buy them, but essentially, they needed to have been made naturally. For them to 'work' they needed to 'come' to the owner. Hag Stone. Emily had never heard the term before. Yet, she knew it. Not only that, but she was now certain she had seen that very stone before. Angelica's room was the most logical starting point.

When the children turned up for lunch, she was pleased to note that everything seemed to be back to normal. Whatever had happened between them all seemed to have been forgotten. Nathan was holding forth, spouting pearls of wisdom, most of them too old for his years. She wondered where he had heard them. Some TV programme no doubt; he kept mentioning Cornelius, and the girls seemed to know what he was talking about although she didn't think that there was a Cornelius in anything they watched.

Once they went out, she returned to Angelica's room and continued her search. As far as she could see, the hag stone wasn't hanging anywhere. She moved books and jars. She moved photo frames and vases. She cleared the entire windowsill, dusted it, and put the items back.

She emptied boxes and drawers, got distracted by keepsakes and photo albums, but didn't find the hag stone. Annoyingly she got brief glimpses of it in her mind but couldn't pin down where or when. Maybe it wasn't even in the house. It could easily be in the garden, or at Lou and Mike's house or even Fare Well Cottage. She knew it was going to drive her crazy until she found it. If she did.

* * *

When Alex came home, he was keen to tell Tansy that she had a riding lesson booked for Thursday evening at the Little Trotters Riding Academy. Emily wasn't certain who was more excited, he or Tansy. The two were soon deep in discussion about a shopping trip for helmet and boots. Jodhpurs, apparently, would come later. Lily and Violet, she was pleased to note, didn't seem bothered that there was nothing for them. The triplets were strangely mature that way.

The meal finished, she left Alex to clear up and headed out to her book club meeting. It was a lovely evening, and the high street was deserted. In the distance she could hear a car, shifting gear as it headed up the hill away from the village. It was rarely this quiet and she liked having the place to herself, heels clicking on the flag stones. It seemed ages since the last meeting, yet it was only two weeks. Feeling uncomfortable, that she hadn't finished the book, she transferred her jacket and bag to her left hand and pressed the doorbell. Soon she found herself, glass in hand, surrounded by people.

The book in question neatly divided the group. Half had loved it and half had hated it. Two confessed to not having finished it which skewed the result somewhat. After a heated discussion as to why some disliked it, which took longer than the positive reasons, things moved on. The hot topic this week was Gemma. Mags was the only person present who had lived in the village long enough to confirm that she was Crystal Winterbottom, and everyone was keen to know what she knew. Discretion being the better side of a glass of wine, and Mags had had two, she told everyone, in confidence, what she knew.

"We were at school together and, let's say, she was very popular with the boys. Forever being called to the head's office regarding 'incidents behind the bike shed', and for insisting on wearing her shirt collar turned up – no reason! It became a 'thing' for a while. Kids took the mick by wearing their collars up – just to torment her."

"When did she change her name?" asked Cheryl.

"I don't know. Didn't know she had until she came back."

"Well, when did she leave?"

"Soon after she left school. There was a circus. Rumour had it that she ran away with them."

"You're kidding. She actually did that! People actually run away with the circus!"

Maggie nodded. "That is what everyone believed, and I can't say I blame her, looking back. At the time we all thought it was funny, but now, well... we were all pretty horrible to her. She was lovely. She was nice and kind. It was her mother. Everyone teased Crystal because of her mother."

"Why, what did her mother do?"

Someone topped up Maggie's glass and passed round a plate of Hobnobs.

"Well, how can I put this politely?"

"Just say it..."

"Well, there was a 'certain establishment' over at Nether Tanning," said Mags.

"No!" said one of the men, "So, what Mr Swire said was true. Crystal's mother worked at Nina Norton's?"

Several people frowned and those in the know sniggered with delight.

"Nina Norton's Knockin' Shop?"

"Er, yes."

"But that wasn't Crystal's fault."

"No, but it didn't stop the name calling and the harassment she got from boys with, shall we say... 'high expectations'," said Mags.

"Maybe the vicar will save her."

"Hmm...," said Mags. "That wasn't all, but I have said too much. No, I'm not spreading gossip. I don't think it was proven."

Despite the uproar this caused, Maggie

steadfastly refused to say any more.

CHAPTER TWENTY FOUR

Emily twirled the bag of bread and wrapped the sticky strip round it. Not much left, she must remember to get another bag out of the freezer.

"James came round last night," said Alex between mouthfuls of toast. "He can't find Gemma."

"Oh, she's still missing?"

"You heard what happened at the beer festival, well, she didn't turn up for work on Monday and he went round to her flat, but she wasn't there and according to the neighbours she doesn't even live there. Seems she gave him a false address."

"No! Well, where does her mother live? I thought she had come back to look after her mother."

"Yes, that was supposedly the address."

"According to Mags," said Emily, removing Snokettee from her chair so she could sit down, "what was said at the beer festival and by Mr Swire, is true. She's put on weight and changed her hair, but enough people are adamant that Gemma is Crystal."

"Really? That is such a shame. James seems to really like her. He is very upset she lied but still wants to find her. I guess he is hoping it isn't true."

A silent figure appeared in the doorway, "Hi, love. What do you want for breakfast?"

"Orange juice and toast," said Violet, "and a cereal bar."

"Why are you all wanting cereal bars all of a sudden?"

"For the stamina."

Tansy and Lily arrived. In the distance the cat flap swung noisily and soon Spider and Marigold appeared shortly followed by Whoops-a-Daisy. Emily stepped over a cat. As she placed a glass of orange in front of Violet she said to Alex, "According to Mags, that isn't all. She just wouldn't say what, but it sounded bad. Whatever it was – they couldn't prove it!"

The front door clicked. Emily briefly registered the arrival of Nathan as she removed Spider from the table. Turning the cat over she pulled a face and plucked a slug from its belly. As she put the cat down, she noticed that the slug had a small fluffy grey feather attached. After depositing the slug in a pot of basil she washed her hands and turned back to the table. A wide-eyed Nathan was standing in the doorway, looking wildly at Violet: the only one paying him any attention.

Alex drained his coffee cup. Then he stood up, gave Emily a quick kiss, and said, "Oh, what happened with the marbles?"

Emily froze.

"You were going to find out how much they were worth. It would be good to have some idea for Saturday, when the Crag money is handed over."

"Oh! I…"

"Anyway," and he glanced round meaningfully at the table, "Have fun. Bye".

Nathan, in the doorway, did a little dance. He looked panicked, uncertain whether to step aside or block the way.

"Daddy, Daddy," shouted Tansy. "The donkeys. Can we get them back today?"

"Just open the gate. They will make their own way back up."

"But they need their feed troughs!"

"I'll move them this afternoon. I promise."

"You said that yesterday," pouted Tansy as Alex 'stared down' Nathan who, with a look of concern on his face, stepped aside. Alex disappeared into the hall.

There was a stifled yell followed by, "BLOODY HELL! What the…"

The kitchen fell silent. All eyes turned towards the door. There were several more expletives. Then three limp, inverted pigeons came into view, held aloft by two outstretched arms. It looked like two of the birds warranted toe tags already and the third a 'Not for Resus' label. "Someone get the back door!" growled Alex.

Emily obliged. As he passed her, he said, "they were in front of the cellar door!"

* * *

James had vacuumed, dusted, and polished the doorknobs, just in case. He sat and sipped his coffee and stared across the table to an empty, lipstick smudged mug. It hadn't been cleared away before he and Gemma had left for the Crag Race, and now he didn't want to move it;   there was something comforting in its presence. A noise from the front door gave him brief hope, which flitted away as something dropped onto the mat. The hall clock began counting to 9. He had 15 minutes before a happy couple would arrive and he would have to smile and enthuse and help them plan and choose hymns.

* * *

With the children out playing, Emily did another tour of the house but couldn't find the hag stone. She had spent a lot of the night lying awake searching her memory. Now she was fairly sure that it was somewhere, above eye level and that it was positioned somewhere slightly darker than its surrounding, maybe in an alcove. She also felt that there was a door, or doorway involved. She visited each door in turn, checking both sides, but there was nothing even resembling a hag stone. Putting on the washing machine she thought back over all the changes that had been made to the cottage that may have caused the stone to be moved, but she didn't think there had been anything that significant and she would surely have remembered a feature like that. Unless, of course, Alex had moved it. They had re-done the outhouse and toilet in the past two years, but she couldn't imagine why anyone would have positioned the stone in there. The more likely place would be the front door, if it was thought to ward off evil. She had searched both front and back porches and it definitely wasn't there. Still, Alex may know.

At a loss, as to where else to look, she decided to make some more of her candles. The Crag Race had been quite lucrative for Heaven Scent, and they had requested more. She was pleased. The extra money could be added to the Crag fund in time for Saturday's hand-over to St Peter's Young Disabled Unit. There was going to be a presentation at the home, with pictures taken of Lady Agnes receiving the cheque, for the local paper. Emily hadn't seen Lady Agnes for a while. It would be good to see her again.

As she waited for her wax to melt her mind went back to the marbles. She couldn't possibly sell them. Somehow, she was going to have to tell Alex about them. She thought that he had forgotten, but apparently not. Then, she realised that she hadn't returned the last marble to its box. She had been so intent on finding the torch and getting out of the cellar that she had forgotten all about the marble. She didn't have a clue what she had done with it. She had opened her hand at the start of the memory...but after that... Was it on the table? Had she dropped it on the floor? She really ought to find it and return it to its box but the thought of going down there again, unnerved her.

* * *

At the forge, Alex was struggling to attach a shoe to a jittery palomino. Its 13-year-old owner wasn't helping matters. She was waving a crop about and shouting at it to stand still and wincing and wrinkling her nose, every time the shoe singed its way onto the hoof. When Nathan and the triplets came into the yard, Alex called Tansy over.

"Tansy, would you like to show Tamara the donkeys?"

As the others looked on, Tansy frowned. Instead, she went to the pony and placed her head against its forehead and whispered to it. The animal quickly settled and was soon standing calmly as Tansy stroked its neck. Violet stared at the pony, enthralled. She had never seen a pink pony before.

The girl slapped the crop against her leather covered ankle a couple of times. "So, where are these donkeys, then?"

Tansy ignored her but the girl was now waving the crop in the air and the pony was warily eyeing her.

"I can manage," said Alex.

So, reluctantly, Tansy led the girl across the yard and over to the field. In silence they trekked across the dry grass. Tansy opened the connecting gate and called. Wonky appeared first, then the other three donkeys. The girl looked them up and down. "What's wrong with them?"

Tansy tried to explain that they were all recovering and explained about the Donkey Sanctuary at High Dudgeon, but the girl wasn't interested. "Can't think why you'd want to show me these. Are we done?" She had now turned the crop round and was slapping the metal tip on her boot. The donkeys shied away.

Tansy snatched the crop from the girl's hand. "Do you know nothing about animals?"

"Give me that back!"

"No."

As the girl lunged, Tansy turned and hurled the crop away from the donkeys and into a nearby tree, where it lodged, out of reach. The girl stood furiously looking up at her crop whilst Tansy stomped back towards the forge.

"You did what?" said Alex.

Lily, and Nathan, who had been milling round the yard came over. Violet was still staring at the palomino.

"She should not be anywhere near animals."

"You go and apologise right now. I've nearly finished here. I'll come and get the crop down."

Tansy scowled: feet planted defiantly.

"Go! Now!"

Tansy stared. She had never seen her father so angry. Her bottom lip came out and she backed away. Tears threatening, she broke into a run as she set off for the field.

"I'll get it Mr Wells," said Nathan and ran after Tansy.

As soon as they approached, the girl started yelling at Tansy, "You owe me a crop. I'll tell your daddy over you."

"He already knows," retorted Tansy, eyeing the other girl's previously pristine jodhpurs and noting green and brown smudges. She studied the tree, tempted to climb it herself, just to humiliate the girl.

"I'll get it. I'll get it," said Nathan, eager to calm things down.

Tamara looked at him with hope, Tansy with disdain. As Lily and Violet joined the little group Tamara looked from face to face to face, scowling. The triplets looked cockily back, united, and Tamara retreated a couple of paces. The first to break eye contact, Tamara turned her attention to Nathan who was now holding his catapult and aiming a stone at the tree.

Tansy opened her mouth, then shut it again

as the stone slammed into the tree branch, and the crop dropped a couple of metres. Not wanting to push his luck he searched out a fallen tree branch and used that, instead of his catapult, to knock the crop to the ground. As Nathan handed the crop to Tamara, Tansy clapped. She was actually impressed, and generous enough to applaud him.

"Gemma gave me lessons," he said shyly.

"Do you think she'd show me?"

"I can ask. I've got more stuff to collect for the charity shop. I can pop round then."

"Is he going to pay you, again?" said Lily, "We're gonna need more batteries soon."

"Yes, it is so kind of you to spend your money on batteries," smiled Violet.

Nathan nodded and looked up. In the distance Tamara had reached the gate and was talking to Alex, waving her arms and the crop in the air. Together they headed to the forge. When the children crossed the lane Tamara, and the newly shod pony were trotting off into the distance.

"You didn't apologise, did you?" said Alex.

"No!" said Tansy, then added, "There wasn't time."

"Well, she has just ridden off without paying. I am now going to have to ring her father and explain what happened and hope that he won't take the same attitude as his daughter."

CHAPTER TWENTY FIVE

As Alex pushed back the large wooden doors of the forge, he was glad that he had moved the donkeys' troughs back to the top field. After the children had left him, he had relented, feeling bad that he had shouted at Tansy. She was only 6 after all and she was just being her usual kind self and doing her best for the animal. She was right, Tamara didn't really care that much about the pony. As far as he could tell, she only had it because her friends had ponies. As he looked up at the clouds, from the shelter of the forge's tin canopy and listened to the drumming overhead, he took a deep breath and let the freshness fill his lungs. Then, reluctantly he stepped inside and set about getting the forge up to temperature. It would soon be stiflingly dry in there.

At 9am he went over to What Sup, enjoying the cool shower on his bare arms as he crossed the yard. He smiled to himself as others huddled in doorways and dashed inside the shops as soon as they opened. Then he remembered that

PAULINE POTTERILL

his new flat tenant was moving in today; she
wouldn't appreciate the rain. The stone steps,
worn deep by generations of feet, could be
slippery when wet. If he had time, he would help
her carry her belongings up.

He sipped his coffee, then wiped his upper
lip with the back of his hand. The yard looked
different in the rain. Light dusty cobbles now
looked black, and surfaces shone. If it wasn't for
the colourful pots of plants dotted round the
yard the whole scene could have been a sepia
faded black and white photo. His eyes travelled
along the shop fronts then up to the roof tops
and along the gutters. His heart sank. Water
cascaded in places it shouldn't and what looked
like buddleia was growing out of an angle in
the forge roof. Yes, he could just pay someone
to sort it out, but that wasn't Alex. If he could
do something himself, he would, even if the
thought of it depressed him. Hopefully some of
the problem could be solved by simply clearing
the gutters, but he wouldn't know until he put a
ladder up there.

Familiar voices, coming through the Ark Aid
entrance, alerted him to the imminent arrival of
the triplets. As three identical yellow raincoats
skipped into view, he was pleased to note that
Tansy was back to her normal self with no sign
of wariness when she saw him. All three came
running over and turned 'cutesy' when they saw
his drink. He tousled the odd damp head and

stepped back inside the shop. When he came out again, clutching three hot chocolates, the girls were happily sitting on wet seats, skinny legs swinging, unused yellow hoods filling with water. He left them, huddled over their drinks, chatting animatedly about the 'arrival'. They lived in their own little fantasy world. A lot of what they said made no sense, but children were like that, and his were no different... Yes, they were. He had to acknowledge that. His were very different. At the forge door, he looked back. All three had adopted airs of sophistication. He smiled, he could see that they all felt very grown-up, watching the word go by from their street-side table. No adult, however, would be content to get wet like that.

At 10.30am when the bell on the forge gate rang and Alex stepped outside to open it, he was surprised to see the triplets still sitting outside the café. He pulled the gate back and allowed his new tenant to drive in and directed her to park under the forge canopy. There, she could sort her things out in the dry. The rain had eased a little, but it didn't look like stopping.

"Hi, I'm Alex. Sorry about the weather."

"Hello, I'm Pauline," I said. "Nice to meet you. Louise told me you own these buildings."

"Yes, I expect she will be here shortly, but I can let you in," and he led the way up the steps and opened the flat door. As we stepped inside Louise arrived, muttering, and shaking drips, and apologising. She turned to shut the door but found three identical children on the threshold, their grins as bright as their raincoats.

"Girls, what are you doing here? Go on. You can't come in," said Alex.

"We are here to help," said one, as the others nodded.

I looked them up and down, and from face to face to face, and smiled, "Hello."

"Girls, please leave, and let the lady move in in peace."

"Are they your girls?" I asked.

"Yes," then realising that introductions were expected, he said, "This is Lily, this is Violet, and this is Tansy. Now say goodbye to Ms Potterill."

A young boy arrived in the doorway, who I later discovered was called Nathan. Louise joined in and together she and Alex shepherded the kids out.

"Sorry about that," said Alex. "I will help you carry your things up. If you like. Then I will leave you to settle in."

* * *

Scraping crumbs and baked bean sauce into the sink, Emily frowned. That old feeling of 'something unsettling about to happen' was back. It had been a while since the children had mentioned The Catolith and the strange cat hadn't been seen for a while, but then she hadn't looked up at the outhouse roof recently; it could still be there. Over lunch however, there had been mention of 'The Cronkler' having arrived; the inference being that this was the third arrival. When she had asked them what they were talking about, they all clammed up again. She also noted, although she didn't see it happen, that most of the fruit had gone and most of the biscuits.

Putting the crockery in the dishwasher she gave Louise a quick call. They chatted for a while. Then Louise had to give her attention to a customer and ended the call. However, a 'girls' night out' had been arranged and Emily felt a little brighter.

"Hello? Hi."

"I'm in here," shouted Emily.

James strolled into the kitchen, looking a little sheepish. "I hope you don't mind, but I wanted someone to talk to."

"Of course, have a seat." As she filled the kettle, he grabbed a couple of mugs and sat down. As they waited for the water to boil she said, "Have you not found her yet?"

He looked slightly surprised, and she cocked her head on one side and looked him in the eye, "Was there another subject you wanted to discuss? Is there someone new that you are moping about?"

"Moping! Is it that obvious?"

"Well, yes. You haven't been the same since the Crag Race."

"Do you think what everyone is saying is true?"

"Well, it does seem that there are enough people who knew Crystal who are adamant that she and Gemma are one and the same. Why she would give you a false address, I don't know, but it doesn't mean that there isn't a simple, innocent reason for that."

"Such as?"

"I don't know. Have you tried looking her up on the internet?"

"Yes. Both as Gemma Modoran and Crystal Winterbottom. I even looked at the church records to see if I could find where her mother lived, although that felt unethical and now I feel bad about that."

"Seriously? AND, did you find out?"

"No."

"So, have you found out anything at all?"

"Only that she lied to me. I really thought that we had something, and now, she's gone."

"Oh, James, I'm so sorry." Emily sat next to him and wrapped an arm round his shoulders, shoulders that had previously supported a whole community and which now sagged and felt so narrow.

* * *

It didn't take the removal men long to unpack the small van and bring in my furniture. Thankfully the rain had stopped by the time they arrived, and they parked at the bottom of the steps. Once they had gone, I unpacked a mug and my kettle. Whilst I waited for it to boil, I emptied my cool box contents into the fridge. With the sun now streaming through the windows it was quite warm, so I opened the front door. Looking down at the What Sup café it occurred to me that I could probably fit a little bistro table and chair at the top of my steps along with a couple of plant pots. It would be a lovely place to sit and watch the world go by and gain inspiration. I planned to start writing again the following Monday but for now I would get to know the area and settle in.

I jumped and turned, a rapping of knuckles on wood alerting me to the figure silhouetted in my doorway. "Hi, I was just locking up for the day but I thought I would come and introduce myself before I left. I'm Jonathan, I have the shop below you, Tempest."

"Oh, hi. Come in," I said. "I'm Pauline, Pauline Potterill. Lovely to meet you. Have a seat." I removed a couple of cardboard boxes and gave the settee cushion a dust with my hand. We both looked at it. I picked it up and shook it. "Hmm…" I found a tea towel, the nearest thing to hand, and draped it over the cushion. He laughed and sat down, carefully hitching his trousers slightly to maintain the smart crease at his knees.

"Can I get you a drink?"

"Thanks, no. I need to get home. Just wanted

to say hello. You'll find we are a friendly bunch in The Ark Aid. If you need any help with anything, just ask. If we can't help, between us we will probably know someone who can."

"Oh, is there anywhere I can get a takeaway in the village? I expect the pub does food, but it has been a busy week and I just fancy a quiet night and no cooking."

"Yes, if you like Indian food there is the Basak's Bangladeshi Restaurant and Take-away. just turn right as you step out of The Ark Aid, it isn't far. Their food is fabulous. Tell Aslam that you have just moved in. I've not been here long but I like picking up a takeaway on my way home. Fortunately, my wife likes it too. So, you're a writer. What sort of stuff do you write?"

"Mainly Romantic Comedy but I am working on a ghost story at the moment. Hopefully it is humorous as well. My writing tends to be somewhat genre-free. After all, life is. We never say, this is my friend Susan, her life is a historical drama, or, let me introduce you to David he is on a sci-fi mission."

"True, very true. I would love to read some of it some time. Well, as I said, got to get home."

After he left I continued with my unpacking and made up the bed, ready for me to fall into later. I had somewhere to sit, a bed to sleep in and the kitchen and bathroom were usable. Everything else could wait. As it was 6pm I set out to find the Basak's."

* * *

"Mummy, mummy, mummy," yelled an excited Tansy as she stampeded into the kitchen. "That was awesome. I rode Comet. He's gorgeous. I did a trot. Daddy led him round but at the end of the lesson I got to steer on my own, just walking, not trotting, but it was brilliant. I can't wait for next week. Daddy, show mummy the pictures."

Alex took out his phone and Emily peered over his shoulder as he scrolled. Emily chewed her lip; Tansy looked amusingly cute in the large helmet which, in a short video clip, seemed to take control of her head as she rocked about on the unfortunate pony's back.

"I am going to get my own helmet on Saturday morning, and boots, aren't I daddy?"

"Yes, love."

Violet looked at the pictures. "I liked Tamara's pony. It was pink."

CHAPTER TWENTY SIX

A t Breakfast Nathan seemed quite sulky. He scowled at Emily and snapped at Violet when she put her hand on his arm in an attempt to comfort him. All the girls seemed puzzled, which in turn puzzled Emily.

When she asked him what he would like for breakfast he replied, "One slice of toast and some orange juice, please."

"Just one?"

"Yes."

For some reason this didn't seem to go down well with the girls. Violet put her hand back on his arm, "You must... for the stamina." Lily and Tansy nodded enthusiastically.

As Emily filled the dishwasher there was muttering behind her followed by an emphatic, "NO!" Nathan left the table. "I'm going to see Cornelius."

"Oh, don't forget to ask Gemma," said Tansy. "Mummy, Nathan is really good with his catapult."

"Yes, amazing," said Violet.

Lily explained how he had retrieved the girl's crop. "He is going to ask Gemma if she will teach Tansy too."

"What? Nathan..." but he had gone. "Does Nathan know where Gemma lives?"

* * *

James was overwhelmed. Clutching his phone to his ear he blurted, "Nathan knows! Where, where does she live?"

"I didn't get a chance to ask him, and the girls don't know but it is somewhere near Mr Swire. Do you know where he lives?"

"Er, No. The other end of the village somewhere."

"Look, I'll get Louise to ask him if I don't see him first."

"What do you think I should do? Should I go round, send a note? I owe her money for the cleaning."

"If it was me, and I was embarrassed, I think I would prefer a note, especially if for some reason she doesn't want you to know where she lives."

"But she's already ignored all my phone and text messages."

"I'm seeing Louise tonight. Hopefully I can get the address from her and see what she thinks too. Are you sure about this though, with everything that people are saying?"

"I don't know, but I have to see her again."

* * *

Overnight, the yard was a quiet haven and I had slept well. Banging doors, opening shutters, and voices had welcomed me to the new day. I lay for a while listening to the sounds until the strong smell of freshly ground coffee beans wafted through my open windows, and I threw on some clothes.

I introduced myself but there was a queue of people, and our chat was brief. The couple running What Sup seemed friendly and welcomed me to the yard. Outside I hesitated. As one of the tables was vacated, I sat. I had intended taking my purchases back to the flat but, despite a slight breeze, it was warm. I parked myself at a table and tore off a bit of croissant. Someone wedged open the door of the charity shop opposite and I found myself swaying slightly to a Trad Jazz classic, which ended before I could put a title to it. A bossa nova took over and I was transported to Ipanema. I wasn't the only one. Consciously or unconsciously people were sashaying over the cobbles, their actions a little slower, their expressions a little brighter and their credit cards, presumably, a little more flexible.

A young lad appeared, dragging a make-shift cart piled high with boxes and carrier bags. It was Nathan, the lad I had been introduced to briefly. A tall elderly gentleman joined him. Despite the sun an overcoat sagged on his thin frame and a cloth cap struggled to keep wisps of white hair under control. Together they unloaded their haul into the charity shop. Nathan waved at me, and the old man winked. Trolley empty, they came over.

"This is Ms Potterill", said Nathan standing tall. "Ms Potterill, this is Mr Swire."

I smiled, stood, and shook Mr Swire's proffered hand. "Call me Pauline," I said, as I squeezed the wrinkled dry skin, the grip frail but firm. "Nice to meet you."

"Cornelius, at your service," he said, placing his other hand over mine. "Welcome to Much Meddling. So... you are the chronicler."

"Pardon?"

Bright eyes looked into mine, searching for something, twinkling. "The Chronicler... the scribe... the writer young Nathan here mentioned."

I looked at Nathan. He was looking oddly at Mr Swire.

"Yes. I'm an author."

"Well, "You won't be short of inspiration here". He put his arm round Nathan's shoulders. Come on me lad, one more load should do it." He doffed his cap.

As they passed the door of the charity shop and headed towards the street, he did an odd little rumba and swung the tail of his overcoat; the whole movement somewhat cat-like.

* * *

Whilst Tansy and Violet distracted their mother, Lily stole down to the cellar where she replenished the man's supplies and removed his rubbish. The collection under the sheet had grown but the man still took care to keep the items hidden and Lily respected that. The time would come. He was stronger now and his leg appeared healed. Fresh air and sunlight would finish the task but first he had his own task to finish and then the purpose of his visit would be revealed.

* * *

When Emily pushed her way through the door of The Three Wells, she stopped short. Friday nights were usually busy, but never like this. Jostled from behind, she found herself being swallowed by the crowd as it edged towards the bar. Clutching her bag to her chest she craned to see over the mass of grey blow-dried heads, scanning the room for Louise's dark hair and Anna's light brown. Podgy arms stuck to hers and she held her breath: Lily of the Valley so strong in the air she could have made posies. There was a shout and a tap on her shoulder and Louise linked her arm and pulled her free, dragging her round the periphery to the back door and out to the sanctuary of the beer garden.

The fresh air came as a huge relief. Emily inhaled deeply. "What's going on? What are all these women doing here?"

"Somewhere, holding court in that heaving post-menopausal mass, is Mr Swire," said Louise.

"It is his 100th birthday," added Anna.

"No!"

"Yes." The three women exchanged a look.

"Anyway," said Louise pushing a large glass towards Emily, "get that inside you."

She took a refreshing swig, noting that a second round of drinks sat at the ready, courtesy, no doubt of Louise.

"So, what's new?" asked Anna.

"Well, the good news is that Nathan doesn't have worms!"

"That's a relief," said Emily. "I did wonder. Especially now that the girls are following suit. They all want cereal bars, for 'the stamina'."

A loud cheer went up from inside the pub, followed by clapping and more cheering. The sparrows, which had been hopping about under the tables, took flight. The pigeons, undeterred, continued with their chip processing.

Louise handed Emily a slip of paper to give to James. It had a map of Gemma's street with her house marked. Nathan didn't know what the number was. The house was opposite the block of flats that James had tried. Anna took a look, puzzled that they should be wanting Mrs Winterbottom's address. Emily kicked herself that she hadn't thought to ask her, but then James should have thought of that too. When they explained about James interest in Gemma,

PAULINE POTTERILL

and the false address, Anna carefully placed her glass down on the table and played with its stem. The others waited, studying her face.

"It wasn't proved, but she apparently killed her husband." She took a sip of wine whilst this sank in. Then continued, "with a knife." She took another couple of sips. "This was about 15 years ago, out in Romania. You know she ran away with the circus that came to the village in the early 2000's. Well, she left and went touring Europe with them. Reporters came knocking on her mother's door when the Romanian Police were looking for her. She wasn't here though, and interest died. If you can speak Romanian, you can probably find stuff about the case online. But, I don't think anything was ever proved."

CHAPTER TWENTY SEVEN

As the assistant checked the fit, rocking the helmet backwards and forwards, Tansy's eyebrows moved up and down with each rock. With difficulty, Alex kept his face straight. He sat patiently through the measurements and then all the motions Tansy was asked to complete to ensure the helmet stayed put, however violently she moved. He could have fit a set of shoes in less time than it took to fit the riding helmet. The boot fitting took less time and he winced when he presented his credit card, thankful that her head wouldn't grow as fast as her feet. However, seeing her so thrilled, was worth every penny.

She cantered her way into the kitchen, eager to show off her gear. The boots and helmet stayed firmly in place all through lunch and only came off when the family pulled up outside St Peter's young Disabled Unit. James was already there, smartly dressed in a suit but wearing his dog collar as opposed to tie.

Lady Agnes, walked across the entrance hall

to meet them, warmly shaking their hands, and kissing their cheeks. Her walking had improved enormously over the past three years. She now carried her stick, rather than used it. After suffering a series of strokes the staff had done a wonderful job of maximising her potential but most of the credit needed to go to Lady Agnes herself, for sheer determination. The one thing that really irked her now was her speech, and she was still self-conscious when eating in company.

The entrance hall was lined with the home's staff and residents. Decorative banners hung from the walls and colourful posters proudly depicted the life and achievements of the home. Sophie sat to one side, Eliza on her lap and Simon and Trevor next to her. Members of the press vied for places.

As James ended his speech and presented the cheque to Lady Agnes, for the money raised by the Crag Race, cameras clicked, and questions filled the air. James did his best to answer, heaping praise on all the contestants and helpers. He and Lady Agnes were asked to turn this way and that, shake hands again, smile. Then, seeing Lady Agnes falter, Sophie wheeled forward and forcefully told the reporters that 'that was enough' and thanked them all for coming.

Once the press had departed and the staff dwindled away, back to their work, Lady Agnes invited James and the Well's family up to her apartment. Laid out, in the turret room at the corner of her sitting room, was a lace covered table. On it, sparkling in sunlight, was a prettily patterned bone-china tea service. Dainty cakes and crumbly looking biscuits sat enticingly on a tiered cake stand. Simon poured everyone a cup of tea and then pointlessly handed round the sugar bowl to the adults. Seeing bemusement on the triplets' faces he used the silver tongues to pick up a cube. Then, after a nod from Emily, he gave the children one each. Violet held hers delicately between thumb and forefinger, rotating it slowly in a ray of sunlight. Lily sucked happily and Tansy crunched into hers whilst eyeing up the bowl.

Emily spotted James, surreptitiously checking his phone. Then it rang and he moved over to the corner of the room to answer it. She needed to get him alone. She had to warn him.

Eliza sat on the floor, an island in a sea of toys. The triplets, who were entranced as always by the small human, vied to engage her in play. Lily and Violet knelt: toes curled under them. Tansy crouched, arms wrapped round the shins of her riding boots, soles firmly planted on the floor. When she thought her parents weren't looking, she used the sleeve of her cardigan to give the toes a polish. Trevor stood forlornly and watched. "So, Trevor," said Alex, "How are you enjoying school?"

The boy brightened a little, "Its okay."

"Have you made many friends?"

"Only, Bryn."

"He is coming to tea tomorrow." said Sophie. "That will be fun. Won't it?"

Trevor nodded but didn't look too thrilled.

Putting his phone away James announced that he had to leave. He needed to see one of his parishioners who was having a 'crisis of faith'. He made his apologies and left. Emily was relieved. The 'Gemma conversation' would have to wait.

* * *

He assured his parishioner, Mrs Prendergast, that God wouldn't mind if she didn't kneel for communion, especially if the action caused her to 'inadvertently blaspheme'. She had tried to substitute other words, but the pain just blotted them all out and she couldn't help herself. Perhaps she was being tested. Did he think she was being tested? He suggested that they pray together. He closed his eyes. There was a thud. As he prayed for her soul, she let out a barrage of ripe expletives and a very contrite, "Sorry vicar, oh God, Sorry God. Oh, No, Oh!!"

Having consoled Mrs Prendergast, he set off on a mission of his own. As he let himself through the small wrought-iron gate he was amazed at the quantity of flowers either side of the stone path. A field of colour, he didn't differentiate between the masses of roses and the dandelions and rosebay willow herb that had taken over the ground. Before he reached the front door, it opened, and he beamed. Gemma stood there looking a little shy, but radiant.

He was ushered into the front room, which smelt of roses, just like the garden. Awkwardly she offered him a drink. Although it made no sense for her to ask tea or coffee, milk, sugar, he was pleased that she didn't. As crockery chinked in a back room, he looked about him. White framed prints, and photos of people, none of whom he recognised, competed to hide the pale pink walls. Above and below, matching flowery borders ran round the room at dado and ceiling height, interrupted by matching curtains. The pattern, he noted, was repeated on the settee cushions. The mantelpiece was hidden under pottery ducks of different styles and sizes and a couple of ceramic candlesticks which, on closer inspection, also had duck motifs.

The tea turned up just as he liked it and with a selection of his favourite biscuits. Once the formalities had been covered, they went back to feeling awkward. Then, to his horror he blurted out, "Why did you lie to me? Why did you give me a false address?"

She hung her head and kind of shrunk into herself. "It was just a job, and I needed it. I thought if you knew who I really was, you wouldn't hire me. I never thought... we would, become...friends."

"And the false name?"

"Gemma is my real name. I got teased so much as a child that I changed it to Gemma, by deed poll."

"And Modoran?"

"That is my married name. I was er... married. He... died."

"Oh, I, I'm sorry," said James.

"That's ok. It was many years ago now and, well, it wouldn't have lasted anyway. Would you like some more tea?" She gathered their mugs and hurried off to the kitchen. A tap ran. A kettle hissed. Another voice could be heard, questioning Gemma: presumably her mother. James couldn't make out any words, just disapproving intonation and much 'shushing'.

As she handed a fresh mug to James she said, "So, how did the Crag Race go? How much was raised?"

"Money is still coming in, but I've just handed over a cheque for £8,300 to St Peter's."

By the time he left things were more or less back to normal between the two of them and she had agreed to return to work on Monday.

When he sat down to write his sermon it flowed easily and he said a heartfelt prayer of thanks.

* * *

Having re-attached the mower's pull cord Alex tried again. He pumped the fuel button and then gave the cord a tug. Nothing happened.

He pulled again. Then again. He pumped more fuel and tried once more. There was a bang and a splutter, and he stepped backwards as a noxious black cloud billowed. As it dispersed, he ran forward holding his breath. The mower was now hurtling across the grass. He grabbed it and swung it round, knocking it out of gear. Eyeing up the peony bush that had narrowly escaped he breathed a sigh of relief. How Emily managed to mow with this thing he had no idea. Putting it back in gear he set off. It didn't sound happy. It travelled about 10 feet and died. He'd checked the spark plug and the filter, confident that he could fix it. Now, he had to admit, Emily was right. They needed a new mower. He had no idea how old it was, but the area code on the manufacturer's label didn't have a 1 after the zero.

He grabbed a cold beer from the fridge and found himself a shady spot under one of the apple trees. Glancing upwards and seeing the cottage gutters reminded him that he needed to do the gutters in The Ark Aid. Then his eyes came to rest on a scruffy looking silhouette atop the outhouse. It was a cat and, from his memory of Emily's description, he believed it to be The Catolith. It was staring at him.

* * *

My first sight of Emily came as she emerged from the candle shop, Heaven Scent. I had been into the charity shop in search of a little table and chair set, to fit outside my front door. They didn't have one but said they would let me know if one turned up. As I headed towards my flat, the three Wells girls surrounded me and started chatting. When Emily appeared they brought her over and introduced me to her. She was as surprised at the introduction as I was but she smiled, slightly apologetically, and welcomed me to the yard. Technically she was my landlady, and I was happy to get to know her. She struck a shy, waif-like figure, and had I been told that she was the mother of three girls I would have been surprised. Surrounded by her brood she seemed to grow in stature. She took confidence from them: patently proud of them. Had I met her separately I would have known she was their mother. Although facially different, the triplets had her expressions and mannerisms.

"I hear that you are an author," she said. "I have never met an author before. Well, not that I am aware of."

She didn't ask what I had written, or comment on my work, so I assumed that she wasn't familiar with it, or had looked me up because she hadn't heard of me and knew she hadn't read any of my books. Instead, she asked me what I thought of Much Meddling. We exchanged a few more pleasantries and she told me a little about the village and the surrounding area. It seemed we shared an interest in walking and she volunteered to take me up to the Crag sometime. For some reason, this seemed to delight the girls. All three appeared keen that their mother and I became friends. It would be a long time before I understood why.

CHAPTER TWENTY EIGHT

With the church bells striking the half hour Emily shouted up for the girls to get dressed. Peering in the hall mirror she ran her fingers through her hair. It needed cutting.

"Perhaps we can have a look at those marbles after church," shouted Alex, from the kitchen. "I'll bring them up when we get back."

Straightening the collar of her blouse, she froze. She didn't want to risk him removing one from a box in the semi-darkness of the cellar. She particularly didn't want him accessing Sarah's memories; some of them were very personal and she hadn't seen all of them. She did a quick sweep through her own memories, the more intimate ones leaping to the fore.

"Are you okay?" asked Alex, "You look quite flushed."

"Yes," she answered, going even pinker and being unable to hide the fact. She was about to blame the weather, but the hall was a bit chilly. "Are the girls ready yet?"

"Unlikely. I'll go see what they are doing."

A little while later the stairs shook as her family descended, then the house relaxed as the front door shut. From the outhouse roof, amber eyes took note as the family disappeared into the church. Shortly afterwards the cellar door opened, and the man let himself out of the back door. He crossed the garden, pausing by the well. He raised the bucket and took a drink. Leaving all as he had found it, he climbed the stile into the wood. He had about an hour to stretch his legs.

* * *

Sliding into a pew, it occurred to Emily that James hadn't asked about Gemma's address. When he started the service, she was pleased to see that he looked a little less serious than he had appeared of late. The thought of ruining that, prayed on her mind all through his sermon. Concentrating on his message of love and forgiveness didn't help; it just made it worse.

As the communion line edged forward, she ran over what she might say to him if he asked. As she moved nearer the altar rail, she looked up in time to see James lunge to his right, arms outstretched. The silver salver flashed as it was tossed into the air sending Communion wafers heavenwards. There was a thud.

In the hushed silence, amid a blizzard of white wafers, there was a howl, then a gasp from those around as James clamped has hand over Mrs Prendergast's mouth, other hand at the back of her head. As he fought to contain them several muffled curses escaped.

When it felt like she had run out of spit he warily removed his hand. "I'm sorry vicar. I'm so sorry. I forgot. You're a saint. He's a saint. Isn't he a saint?"

After a brief hiatus James returned from the vestry with a washed salver and more wafers. Starting where he left off, he handed out a wafer. It was inspected and a declaration made, "I'm not eating that."

"I have thoroughly washed my hands and the salver, and the wafers are fresh out of the box," whispered James.

"I don't care. I'm not eating that. It's gluten free!"

"It is all we have left."

"I'll pass thanks."

* * *

Back home the triplets ran off upstairs, Alex headed into the kitchen and Emily made a beeline for the cellar, eager to get the marble boxes and bring them up to the light before Alex thought about going down there. She flipped all the light switches and skipped down the stone steps, hand firmly on the handrail. Eyes on the boxes she didn't see the marble lying on the floor. She felt it though, as she kicked it with her open-toed sandal. The glass sphere shot noisily across the stone slabs and ricocheted between the packing cases at the end of the cellar. Unable to see where it had gone she moved first one packing case and then another, but she couldn't see it. There was a heap of clothes on the ground in the space behind the packing cases. She carefully lifted an edge so as not to displace the marble if that was where it had rolled. It hadn't. What was there, was a hand. As Emily stared, it trembled slightly. Emily screamed and launched herself backwards and kept on screaming until Alex arrived and found her sprawled on the floor.

"Emily, Emily. What's happened? Are you okay? Are you hurt?"

She said nothing, silent now, just pointing towards the corner of the cellar. He looked but couldn't make out what she was looking at.

"There is a body," she managed. "It's moving!"

Alex grabbed the packing cases and slid them forcefully to one side. Then he kicked the heap on the floor. It moved. He stepped backwards and picked up the first likely item that came to hand; a broken chair leg. "Get up. Get up, I said. Move!"

The man slowly moved into a sitting position, blinking up at the light, eyeing the lump of wood Alex was wielding.

"Who are you?" growled Alex. "What the hell are you doing in my cellar?"

There was a commotion behind him as several cats and the triplets arrived, "Daddy, Daddy," yelled Lily.

"Get back girls. Get back up stairs. Emily, call the police."

"No Daddy."

"Do as I say. Get back upstairs. NOW!"

"No, its okay."

"Daddy, don't hurt him."

Alex didn't have enough arms to control all three as they placed themselves between him and the man. As Lily and Tansy stood fiercely barring his way, Snokettee and The Catolith joined them. Violet crouched down and held the man's hand, telling him not to worry as Marigold, Whoops-a-Daisy and Spider milled around and over him.

Behind Alex, Emily found her voice. "You knew he was here. Didn't you. You've been feeding him. That is where all the food has been going..."

"Yes," said Violet. "We have. Nathan will be pleased that you know. He won't need to get his bottom looked at again!"

The girls helped the man to his feet and sat him at the table in the centre of the cellar. Alex looked on uncertainly, clenching and unclenching his hand on the chair leg, eyeing up the frail, elderly man in their midst. Emily, calmer now and with trust in her girls, pulled out a chair and joined the little group at the table. Then she motioned to Alex, and he sat too. As the tension eased The Catolith jumped up on the table and allowed the man to stroke him. As Alex and Emily mentally processed this relationship, the man spoke.

"Yes, the girls have been feeding me and looking after me. I am The Stone Carver."

Emily and Alex looked at one another and then back at the man.

"So, you are the arrival, heralded by... The Catolith," said Emily. "One of three?"

Alex looked at her in puzzlement. His girls were nodding.

"Yes. I have nearly completed my task. Then I will go. Girls, will you leave us please. I need to speak to your parents alone." At this, all three happily disappeared off upstairs and shut the cellar door. With the children gone the man looked visibly younger and far less frail. The man who had been helped to his feet, timid and weak, was gone. The new version, confident, articulate and purposeful, would have greatly surprised the triplets.

"As you are no doubt aware, your triplets follow a long line of triplets all of whom have lived to be 100 years old and all of whom have been blessed with 'generational knowledge'."

"Generational. I don't understand," said Emily. "They aren't direct descendants."

"No, but their father has Well's blood, and this house, this stone carries it."

"What does that mean?"

"It means," said the man, "that knowledge and wisdom, built up by previous generations of triplets is passed on. They both inherit and absorb it and it builds over time as they grow. I am here to test them. Normally this wouldn't happen until they are older but the world is changing and they need to be ready." He paused, letting this sink in.

"Ready! Ready for what?" said Alex. "You expect us to believe all this...rubbish. You turn up in our cellar making claims about the girls..."

"Alex," said Emily, laying a hand on his arm. "Let him speak. You know the girls are different and it isn't just because they are triplets. You knew your great great aunts. You know you couldn't rationally explain lots of what happened. Please, listen to the man..."

"Maybe this will help..." and the man got up and walked over to the dark corner of the cellar and collected the bundle from the floor. Sitting back down he placed the cloth on the table, positioning it under the ceiling light, and began to carefully unwrap the contents. Alex and Emily leaned forward. Behind them a tiny drop of liquid fell from stalactite to stalagmite: a barely perceptible 'plip' of time, in the cavernous space. As the last of the bundle was unfurled Emily gasped and the craftsman in Alex looked at the contents in awe. "They aren't finished yet. I just need another couple of days." He looked at Alex and appraised his reaction. Alex was lost for words. He stared at the items before him, disbelieving of what he saw: shapes so delicate and complex and so ethereal. The man could see that Alex, if not convinced, was accepting of the possibility of what he had been told. "Alex, I need to speak to the triplets' mother. Would you mind leaving us please."

Quietly Alex got up and silently followed the triplets upstairs. At the top, he closed the cellar door.

"Emily, your triplets, out of all the triplets that have gone before, are special. You know, having experienced some of the memories," and he glanced in the direction of the marbles, "that Wells triplets are capable of more than normal people. They have a depth of human knowledge which gives them great intuition and great understanding of others: empathy, which borders on telepathy. They have other abilities too, as you will be aware."

"Like with metal," said Emily, not wanting to meet his eye, feeling naked on Sarah's behalf.

"Yes. Their knowledge of structure and form, or what you would describe as chemistry, physics and other sciences, is inherent and will grow."

"You mentioned testing."

"Yes. They are young yet, but their problem solving is strong, and they intuitively know to keep their abilities to themselves. Besides you and Alex, only the lad, Nathan, knows that they are 'different'."

"Why are they 'special'?" asked Emily.

* * *

Once the service was over James dashed back to the vicarage, showered, ironed a shirt, slapped on some aftershave, checked his 'abs' in the mirror and got dressed. All the running he did kept him physically fit and he hoped that it applied to his physique too. He believed that he looked good in a shirt and liked to think he would make a good secret agent, if he ever got the opportunity to wear a tuxedo. He put on a watch: his expensive one with the fire service crest. Then he inserted cufflinks, with the same matching crest. He combed his hair, then thought better of it and went for the 'tousled' look.

Climbing into his car he regretted not having cleaned it. Glancing in the backseat, he got out and opened the boot. Then he gathered up all the rubbish from the car and shut the boot lid on it. He then took a look at the passenger seat and dashed back inside the house for a brush. Once he had decrumbed the seat he set off, annoyed with himself for not having thought about it earlier. What he had done was barely adequate. It would have to do. He did not want to be late.

When he pulled up at her front door Gemma opened it and stepped out. James' heart skipped a beat. She looked stunning: really classy in a simple light blue, fitted dress, and sandals: a yellow and blue cardigan over her arm. As she climbed into the car she smiled at him, flawless make-up making her look radiant and a gentle hint of perfume very welcome in the hastily cleaned interior. He helped her with her seatbelt. Rarely used; its catch was stiff. He hoped that it would unfasten again. He turned the car round and embarrassed himself, bumping the pavement twice, during his four-point turn.

As they drove through the countryside, he enjoyed the companionship and the warm feeling of having someone at his side and the sheer novelty of being a couple. He hoped it would last. When they arrived at The White Horse, chosen because it was away from Much Meddling and his gossiping parishioners, Gemma's safety belt behaved itself and released her. James got out and opened her door. As they crossed the carpark Gemma linked her arm with his. Her skin was warm through his shirt sleeve, and he felt little tingles of electricity every time she changed her grip.

He held open the heavy pub door for her and pulled out her chair when they reached their table. She appeared comfortable with this attention, and quietly appreciative of his manners. He berated himself for thinking that maybe she lacked sophistication. She seemed completely unfazed by the menu or wine list and at home with the array of cutlery. He was shocked that he was being so judgemental. He knew so little about her but then, she had a lot to learn about him. It would be fun finding out.

* * *

When Emily finally came up from the cellar, she brought the man with her. After a brief chat with Alex, she went upstairs and prepared the guest room. Alex still had his reservations but, deep down he too trusted the girls' instincts and agreed that the man could stay.

Over dinner that evening the delighted triplets, relieved of their secret, happily related how they had got the man from the woods to the scout hut and then into the cellar. Alex and Emily were incredulous. The girls, and Nathan, had achieved all that without either of them having any idea. However, little memories were beginning to surface.

"So, the dead pigeons in the hall…," said Alex.

"Well, Lily did roast pigeon for him, with the ones the cats brought to the scout hut. So, they probably thought more would be welcome," said Tansy.

Emily turned to Lily. "You know how to roast pigeon?"

"And this Gemma has taught Nathan to use a catapult accurately?" asked Alex.

"Yes, and she is going to teach me."

"No!" said Emily, a little too fiercely. "I don't think that is a good idea." After a brief argument, because Emily's only retort consisted of 'because I say so', Tansy sat and sulked.

CHAPTER TWENTY NINE

At precisely 9am Gemma parked her bicycle at the side of the vicarage and let herself in. Cycling through the village there had been a couple of unfriendly looks. Maybe it was paranoia, but passing a little group standing outside the store, she saw heads move closer together and felt their eyes on her back as she turned into the vicarage, certain that she was the topic of their conversation. She was glad to close the door and shut the world out. If this was how it was going to be she wasn't sure she could cope. Memories of her teenage years came flooding back and she felt 15 years old again, running the daily gauntlet of nasty comments from girls and 'pawings' by the boys. This time though, she couldn't leave; her mother needed her.

James met her in the hall and stopped as she held up both hands and looked him in the eye.

"When I am here working," she said, "I think we should be strictly professional. I am here to clean. So let me do my job."

"Oh, okay."

"Things could get complicated otherwise." Seeing James processing this she added, "I had a wonderful time yesterday. I hope we can do that again."

"Yes, I'd like that."

"Right, out of the way and let me get the vacuum."

James retreated to his study and attempted to type a letter. It wasn't long before Gemma popped her head through the door and said, "You've been cleaning, haven't you! I can tell because there is no cap on the polish and there are streaks on the coffee table and all the ornaments on your mantelpiece are in a different order. Not only that but I believe that you did that just before I came..."

He stared at her, wanting to deny it but not wanting to be caught out in a lie, especially whilst wearing his dog collar.

She grinned. "The top of the aerosol is still wet."

"Oh..."

"What appointments have you got this morning? There is something I want, need, to tell you."

"Er, I'll be free just after 11. We could have coffee, but then I will need to go over to the vicarage for a pre-Christening meeting."

As he returned to his writing, he was a little worried, she had seemed so serious, but she was busy singing, so maybe he needn't worry.

* * *

At Wishing Well cottage the man was tucking into a cooked breakfast. After the diet, to which he had been subjected, Emily felt obliged to make amends. He poked the corner of his toast into the centre of an egg and swirled it round, then popped it into his mouth and took a swig of tea. Engrossed in his food, and unnerved by the radio, he didn't immediately notice when Nathan walked through the door, but the boy's gasp of surprise, provided a suitable interruption.

The girl's quickly explained the man's presence in the kitchen and Nathan was patently delighted that his covert days were over. There were still complications and he had many questions, but he was off the hook as quartermaster. What he could say, and who to, he determined to simplify by saying nothing to anyone, if he could possibly help it. He was traumatised enough by having lied to the doctor.

As the girls settled to play on the rug, waiting for Nathan to finish his breakfast, Emily wondered what she was going to do all day. She needed to go out but felt uncomfortable leaving a stranger in the house, with or without her children. He had been in the house, unattended for the past few days, but it still didn't feel right.

Nathan scraped his spoon round his bowl, and downed the last dregs of his orange juice.

As he pushed back his chair the man took hold of his wrist. Nathan froze, staring at the man. Then he relaxed and looked him in the eye. The man smiled and The Catolith transferred its foot circling to Nathan's ankles.

"Thank you, Nathan. I know this hasn't been easy for you, but you are a worthy young man, and the triplets are very fortunate to have you as their friend and guardian."

Emily was jolted by the last word. There was meaning in it. The emphasis had been subtle, but it was there. She looked at Nathan, remembering what the man had told her, and fingered the silky-smooth calcite at her neck.

"I must return to my work."

"You can work here," said Emily. "I'll clear some room on the table."

"No. I have all that I need in the cellar. Thank you. It is where I need to be."

Whether it was because Nathan had finished his breakfast or because the man had gone back to the cellar, Emily didn't know, but the children decided that it was time to go out. Soon Emily found that she and Snokettee were on their own, with yet another messy table to clear. She took the kettle off the range and poured hot water into the grill pan followed by a squirt of washing up liquid. As she worked, her thoughts kept her mentally occupied. She really needed to tell James about Gemma. It was unfair to keep him in the dark and she felt bad that she had been avoiding him. Well, not avoiding him exactly, a lot had happened to prevent her contacting him, but she had been glad of the excuses. Then it occurred to her that he hadn't been in touch with her either. There had been no visits, no calls, no texts.

* * *

At 11am Gemma could hear that James was still on the phone and it didn't sound like the conversation would be ending soon. She took a mug of coffee in for him, but his raised eyebrows and body language told her that he didn't have time for a chat. When he finally finished, he took the phone, grabbed a folder and headed for the door.

"I am really sorry but I need to get over to the church. I'll be back in about 30 minutes, but I won't have much time. That was Lesley on the phone, my previous housekeeper. Her mother has died, and she wants me to do the funeral. It is in Scotland, so I have arrangements to make and appointments to rearrange…"

"Oh, I really need to talk to you."

With the door half opened he turned, "Will it take long?"

"Maybe. It depends."

"Can we do it on the phone?"

Gemma hesitated, "No, I'd rather not."

"Look I really need to go. You and me, we are okay, yes?"

"Yes, it is nothing like that."

"Then, will it wait until I get back?"

"I suppose so, but... James, just... please trust *me*, before anyone else. Promise me that."

A couple of steps and he was facing her. One eyebrow went up, and his eyes twinkled as a huge smile spread across his face. "I promise." As she stood, bucket in one yellow hand, bleach in the other, he took her face in his hands, gently tilted her head back and kissed her firmly on the lips. Then he was gone, and she was left staring at a door, lips tingling and a warm glow spreading a delicious longing through her body.

As she finished off the cleaning, she considered telling him over the phone, but she needed to see his reactions to know how to react herself. If he was going away for a few days, it was less likely that he would hear it from anyone else. No-one had told him so far.

* * *

Taking a break from my writing, I took a chair and placed it outside my front door. I made myself a cup of tea and sat, sipping, observing the world from my lofty position. Sadly, it failed to 'hit the spot' as they say, and I found that the strong smell of coffee repeatedly drew my attention to What Sup. If I wasn't careful, the shop could turn into an expensive habit. The clientele, however, could be a profitable source of characters. My latest work, a ghost story, needed some quirky individuals to add interest and I was on the look out for character traits. Observing the What Sup customers from my elevated vantage point was fun. People didn't tend to look up and those that did quickly looked away again.

A doorbell tinkled and Cornelius, the elderly gentleman that the boy Nathan had introduced to me, stepped out of Tempus clutching what looked like a receipt. He folded it and placed it in an inside pocket of his coat. Doffing his cap at a couple of people he disappeared through the archway to the high street.

* * *

After lunch, Emily deciding that she couldn't put it off any longer, went in search of James. His door was locked and there was no answer to her knocking. She went round the side and peered through his office window, but there was no sign of him. She looked inside the church, but he wasn't there either. As she headed home she texted him, 'Hi, need to talk to U. Please call.' There was no immediate response and as the afternoon rolled on, she grew concerned. He always carried his phone with him and, even if he was with a parishioner would respond within an hour, 2 at the most. It was so unlike him. She went back to the vicarage and peered through all the downstairs windows, but there was nothing amiss. In fact, it was all very tidy; not even any washing-up visible on the drainer. Then her phone 'pinged'. Retrieving it from the pocket of her shorts she was relieved to see it was a text from James.

'Hi, on my way to Scotland. Lesley's mother died last week. She wants me to do the funeral. Just leaving Tebay services. Traffic dreadful. Call you from hotel later, James.'

She quickly texted back, 'My condolences to Lesley. No need to call; it can wait until you get back. Emily x'

CHAPTER THIRTY

For me the week passed quite quickly. My writing happened in bursts, flowing nicely. Then some plot construction would bring me to a halt, and I would make myself coffee and sit on my little perch and study the goings on in the yard below. I decided that Friday would be my treat day, a coffee from What Sup signifying the end of my working week. I also endeavoured to go for a daily walk and get to know the surrounding countryside. The triplets' mother, Emily, popped by on the Wednesday when she visited Heaven Scent and saw me sipping my cuppa, and suggested that we went for a walk up the crag on the Thursday morning. I was pleased; it hadn't just been something polite for her to say when we first met.

* * *

When Alex spotted that Emily was again wearing the periapt, he wasn't pleased but decided not to comment. He had always said that it was her choice, and he knew that her decision to put it on again was due to her talk with the man in the cellar. He didn't like him being there and would be glad when he had gone. It wasn't that he didn't trust him, he did. He trusted his girls' judgement, and Lily's in particular. However, as their father that just made him feel inadequate; they were 6 years old; they should be relying on his judgement. He thrust another piece of metal into his furnace and held it there until it glowed.

* * *

On the Wednesday morning, as the man wiped egg yoke and ketchup from his plate with a slice of toast, he announced that his work was nearly done. This would be his last day. Emily was surprised at the lack of ceremony. However, he said that when he presented the items that the whole family needed to be there. So, as Alex needed to go to work it was decided that the event should take place that evening.

With the man back in the cellar Emily went to work in Angelica's room. Collecting a bunch of candles that were dangling over her wax bath she sat at her table and proceeded to trim the wicks. Fingers occupied, her mind went back to what the man had told her on their first encounter. She had had so many questions, but all his answers had been cryptic. He had said that the girls were being tested but he wouldn't say how, only that they had passed everything, so far. When she had asked what would happen if they failed, he had said simply, 'Then you all fail'.

Once she was satisfied that the wicks were all the same length, she boxed up the candles and stacked them ready for delivery. After lunch she trundled her collection over to Heaven Scent. A child stood stoically as a woman wiped at the ice-cream adorning his T-shirt. Emily negotiated the pair and wove her way to the shop. Inside she nodded to the woman behind the counter, who smiled. As she deposited her wares in the back room the till rang repeatedly. She let herself out and, struggling to make headway with her trolley she left it at the forge for Alex to take home. She had considered heading back along the back street, but she had noticed me sitting on my little balcony so climbed the steps.

* * *

Mr Swire frowned at the crowd, but pushed his way through. A quick glance in St Peter's Charity shop window brought a smile to his face. A mannequin dressed in purple paisley shirt with yellow kipper tie and green corduroy bell-bottoms, stood, hand outstretched and palm upwards, a selection of other garish ties dangling from it. How ridiculous he must have looked with his long hair and huge sunglasses. He would have been in his 40's by then, just an old rocker trying to stay 'hip'. He'd loved that shirt.

He stepped into Tempus and thankfully closed the door. A number of customers were wandering round the shop. He waited impatiently to be served. When his turn came Jonathan reached under the counter and pulled out a leather box. Opening it he reverently lifted out a gilt metal and silver pocket watch, approximately 3.5 inches in diameter. The casing was delicately engraved, the back depicting floral swirls and Tudor roses, the front similarly decorated but with circular holes to allow the single watch-hand to be seen without opening it.

"I did a bit of research to be sure, but as I said the other day, this appears to be an original Newsam made in the 1560's." Taking a quick look round the shop Jonathan slid a piece of paper across the counter. On it was written – 'At auction'. Mr Swire took the paper, unfolded it and looked at the figure written inside. He raised his eyebrows at Jonathan and said, "It isn't for sale. Thankyou for servicing it. The other matter?"

"That is coming along nicely. I should have it finished by next week."

"Excellent. How much will that be? I'll pay you now."

"Oh, that is okay, you can pay me next week."

"Thank you but I'd rather pay now."

Outside the shop he paused and pulled his cap from his pocket. The Tempus doorbell rang and Jonathan called, "Mr Swire, your change."

"Mr Swire flipped his cap onto his head and turned, "Keep it, I don't need it. I've now done all

I need to do. Wishing you well."

* * *

At my side Emily gasped. She had gone white as a sheet. I stood and begged her to sit. She was still staring down at the old man but now shaking her head, saying, "No, No, No!" When I asked her what was wrong, she just shook her head more violently. When she had recovered a little, she chatted distractedly for a while and took trouble to confirm our crag walk for the following day. Then she made her excuses and left, purportedly on her way to her friend Louise. Hopefully she would feel able to confide in me on our trip up the crag. I watched her walk away. She looked so fragile. The transformation had been so sudden, and I was at a loss as to the cause.

* * *

The door of the estate agents crashed back against a filing cabinet, its hinges straining. What had been a calm quiet afternoon, now wasn't. In the doorway stood Emily. She pushed damp hair from her forehead and scanned the office. Gerald called over his shoulder, "Louise, would you come here please?" Something in his tone brought her running. She took one look at Emily, wrapped an arm round her shoulders and took her through to the staff room at the back of the building. Louise moved aside a stack of brochures and sat her friend down.

"Talk to me," prompted Louise.

"He's gonna die. In the night. He's gonna die."

"Who?" said Louise, slightly annoyed by the drama, but with a nagging feeling that they had had a similar conversation before, when Emily first moved to Much Meddling. Bit by bit, Louise coaxed out of her what Mr Swire had said.

"Look, 'Wishing you well' is a common phrase round here and besides he is 100 years old, he is going to die sometime. He can't live that much longer."

A stiff coffee and a couple of biscuits and Louise eventually got Emily to calm down and accept that, even if he did die in the night, no one was going to blame her.

* * *

With dinner over, the family followed the man down into the cellar and gathered around the table. In its centre, under the glare of the ceiling lamps, lay a cloth. Beneath the cloth 3 small objects and 1 large one, waited. There was a shuffling as the gathered group settled, then an impatient silence as they all craned for their first glimpse of the hidden objects.

Alex was keen to see how the man had improved the item that he had already seen, which the man had said wasn't finished yet. He had been stunned by the delicate and intricate interlocking carving of calcite. If it had been produced by a laser printer he would have been impressed: the only way, he would have thought it possible to produce such a shape.

The man interlocked his fingers and waited until all eyes broke contact with the cloth and looked at him. A slight echo was heard as he cleared his throat.

"I can't tell you what will be. I can't tell you what you will need to do. I can only tell you to be ready for the times to come.

"Alex, this is for you." He reached beneath the cloth and pulled out the largest of the items. He handed it to Alex who took it and cradled it in his cupped palms as gently as one might hold a butterfly. Slowly he rolled it, inspecting each angle. 5 interlocking rings, each with a different pattern shone in the light, their inner surfaces silky smooth.

"The rings each represent a member of your family. Place it at the base of the stalactite from which it was cut. I have created a plinth for it. It will keep you safe. Over time it will be absorbed, becoming one with the earth, once again."

With a gesture instructing him, Alex rose and walked over to the stalactite. On the stalagmite beneath it, was a small carved depression. Reverently he placed the carving on the plinth in the tiny pool that had gathered. It rolled briefly then lay still, damp already. As Alex stood back a tiny prism dropped from above, every colour of the spectrum briefly visible, the earth laying claim once again.

As Alex sat back at the table the man turned his attention to Emily. "You have had your periapt all along. It will keep you and Alex safe, wear it always. The 2 interlocking circles of life represent the pair of you."

Emily reached out her hand and found Alex's reaching for hers. As their fingers entwined and she felt the familiar warmth spread through her she also felt his acceptance; he no longer resented the periapt's possible interference in their lives. They loved one another and it didn't matter why.

"Girls, you are each to receive a periapt, each of which is unique." He reached forward and peeled aside the cloth. Three apparently identical stone carvings lay perfectly spaced and perfectly aligned on the table in front of them. On closer inspection there were subtle differences. Roughly hemispherical each had a tiny sphere encased within it but in different positions. He picked up the first and held it out to Violet, saying, "Of the earth, to the earth."

She took it and stared at the tiny carving. The detail was like that of Alex' periapt but the shape very different. With a flat back it was meant to be worn as a pendant, but the hemispherical front was hollow, tiny slivers of calcite shaped to hold the pea sized sphere at its centre.

He handed the next one to Lily, "Of the earth, for the earth." This one held its pea-sized stone flush with its surface.

Finally, he handed the last one to Tansy. As their hands touched, he almost dropped it. Tansy's head shot up and they looked each other in the eye. Meeting her gaze, he appeared to challenge her and then back down. Tentatively he leant forward and placed the periapt in her outstretched hand, taking care not to make skin contact. Lily and Violet shot a look at Tansy, uncertain what had just happened. The man continued to stare at Tansy. Almost as an afterthought he said, "Of the earth, from the earth." She held his gaze a little longer, then set him free and inspected her periapt. The sphere in her carving was held proud, in a semi-complete dome, and glowed almost red. She looked quizzically at the man. He looked away. Neither spoke. Excluded from this exchange Lily and Violet looked to each other for answers, but got none.

CHAPTER THIRTY ONE

As per instructions Nathan let himself through Mr Swire's gate and headed round the side of the house to the plant pot under which Mr Swire kept his spare key. Any task for Mr Swire, or Cornelius as he now called him, was welcome. It wasn't just the money that he liked, which he no longer needed to hand over for food or batteries, but the old man's company. Cornelius talked to him like an adult. They were friends. He also liked Gemma. It was she who had provided the pram wheel to fix his trolley.

He crouched down and tipped over the plant pot. The key was there, but beside it was an old leather box with an envelope on top, addressed 'To Nathan'. The envelope had a lump inside it. Puzzled, but curious about the box, he put the envelope to one side and lifted the box lid. It seemed to be stuck shut. Sitting back on his haunches he turned the object to and fro, inspecting it. Then, he tried pressing the metal lump below the lid and it sprung upwards. What he saw both delighted and alarmed him. Inside was a very old watch with a chain. It was cold to touch and heavier than he expected. He hefted it in his hand and turned it over. Precious and beautiful, it surely wasn't for him. Guilt and fear of being caught crept up on him and he lay the watch back in its box, glad to shut the lid. The envelope, though, was most definitely for him. 'To Nathan' it said. Slipping a finger under the flap he gently unstuck it and tipped out a ring. He froze. This wasn't right. Not wanting to know but unable to stop himself he picked it up and turned it over; the figure of a cat lay embossed on its surface. His bottom lip began to tremble. He pulled the crisp cream paper from the envelope and unfolded it. His eyes started to mist.

Dear Nathan,
This watch is for you. Keep it safe. It is nearly 500 years old and valuable.
Remember what we talked about.
This ring is for you. Once it fits, you must wear it.
Thank you for all your help and your friendship. I have enjoyed our time together.
I ask one last thing of you, and it is very important. Do not go in the house on your own. Get an adult.
Your friend,
Cornelius

Nathan stared at the page, then part of the ink started to run. He held it away from him and screwed up his eyes. No, this couldn't be. He stuffed the ring and box in his pocket and folded the sheet. It crumpled slightly as he fumbled it into the envelope. He grabbed the key and ran to the door and stopped, fear and obedience halting him in his tracks. Bumping a fist at his eye he startled a robin, hopping about the path, as he ran blindly into the street.

The sound of a familiar bicycle bell slowed him down and he turned as Gemma called out to him, "Nathan, are you alright? Stop. Wait for me."

He stood clutching the key. Through her gentle coaxing he managed to explain. Together they headed back to Mr Swire's house. At the door he handed her the key. When she told him to wait, he did: fear and denial rooting him to the spot. He listened, praying for a response to her calls as she moved about, first the ground floor and then the upper one. There was none. When she finally came out, he took one look at her and burst into tears. She was still hugging him when the ambulance turned up, and a Police Officer. Despite calling the doctors' surgery they had insisted she call an ambulance – just in case.

When the doctor arrived to certify the death a little crowd of elderly women had gathered in the street, news of the ambulance having spread. By the time the undertaker arrived the group was considerable.

'Let's go and tell the vicar," said Gemma, "he should be back by now. I don't know why he isn't answering his phone. He will need to know."

Locking the house, they fought their way through the frosty faced women in the street, Nathan acting as an icebreaker. Some smiled sympathetically at him, others glowered at Gemma. Together the pair marched up the high street. At the estate agents Gemma steered Nathan inside and explained to Louise what had happened. Then Gemma set off for the vicarage, checking her phone. Louise watched her leave, glad to be rid of her. If the woman had killed her husband, she didn't want her anywhere near her little boy.

* * *

James, having been stuck in traffic on the M6, had gone straight to bed when he finally made it home at 2.45am. After a lie in he had eventually surfaced around 11am, had a shower and some breakfast, put his phone on charge and headed over to check the church. He had a problem, and he didn't know how to resolve it. With Lesley's mother now dead and buried, there was no need for her to stay in Scotland. She had intimated that once she had sold her mother's house she would be returning to Much Meddling. He couldn't employ 2 housekeepers. This dilemma occupying his thoughts he entered the church.

* * *

Emily arrived spot on 10.30 and we wove through the shoppers and out into the high street. I was struck by the change in her. When we had last parted, she had been almost frantic as she fled down my steps on her way to her friend, Louise, who she now confirmed was my estate agent. She was brighter and possessed a confidence that hadn't been there before. Well, perhaps confidence wasn't the right word. Maybe wiser, fitted better, although I had no idea why.

We soon left the high street and walked down one of the side roads. At the end was a stile, which wasn't noticeable from the high street, and she led the way over. The stone steps were worn, and I wondered how many generations of feet it had taken to create such depressions. The rows of houses we had just passed were probably built in the mid 1800's, but the stile could be older than that.

She asked me how I was settling into Much Meddling and who I had met. It was an easy entry to our conversation and I told her of the people I had spoken to in the yard and some of the shopkeepers on the high street. She seemed pleased when I told her of my takeaway from the Basak's and told me how Louise had been responsible for their arrival in the village.

I asked her how long she had lived in Much Meddling. I didn't know it at the time, but this would be the start of the story I was to write. It was a very abridged version. It would take time for her to trust me with the fuller truth.

The transition from the woods to the lower slope of the crag was a surprise to me. From the enclosed passageway through the trees, with its full canopy of leaves, to the bright, barren, scree strewn slope topped with rock, was blinding. I slid my sunglasses down, from the top of my head, and still squinted. The ground was steeper now, but Emily strolled effortlessly upwards. Realising that she was talking to herself she stopped and waited.

"Sorry," she said. "I forget others aren't used to the climb."

She led the way along the slope to the base of the crag. I glanced sideways at the view and when I turned back, she had gone. Puzzled I took a couple of steps and saw that the path disappeared between the rocks. There were steps hewn in the gully and Emily was half way up. I followed and as we emerged onto the top of the crag she told me not to turn until we reached the cairn. I did as I was told. At the pile of rocks I reached out and placed my hand on the little makeshift monument. It was warm. It made me wonder how many other hands had rested there? Then I turned and refocussed. Below was an expanse of vivid green, moving gently in the light breeze. To the right, almost hidden, was the top of the church, its stone matching that of the crag. Below and left, little sections of roof could be seen, marking out what I took to be the rooftops of the high street. Beyond were rolling hills, purple, brown, and green, with higher hills forming the distant skyline, their colours muted.

"This is one of the best times of day to come here," she said. "The view changes with the light but right now, with the sun virtually overhead, you can see all around."

I turned through 360 degrees. She was right. It was truly spectacular. Oh, for the ability to capture this in watercolours. For me, pixels would have to suffice.

We sat for a while chatting, and for some time in silence, both of us enjoying the view. There was a sense of peace here, the world spread out below us, revolving through space.

Then Emily's phone rang.

* * *

Louise was going to take Nathan home, but then thought it would be better to take him to Emily's. They could tell the girls together and hopefully their company would help him, and she needed to be there when Emily found out. As she tried to re-organise her work, giving a list to Gerald, of what she had done and needed to do, he told her to just go, he would deal with whatever needed doing, "Look after Nathan."

She appreciated that. He was a good man. She really wished he could find someone.

As the door closed behind her, she tapped her phone. "Hi, Em. Are you home? There is something I need to tell you, but I want to tell you in person."

"What, what is it?"

"I'll tell you when I see you. I'm on my way over."

"It's Mr Swire, isn't it? Tell me."

"Emily, where are you?"

"He's dead, isn't he?"

"Look, I'll see you at yours."

"Just tell me."

"Yes."

Placing her phone in her bag Louise became aware of voices, getting louder as she and Nathan approached the village green. In full foliage the weighted branches of the oaks and sycamores blocked the view of the far side of the pond. Slightly ahead of her, Nathan started to jog, and then broke into a run. Heels tapping noisily, she failed to keep pace. As she grew nearer and the branches thinned, she could see a large crowd gathered at the far side of the pond, blocking the vicarage gateway. Raised voices, angry and shrill were competing to make themselves heard. Arms were being waved and fingers pointed.

Arriving at Nathan's side, heels sinking into the soft ground at the water's edge, she stood and took in the scene. Across the water a group of about 50 people, mainly women, had wound themselves up into a 'lather'. The occasional phrase escaped from the melee. "Murderer," "Stay away from our vicar" being the most politely phrased.

Then, the mob started to part and Gemma backed towards the water, arms raised defensively, head moving from side to side as she scanned the crowd for help.

* * *

As Emily ran down the scree, jumping and sliding I did my best to keep up. I was afraid she would fall but she kept her feet and somehow we arrived at the wood in one piece. I called for her to slow down, afraid I would lose her. She made so much noise though, that I wouldn't have got lost. As we neared the back of the church, voices could be heard, shouting and screaming what sounded like accusations. Despite her desperation to get home Emily slowed her pace and listened. Before I could reach her, she changed direction and darted through the undergrowth. I followed, brambles grasping at my clothes and ripping my arms and legs. At the church wall she scrambled over. By the time I had negotiated it she had disappeared round the side of the church. At first, I couldn't see her. Then, separate from the crowd, I saw her moving sideways round the pond, scanning the people as she went. It seemed to me that most of Much Meddling's population had gathered. Arriving by her side I looked across the water. Amid the throng, a woman was being hounded towards the water.

* * *

James strolled through the church, straightening the odd pew and re-hanging kneelers on their little hooks to keep the tiny group of volunteer cleaners happy. Everything that should be locked was locked, and all was well. He knelt at the altar and prayed. As he stood and stepped back, a clamour from outside the church broke into his day. The church walls were thick and the windows high; external noises weren't normally heard. As he headed down the aisle a growing sense of dread quickened his pace.

* * *

Nathan was yelling at the crowd. Unable to get near Gemma he stood helplessly at the opposite side of the pond. Louise pulled him back from the water's edge, his feet already wet.

"Who else are you gonna murder?" shouted a severe looking woman in an overtight red dress and large white ear-rings.

"She's not a murderer, she's not," yelled Nathan growing hoarse.

"Go on, get back to your circus. You whore," yelled another. "We know what you did…"

As Gemma teetered on the edge of the water, visibly shaking, Tansy arrived at Nathan's side and spoke in his ear. Louise didn't hear what was said but suddenly found herself standing on her own. Nathan and Tansy darted away, ferreted on the ground under one of the oaks and returned to the water's edge. Before anyone could intervene the two children pulled out catapults and took aim. Stone after stone hit the water sending curtains of water skywards. Within seconds, those on the other edge of the pond, either side of Gemma, were drenched. As the crowd fled the splash zone Lily and Violet ran and stood in front of Gemma, glowering at the mob. Then Tansy and Nathan ran round and joined them, reinforcing the defensive wall.

Slowly the shouting died, and the women backed away, cowed under the glare of the four children.

Somewhere at the back of the people a disturbance was noted and people started to turn. A murmuring ensued and a gap began to appear to allow passage. James stood at the end, a bemused look on his face. He began to walk forward, all eyes now on him, and not Gemma.

"What is going on?"

"Stay away from her vicar."

"What do you mean?"

"She murdered 'er last 'usband. You want nothing to do with 'er."

"And now Mr Swire is dead! We saw her, coming out of his house."

James looked at Gemma, then at members of

the crowd, then back at Gemma. Bewildered, he stared at her.

Finding her voice she said softly, "That is what I wanted to talk to you about."

He shrank backwards. Everyone saw. Several expressions crossed his face. He tried to rally himself, "Yes, we need to talk," he said, but it was too late; the look on his face, the tone of his voice, but mainly... the hesitation. Slowly Gemma turned. She took a step, and staggered slightly, then another. Gathering momentum she broke into a run, battered her way through the edges of the crowd and fled down the road.

Nathan was livid. It was so unfair. She was so nice. None of this could be true. "She's not a murderer, she's not." With Louise in tow, shouting at him to stop, he set off after his friend.

With Gemma fading into the distance people started to shift into little groups and a general murmuring began. Lily stepped forward, hands on hips and, flanked by her siblings, hollered "STOP!" Once she had everyone's attention she began, "She is a good person. She is helpful and kind. You are not. You don't know her. You don't know what the truth is. You gossip and believe what you want to believe. The truth doesn't matter to you. I thought you were all better than this. You should be better than this. Much Meddling is better than this. What you did was wrong, and you know it. You are all bad people."

On a bench, beneath a sycamore, the man chuckled to himself and stroked the head of the Catolith. It was time for them to go.

CHAPTER THIRTY TWO

Emily put her arm around the vicar and guided him to her house. I followed at a short distance, uncertain what to do. After her reaction to the news of Mr Swire's death, I was concerned for her. I too felt disturbed by his passing. I had only met him a couple of times but had found him likeable. Now I wasn't sure whether to stay or go. The front door was left open, so I ventured in and followed her voice to the kitchen.

She sat the vicar in a chair and held the kettle under the tap.

"I'll just say goodbye," I said. "I enjoyed our walk."

"No, please stay and have a cuppa. Tea, coffee, fruit tea?"

I attempted to make my excuses, but she insisted I stay. I am not sure the vicar, James, wanted me to. She introduced me to him as The Cronkler. Apparently, this is what the children had called me. No doubt Nathan had repeated what Cornelius had said. I recalled him referring to me as The Chronicler. I would miss the old man.

"Well," said Emily as she placed mugs on the table and slid the sugar bowl my way. "I am sorry James. I didn't want you to find out like this. I tried to tell you last weekend but then you went away and I was happy to put it off. I am sorry."

"So, you are telling me that it is true?"

"Anna said…"

"Anna, she knew?"

"Yes, she said that Gemma had killed her husband with a knife. She didn't know any more details, but it apparently wasn't proved."

"I need to go see her. I need to know the truth. There are all sorts of reasons… she may have been defending herself. She had wanted to talk to me before I went away. Maybe she was going to tell me about it."

* * *

Gemma shut her mother's front door and bolted it. She rested her head against the glass, gathering herself. The memory of James' expression seared into her soul. The look of hurt and horror so apparent as he shrank backwards, "Yes, we need to talk…" The phrase had been so formal, like he was suggesting confession, his black-sheeped flock closing around him.

A noise outside caused her to peer through the frosted glass. The blurred shape of Nathan was there. She reached for the bolt but another, taller figure appeared, and Nathan was dragged protesting, back into the street and away.

Behind her, a voice, "Gemma, I'm cold. Put the fire on and get me a cup o' tea."

She gathered herself, reluctantly stuffing her emotions back down, deep inside her. Nothing ever changed. She should have learnt that by now.

* * *

The door crashed open and in ran the triplets. They beamed at me and then threw their arms around James. He seemed grateful for their attention and unreservedly hugged them back. Letting him go, they stood back.

"It will be alright," said one of them. "Gemma or Crystal, she is still the same person."

Then she said something really strange, "Tansy chose her for you. She didn't get it wrong."

Even stranger, neither Emily nor James showed any indication that they too thought it odd.

"Uncle James," said the quietest of the three, "Gemma is really upset."

More sounds from the hall and in walked Nathan and Louise.

"Oh," said Emily, seeing Nathan's face, "I haven't told them yet." In the silence that followed she shepherded the girls to the sofa and sat them down. She looked at each in turn, "Violet, Tansy, Lily… something sad has happened."

They stared at her wide eyed, casting sideways glances at Nathan's puffy eyes.

"Mr Swire has died."

There was a sigh from James and a sniff from Nathan. Violet got up and went over to Nathan. Taking his hand she said, "I'm sorry. Cornelius was a good friend." As Lily and Tansy sat him on the sofa Violet turned her attention to James and threw her arms round him. Then she stepped back and looked him in the eye, "He was a 100, days ago. It was time."

* * *

The crowd had quickly dispersed and was no where to be seen as James headed up the high street. It didn't take him long to reach Gemma's road. His mind on one thing, the walk was a blur. He rapped on her door, politely at first, then with more urgency. There was no reply. He took out his phone and called her, but she didn't answer. He left a message, garbled and crass, and instantly regretted it. He knocked again, but to no avail.

Back home he sat and poured his heart out in an e-mail and prayed she would respond.

* * *

This week's pony was called Pepper, and Pepper was a bit podgy. Tansy's legs stuck out sideways, and she had difficulty getting her shiny new boots to make contact with its sides. She sat up straight, proudly sporting her new helmet. Alex smiled; she really looked the part. She had a lot to learn but was quick to take onboard the instruction she was given. Apparently she was 'a natural' and he swelled with pride. Glancing round at the class he had to admit, that she was better than the other students. Then he caught her looking at the other riders; was that smugness or disdain? When she looked at the teenager, giving the lesson, it was with a definite 'told you so' attitude. Her refusal to carry a crop was having no effect on her ability to control the animal. Hopefully that argument wouldn't be repeated.

CHAPTER THIRTY THREE

T he next 2 days were torment for James. He tried time after to time to make contact with Gemma, but none of his efforts elicited any response. Finally he texted saying, 'Please, just let me know you are alive before I call the Police to break down your door." There was a ping, 'I'm alive.'

He had no idea how to resolve this. If she wouldn't see or speak to him, he was at a loss. His plan to send Nathan was scotched as Louise wouldn't let her child anywhere near 'that' woman. If Gemma wouldn't speak to him then perhaps finding out the truth would help him work out some way to get through to her. He called Anna to ask if she had any further information. She couldn't add anything to what she had told Emily and Louise and couldn't think of anyone else, who had been around at the time, who may know any more.

He had a sermon to write and some forgiveness to seek. His thoughts towards his parishioners were less than charitable. Lily was right, they were bad people. His congregation were bad people. Was he to blame for that? Had he taught them nothing? He pulled off his dog-collar and held it in his hands. Maybe he needed to do something else. Maybe he wasn't cut out for this.

There was a clunk from the hall as a stack of mail got pushed through the letter box. Then a 'thud' as it hit the mat. He smiled. Was he being tested? Perhaps some fresh air would give him a fresh perspective. Running gear on, he headed for the crag.

* * *

Gemma hauled her mother to her feet, arranged the elderly woman's underwear and straightened her skirt, then reached back and pressed the flush handle. She watched briefly as the water swirled, taking her dreams away with the contents. She steered her mother over to the sink and soaped her hands. Glancing up at the mirror over the sink she stared herself in the face. It was no longer pretty. Her high cheekbones, which once gave pleasing structure to her face now just provided a platform for the bags under her eyes. She was going to have to rethink her make-up. Make-up? What was the point. Glancing at the reflection by her side, she realised that the similarities between her and her mother were increasing, and not in a good way.

Her mother met her eyes, and in a rare

moment of clarity, said, "You're better off without 'im. A Winterbottom and a vicar. Pah!"

Stacks of cucumber sandwiches suddenly popped into her head. Had she really considered that life? Even if she could get past the look on his face; the way he had recoiled; the crowd claiming him and protecting him from her, she just couldn't live here. She'd never belonged here. She hadn't before and she didn't now.

She dried her mother's hands. Then she stood back and watched impatiently as the Zimmer frame was crashed into the door frame. Freed, it headed down the hall. She finished drying her own hands and placed the towel on the radiator. Then she switched off the light and, with a soft click, shut the door.

* * *

Nathan had had a rough 2 nights. Louise had sat with him and held him and tried to get him to talk but he had clammed up. He was so grief stricken that she was considering taking him to the doctors, but memories of his last visit, held her back.

During the day he was desperate for the girls' company and she was glad of that. Perhaps they could help him. However, there was a sort of manic urgency present in his need to get out of the house. He seemed to have aged, burdened by a responsibility she couldn't fathom.

Now, he ran down the high street, aware that

his mother was watching him go. Once out of sight he took the next side road and climbed the stile at the end. When he arrived at the clearing, he waited, and listened for their arrival. He always ate much faster than they did, and today he hadn't been hungry. He pulled out his catapult and searched out a selection of stones. Then he sat and took aim. It was harder sitting and his aim was off slightly, but he could work on that. Out of ammunition he collected more. Then he set three large pinecones on a tree stump and stood back. If he could knock all three off in succession he would be happy. He missed with his first stone, which thwacked into the rock outcrop behind. His second stone hit the stump in front of the target, shot sideways and took out the middle pinecone. He aimed again, successfully. He did a little jig but was annoyed with himself for changing his position. He settled himself again and aimed at the third target. The stone hit the rock wall.

The triplets heard a resounding "Yes," as they threaded their way through the undergrowth to the clearing, Marigold, Whoops-a-Daisy and Spider dashing madly around. Violet was delighted to see him mid victory jig as they stepped into the make-shift arena. Proudly he set up his pinecones, stood back and took aim. Tansy provided a drum roll, beating sticks on a hollow trunk, and then he let rip. The first cone went down, then the second, then the third stayed where it was. "Bugger!" said Nathan.

Violet clapped anyway. "You'll get there. That was really good."

Lily and Tansy said nothing but sidled off to activities of their own. Lily stepped up onto a tree-stump and stared across to a similar one opposite. Then, arms outstretched, she stepped forward onto a rope which stretched between the stumps. She managed 4 steps before she lost her balance and had to leap to the floor. She returned to the stump and tried again. This time she managed 6 steps but the further along she went the greater the movement in the sagging rope. Whilst Lily practised, Tansy trotted round in circles, arms out for balance, "Yes, Silver, good girl Silver. Now canter, left circle...and right circle."

Violet heard it first. Something, or someone was working their way through the wood towards them. All four children stopped and looked towards the sound. Nathan moved and positioned himself in front of the triplets, left arm outstretched, the other taking aim. Through the branches they could see movement. It was an adult, carefully moving aside brambles and, by the sound of it, not too successfully. Between snapping back of foliage, yelps could be heard.

"Uncle James," called Lily as the others echoed her cry and Nathan lowered his catapult.

He stepped into the clearing inspecting his limbs and wiping at some red dribbles on his legs. Spider rubbed round his ankles, smearing the blood. "Hello, you lot, what are you up to."

Laid out before him was a ring of stones and logs. In it was Nathan's target station, Lily's tight rope, and a selection of planks, buckets, and other items.

"Is this a circus? Wow."

"I can juggle," said Violet and picket up three stones. Deftly she tossed them in the air and kept them moving in a circular motion. Then she dropped one but caught the other 2. "Just watch Nathan, he is really good."

Nathan set up his cones and gathered his stones. Then he took a deep breath and took aim. The first cone fell, then the second. He held his breath, then let it out slowly and aimed at the third. He fired. The cone fell. Nathan gasped and turned as James and the girls clapped madly. He had done it, and with an audience.

Tansy gathered the cats on the end of a log and took a handful of treats from her pocket. She held one up to gain the cats' attention. Then raising her hand, she told them to stay whilst she placed the tiny biscuits at the other end of the log. Getting the cats to stay was incredible enough but then James noticed that the log had wire obstacles along it, hoops and hurdles. One by one she got the cats to negotiate the obstacle course ensuring that they got a treat at the end. "I am the lion tamer," she stated, "and the bareback rider." Now she cantered off in a circle round the perimeter of the ring.

"Uncle James, Uncle James, watch me." Attention now on Lily he frowned as he watched her struggle to balance on the swaying rope. She made it halfway across before she fell. "Wait, I can do it," she said getting back on the stump.

He watched a couple more times, then asked if it was okay if he made a suggestion. She nodded. "You know that I used to be a fire fighter. Well, I am good with ropes. Let me tighten it for you." A bit of effort later and the rope was taught. He then sought out a branch and stripped its bark. She held it and agreed that it wasn't too heavy. "Right, now try," he said.

Holding the branch for balance, she set off along the rope. This time she made it beyond halfway before she fell off, but encouraged she tried again. At the 4th attempt she made it all the way. "Well done, Lily. Well done all of you. Practice, practice, practice. If you want to get good at anything that is what you need to do. Nathan I can see that you have been practicing a lot."

"Gemma taught me," said Nathan proudly. "She was in a circus."

"I know," he gulped. "Right, I'd better be getting back. Have fun." He was about to plunge back into the woods but then turned and addressed Nathan, "You don't know the name of the circus do you?"

"No," he said. Seeing the disappointment on

James's face he added, "It was something foreign. 'Com' something."

"It will be alright, Uncle James," said Violet. "Tansy chose her for you." By her side Lily nodded.

* * *

Back home James waited impatiently whilst his computer woke up. He made himself a cup of tea and sat facing the screen. First he tried 'Much Meddling + Circus' but this gained him lots about Much Meddling but nothing related to a circus. Then he wondered where in the village the circus would have been sited. It would have been more logical to site it at Prior Meddling as it was better located for the surrounding villages. 'Prior Meddling + Circus' brought up 2 newspaper articles and 3 adverts for circus visits and one of them was Comaneci's Circus. It looked like Nathan was right with his 'Com' something. He then tried searching on 'Comaneci's Circus' but this just produced a number of reviews of the circus's visits to other parts of the UK. He then tried 'Romania + Circus' but this gave him lots of articles about the state circus and nothing of use to him. He tried adding Gemma's name plus her maiden and married names and Crystal Modoran. This got a hit, with a photograph. He enlarged the image as far as it would go, but it may have been a younger Gemma, equally it may not. However, her name was there and was repeated in the article. The article, however, was unintelligible to him. He needed someone who spoke Romanian.

Taking a copy from the printer he searched his contacts list for an interpreter. The church had an extensive contact list and he knew that he shouldn't be making personal use of it but he just had to find her. Besides, she was distressed when she left, and he was meant to help people; it was his job.

* * *

Alex, lifted the new mower out of the back of the Range Rover and trundled it round to the back of Wishing Well Cottage. The lawn had grown quite long and he wasn't looking forward to the task ahead. He coughed and snorted, as petrol glugged into the mower's tank. Tank filled, he pumped the petrol button several times. Then he pulled the starter cord. Apart from a disgruntled 'chuff' nothing happened. He stripped off his T-shirt and tried again.

"Aren't you meant to read the instructions first?" said Emily.

"It is just a petrol mower."

"And, I'd raise the blade if I were you."

"Do you want to do this?"

"That, no, but this... I'm happy to do," she said jiggling a bottle of sunscreen in front of him.

"What? I don't need that...Oh, alright then."

She smothered her hands with cream and

proceeded to slather it all over his chest. He flexed his 'pecs' under her fingers and as her hands moved down, he grinned and rippled his 'abs'. As she spread the cream up to his shoulders, he put his hands on her hips and pulled her to him.

"No, you'll get it all over my clothes," she wailed pushing him back to arms length.

"Not if you take them off..."

Looking him in the eye she bit the corner of her lip, then slowly crossed her arms in front of her. Taking hold of the sides of her top she began to lift. She stopped tantalisingly, in stages of reveal. She hadn't planned this, but she was wearing her good bra. With her top at shoulder height, she grinned and turned her body towards the back door, lifting her arms above her head and enticing him to follow. Just as her vision was obscured by a piece of lemon coloured cotton interlock, she saw a shocked James stepping out of their back door. Arms stuck above her head, the disruption in the manoeuvre ruining the flow, they stayed there. she fought frantically to get her top back down, but at the same time happy to keep her face hidden. He stepped aside, eyes averted, as she crashed into the porch and disappeared, pinball like, into the house.

Alex roared with laughter and James started to laugh. When the 2 had settled down Alex offered James a beer. "It's good to see you laugh again, mate."

James nodded, jealously eyeing up Alex's greasy torso. He wanted a relationship like theirs. He wanted someone to smother him like that, and no-one but Gemma would do.

When a pink faced Emily reappeared James announced that he wanted their help, well, Emily's mainly. After explaining about his internet search, he told them that he had got an interpreter to do a search for him on Romanian websites. What he wanted from Emily was a way of getting Gemma to talk to him. He needed to make a grand gesture to show her how much he cared. He needed ideas. He thought of watching a load of romantic movies but that could take ages. Had Emily seen any good ones? Perhaps she could talk to Lou and Anna for their advice.

"Mate, what if it turns out she did murder her husband, what then?" asked Alex.

James looked stunned, "No, she couldn't have done something like that. She just couldn't."

"Not even if he was a right bastard and it was her only way out."

"No, I don't believe that."

"Not all men are like you and I. Some treat women as punchbags, physically and psychologically."

"No, she couldn't do something like that, not with a knife."

"You just don't know, what the most unlikely people are capable of."

CHAPTER THIRTY FOUR

James threw back the crumpled sheet, hauled himself out of bed and headed for the shower. The water was cool and refreshing. He lingered, not relishing the thought of donning his robes and walking across to the church. He wrapped a towel round his waist and flip flopped his way to the kitchen. As the kettle boiled, he reread the words of his sermon, memorising them as best he could. His delivery was better if he didn't have to read it verbatim, and he needed his delivery to be good; he had a message to get across to his wayward flock. He prayed for the strength to deliver it calmly when what he really wanted to do was scream and holler at them, old style. Those old preachers really commanded an audience with their threats of fire and brimstone, pointing and accusing. These days, just 'steepleing' his fingers and pursing his lips could put him in danger of bullying and harassment accusations.

He made his way across to the church a little earlier than normal so he could hide away in the back until it was time for the service. He didn't want to make small talk with any of those he was about to 'enlighten' before he delivered his 'suggestons'.

When he made his entrance, he was a little taken aback by the number of people present. Then he took in the fact that apart from the regulars, they were nearly all women. It seemed that Mr Swire could still command a following.

When he announced Mr Swire's death, there was audible sobbing. He hoped the hassocks wouldn't rot. When he announced that the funeral would be on the following Thursday some muttering could be heard, apparently not everyone was happy with that date. No doubt he would hear why. Thankfully it wasn't his choosing and he would only have to defend it not explain it, or try to change it.

His sermon was listened to attentively and with complete oblivion. He looked individuals in the eye as he spoke, moving from face to face, but they all looked back confidently meeting his gaze. Not one showed any sign of remorse or the slightest tinge of guilt. They had cast out the sinner and were perfectly content with their actions. He gripped the edges of the pulpit and scanned his congregation. He easily found Alex, head above the rest, and Emily by his side. The pair were looking back sympathetically. At least someone understood. Then, between the rows of bodies, he saw Violet's little face. She had her head on one side peering through the gap of shoulders. She smiled at him, and he felt a whole lot better. He was silent for a moment, taking strength from above, then continued.

Outside he was immediately assaulted by those not happy with the funeral date and others keen to pat him on the back and tell him he was well rid of 'that woman': all the vile, derogatory terms, that had been hurled at Gemma by the pond, absent in the church yard.

"You are all bad people. That sermon was meant for you." A furious Lily stepped in front of James and pointed. "Gemma is a good person. You don't know her, but you accuse her. If we hadn't stopped you, you would have pushed her into the pond. Did you want her to drown?"

Tansy and Violet moved to flank Lily again, this time shielding James. Only the birds and the gentle rustle of dry leaves, could be heard. James put his hands on Lily's shoulders, "Its okay, girls."

"No, it isn't." Alex stepped out of the crowd and moved alongside James. Emily's heart kicked up a gear as all eyes fell on her husband. "I will say, what maybe James can't." He swept an accusing finger at the mob, "You should be ashamed of yourselves. All those of you who were here on Thursday, shame on you. You hounded and terrified a woman based on nothing more than gossip. You have no proof. You drove her out of the village 20 years ago and now you are doing it again. She has done

PAULINE POTTERILL

you no harm and you have no proof that she has harmed anyone else. It is just a witch hunt." Now the crowd looked cowed. Being boomed at by the large, normally affable blacksmith, was a shock.

* * *

After lunch the family piled into the car and set off. Just beyond Prior Meddling James turned down a side road, at a brown sign stating Bracken Lea Water Mill. Crunching to a halt under an oak he switched off the engine.

A chipping path wound its way between a young alder hedge to a pale green kiosk. They joined the small queue and waited their turn. It didn't take long before someone noticed and all heads turned to look at the triplets. The girls smiled brightly. Once through the turnstile the girls headed straight for the play park and began to climb. A series of wood and rope structures stood on a patch of bark chippings, blending beautifully into the surrounding trees. Lily quickly found a beam walkway and impressed her parents by walking the full length of the 5 sections with ease. As Violet kicked off on one of the swings there was a call from on high.

"Watch me," yelled Tansy.

Before Alex or Emily could react Tansy launched herself from a 10ft high platform at the top of a fort-shaped structure. In mid-air she wrapped her arms and legs round a metal pole, her body crashing into it. She rotated slightly then, with a squeal of plastic sandals, she slid to the ground. Emily and Alex looked at one another and sighed as their daughter ran away, bark chippings flying, to the scramble net which led back up to the top of the tower.

The water wheel, when they finally got the girls there, was impressive. "The Victorians really knew how to build," shouted Alex inspecting the metal work. The triplets capped their hands over the top of the wooden guard rail and stood on tiptoe. Peering over the edge they stared down at the swirling water. As they moved past the wheel Violet clapped her hands over her ears. Moving through the building they saw the massive mill stones driven by the wheel, and watched as milled flour spat out and dropped for collection. In the shop Emily bought a bag of flour, her intention being to get the girls to make some bread when they got home. Then, maybe they could help with all the bread making that would be needed next time the Well Blessing Ceremony came round.

* * *

Back home, with the children off somewhere in the woods and Alex busy mowing the lawn, Emily stripped off the bed which the man had used. He hadn't said goodbye, but he had done what he needed to do and all his belongings were gone. She bundled the sheets into the washing machine then headed down to the cellar. There was something that she needed to check. With all the lights on she removed all the marble boxes and placed them on the table. Then, one at a time she lifted each lid. Each box had a full set. 6 boxes each containing 3 trays with 36 marbles in each. The man had been very clear. These memories were for her, as the mother, to help her understand and as a record. She must 'find a way of preserving them for the next world. Help is at hand'. She ran her eyes over the marbles. Why hadn't she asked any questions? Why had she sat there mute and just nodded? At the time the surreal comments had seemed reasonable. Had, 'preserve them for the next world' been his exact words? She knew they had.

* * *

"Crystal…"

"Yes, mother?"

"Make me a cup of tea, love."

"Okay. Just let me finish the washing up."

"But I'm thirsty now."

Gemma placed a pan on the drainer and briefly watched as it dripped. Then she dried her hands and switched on the kettle.

"Crystal…"

"Yes, mother?"

"Make me a cup of tea."

"I'm making you one."

"What?"

"I said, I'm making you one." Gemma got a

tea bag out of the cupboard and eyed up all the other ingredients in there…

"Crystal…"

Gemma slammed the cupboard door, placed the bag in a mug with 2 spoons of sugar and rapped her nails on the kitchen counter until the kettle boiled.

"Crystal…"

Robot-like she took the mug and a couple of biscuits through to the sitting room, and yelled, "Mum, no…" She quickly placed the items on a table and leapt at her mother, steadying her before helping her back into her seat. "Please don't try standing on your own. You know you aren't steady. Look I've got your tea and some biscuits." She retrieved a tartan blanket from the floor and placed it over Mrs Winterbottom's lap, tucking it firmly down the sides of her chair. She tested the temperature of the tea then placed it in the old woman's hands. The biscuits she placed within reach. Her mother now occupied, she returned to the washing up. This couldn't go on.

* * *

A ping from his phone alerted James to an e-mail from Emily. He smiled. There was a hastily compiled list of Romantic Comedies with rambling details of their 'happy endings'. Awkward to view on his phone he switched on his computer and got himself a cup of tea.

CHAPTER THIRTY FIVE

G emma woke with a start, prodded by the familiar sense of dread that accompanied her every waking moment. There was silence as she grasped desperately at the dissolving memory of her dream. Then, it was gone, like cream stirred into coffee, by the teaspoon that was her mother.

"Crystal…"

Gemma rolled onto her side and looked at her alarm. 7.25am – 2 hours sleep.

"Cryyyystaaalll!"

Gemma threw back the covers and reached for her dressing gown. She rubbed her face with her hands and took a deep breath.

"Crystal, where are you? I need to go again."

Silently Gemma turned back her mother's sheets and moved the woman's feet to the edge of the bed. Physically it was a little easier, this now well practiced routine, but her brain was screaming. It was like she was two different people. The physical Gemma was calm and reassuring. The mental Gemma was smashing rocks. Then there was a third Gemma, who stood aside and observed them both. Gently she manoeuvred her mother to a sitting position and placed the Zimmer in front of her. Pushing a rising fear of panic, deep inside, she took her mother by the arm and helped her to her feet. Together, the two of them moved, zombie-like to the bathroom.

She was just helping her mother back into bed, debating whether to get her up and dressed now or leave her in bed for another hour or so, where she would be safe and Gemma could get on with the day, when a noise from outside drew her to the window. It was singing, and close by: the beautiful close harmony singing of a barbershop quartet. Mystified she pulled back the curtains and looked out. In the street, below her mother's window, was a group of 5 figures all looking up at her. Shocked, she clutched at her robe, and shrank backwards into the room. Robe suitably arranged, she cautiously returned to the window and peered out. Below stood 5 beefy men in gold trousers, each with fluorescent strips down the sides and round the ankles. Each man clutched a bright yellow helmet to his black t-shirted chest, muscles clearly defined in the early morning light. They sang in perfect harmony, their chests expanding and contracting as they breathed. Her mind raced. This was obviously for her. Was this James's doing? The barbershop singing continued, and she scanned their faces. At first, she didn't recognise him. The tight t-shirt, the well-honed physique and strong arms. When she spotted him, her stomach flipped. She had never seen him like this. This playful version of the vicar she knew. There, front and centre was James. Her James, clutching a rose. As she watched he went down on one knee, kissed the rose and raised it to her. The other firemen spread out their arms, framing James with 'jazz hands' as the singing came to an end. She beamed back at him shaking her head in amusement.

Below, James thanked the men and as they headed off up the street, Gemma closed the curtains and James walked up to her front door, where he stood nervously clutching his helmet. As his mates disappeared into the high street James waited. Perhaps she was getting dressed. Yes, she'd be getting dressed, before opening the door: making herself presentable. He waited. Finally, after 30 minutes, he realised that she wasn't going to open the door. He knocked once. Waited again, then fed the crumpled rose through the letter box.

* * *

At Wishing Well Cottage Emily was washing the cats' dishes when the doorbell rang. On the step was Jonathan from Tempus.

"Oh, hello," she said.

"Hi, erm..." he reached behind him and

manoeuvred a leather bag, which hung from his shoulder, round to his front. He opened the flap and began struggling to remove a large brown parcel.

"Would you like to come in," she offered.

Whilst the kettle boiled, he sat and carefully worked the parcel out of the bag and placed it on the table. It rattled slightly. Emily's heart beat a little faster; there was something familiar about that sound. She placed two mugs on the table and sat opposite him.

He placed his hands on the package and looked up at Emily, "Before he died, Mr Swire commissioned me to make this. He said it was for you, and you alone." He gave the item a couple of affectionate pats and then slid it across the table.

Emily took it. The size was familiar. The weight was familiar. The sound was familiar. Tentatively she unwrapped it. Despite being no surprise, it was still a shock. A brand-new oak box sat before her. With shaky fingers she lifted the lid. Inside she found 3 trays each with 36 amber marbles with black strips at their cores. An envelope, addressed to her was also in there. She lifted it out and turned it over. A bright red wax seal kept the contents secure. Briefly she ran her fingers over the indentation, unable to make out what she was looking at. Tilting the envelope slightly to catch the light she saw the impression quite clearly; it was an imprint of a cat.

"Are you okay?" asked Jonathan.

"Sorry, yes," said Emily realising that she had been staring at the seal for some time. "Sorry, I liked Mr Swire. He was a bit abrasive, but you knew exactly where you were with him." She inspected the box. "This really is impressive. You have done a wonderful job. It is so beautifully made."

"Well, I enjoyed making it. I felt quite inspired. I have no idea what is so special about those marbles, but he was very insistent that they had a good box and very specific about its dimensions. Anyway, I have done as he asked."

With Jonathan gone she took the box and a torch down to the cellar. She sat and removed a marble and switched off the torch. Nothing happened. She tried another. Again, nothing happened. The marbles were blanks.

* * *

James threw open his fridge door and pulled out a can. He ripped back the ring-pull and took a swig. Then downed the lot. He pulped the empty can and slung it in the bin. He was about to reach for another, but he knew that wasn't the answer. Maybe fresh air and a run would help. Upstairs he caught a glimpse of himself in the mirror, as he stripped off his fire fighter's clothing, and felt a fool. Had he been recognised? People had opened their windows to watch, and people had stopped in the street, clearly enjoying the show. They had drifted off when the singing stopped but now, suddenly, he had a vision of the local paper with the headline 'Much Meddling Vicar Moonlights as Stripper-gram'. What had he been thinking! It was totally inappropriate for him to behave in that way. Wasn't it? What if someone had filmed him? He got one trainer on then realised he just couldn't face meeting anyone: couldn't trust himself to maintain his composure. Instead, he went to the kettle.

Steaming mug in hand he sat at the kitchen table and hung his head. Opposite sat a mug with red lipstick. He knew it was there, but he couldn't bare to look at it.

* * *

When the children came home later that afternoon Emily sat them down. They settled immediately, as if they had been expecting this. Lined up on the kitchen sofa, faces expectant, they looked at their mother. She looked at each inscrutable face, and smiled. She loved them unreservedly, but she also feared them, but more than that she feared for them. She had always known they were different to other children. Now, she knew they were different to all the other triplets that had gone before. Did they know it? Did they know what was to come, in the years ahead?

"Girls, some time ago you mentioned that the Cronkler had arrived." She waited, would they respond or clam up?

They nodded. Good. "The Cronkler being Ms Potterill?"

They nodded. "You also mentioned that she was the third?"

They nodded. "If the man was the first, who is the second?"

As one they replied, "The Wood Carver."

"Jonathan at Tempus?"

They nodded. Then Violet stood and, counting off on her fingers, said, "The Stone Carver, The Wood Carver and The Cronkler."

"Has the man gone?" asked Emily.

"Yes, he'd done what he needed to do. We won't see him again, or The Catolith."

Emily pondered this. It seemed they had passed their test. The children rose, the interview apparently over. As she watched them go, and then listened as they climbed the stairs, she wondered what was to come. The man had been impressed by Lily and Violet, but he had singled out Tansy. He seemed surprised at the potential she displayed. He had also hoped that it would be enough.

* * *

James waited impatiently whilst his printer spewed out several sheets of paper. Then he took the pile and settled himself in the corner of his settee, long tanned legs stretched out on the cushions. On the coffee table to his right was a cork coaster and a crystal glass. He noted the irony, took a sip of the rich amber liquid, and stared at his white feet. Perhaps he needed to wear sandals for a while, or go barefoot. The liquid coursed through his body, warming and numbing, but not consoling. He picked up the pile of papers. His Romanian interpreter had really done, what appeared to be, a thorough job. He had skim read the report but found it easier to read the detail as a printed sheet: his computer not being that reliable. He took another couple of sips, then reached for the bottle and refilled his glass.

CHAPTER THIRTY SIX

When James pulled back the curtains on the morning of Mr Swire's funeral he was greeted by dark clouds and a steady drizzle. No, he didn't want this for Mr Swire although the thought of rows of soggy black fascinators did lighten his spirits briefly. Memories of other rain soaked funerals sprang to mind. Rain hitting canopies of umbrellas, drumming like arrows at the Battle of Hastings, and drowning out his words.

However, his prayers must have been answered because by the time he headed over to the church there wasn't a cloud in the sky. Early arrivals nodded to him and parted to allow him passage. No one mentioned singing fire fighters, and he breathed a sigh of relief. The church filled quickly. He wished it could always be like this. He looked round the faces, many shiny damp around the eyes. There was the odd audible sniff and, as he began the service, a stifled howl.

Mr Swire's 2 relatives, a great niece with her husband, and a great nephew, sat in the front row. He nodded to them, acknowledging their presence. They sat impassively. He had spoken to them briefly on the phone but hadn't met them before. They were clearly a little bemused by the number of mourners for this man they had never met.

James spotted Alex and Emily and the girls, Louise and Mike and Nathan, Richard from the pub, Anna and Sasha and several other familiar faces. As he spoke the familiar words of the funeral service, he continued to look at his congregation. Then he felt a little jolt of recognition and quickly returned his gaze to a face in their midst. He faltered slightly and had to refer to the order of service in his hands. He took a quick look and was certain. There, black hair framing her face, dark glasses hiding her eyes, was Gemma. It was either a wig or she had dyed her hair but it was definitely her. Mind racing, he returned to the service, flustered but a little happier.

The eulogy was delivered by the star of Much Meddling's amateur dramatic society. Many had fought, very nearly physically, for the honour of delivering it. James had intervened; only one of them should do it and as she had the best 'projection' of all of them, it was appropriate that she be the one: there being no microphones in the church. James secretly felt that Mr Swire, with his wicked sense of humour, would approve. The woman had had the audience in stitches with her performance as Lady Macbeth. It had been the longest death scene that Prior Meddling's stage had ever seen and surprising as the only time Lady Macbeth had died in full view of an audience. The Physic and Gentlewoman had attempted to stick to the original script by taking an arm each and dragging her off to the wings. A mistress of improv. she had fought free and to settle the long-standing thespian debate, once and for all, proved Lady M. hadn't died at her own hand but was strangled by the Gentlewoman as the Physic sat on her.

Disappointingly, the eulogy went flawlessly, and James led the way outside, the coffin and mourners following behind.

As people filed past and scattered handfuls of earth into the coffin hole, James stole glances at Gemma. She stood silently staring at the hole, until it was her turn to add some earth. Then she walked by, genuinely upset at Mr Swire's passing. He had been one of the few people in Much Meddling who had been welcoming and kind to her.

The service ended and people began to drift away, mainly in the direction of The Three Wells where the wake was to take place. With those that remained, conversation moved on, on to Gemma. James heard them, the same nasty comments, 'whore', 'murderer'. He was livid and glanced round anxiously to see where she was. Had she heard? Then he spotted her heading out of the church gate, head down and hurrying, heading home. He made to go after her, but was stopped by a woman congratulating him of being rid of 'that woman.' He was furious. He opened his mouth to let rip but was swept forcefully to one side. Alex was steering him back towards the church. "I'll deal with this. You go change and go after Gemma."

James hesitated. So, Alex had spotted her too. Gratefully he ran into the church, whipping his Cassock and Surplice over his head as he went.

Free of his vestments he darted through the church yard, cutting off the angle. Dodging the grave stones and giving the compost heap a wide birth he vaulted the wall into the street. He landed badly, jolting a knee and his back. In the far distance Gemma could be seen, jogging awkwardly up the street, stilettoes clicking furiously. James sped along the high street, skidding as his leather soled derby shoes failed to provide grip on the flagstones. Even so, he was gaining on her. Had there been another 50 metres he would have reached her, but there wasn't. As he rounded the corner of her street she turned into her gate. He called out her name. She glanced back but kept going. By the time he reached her door, it was firmly shut. Desperately he yelled through the letter box, begging and pleading for her to come talk to him. Eventually, emotionally drained and hoarse, he conceded defeat. Miserably, he made his way home.

* * *

The Three Wells was stifling. Drinks were passed over heads and out through the doors. People sat uncomfortably on the beer garden wall thankful for the ice cold ale. A shout went out for more glasses and a steady stream of sticky pint pots made their way back over heads to the dishwasher, dripping nastily as they went.

"James, come join us," yelled a man waving a frothy topped glass. Across the green, James kept his head down and disappeared through the vicarage gate.

"I am so glad that Crystal woman has gone. Hopefully we won't be seeing her again," chipped in a woman sipping a glass of iced water. "I really don't know what he was thinking."

"Well, if Much Meddling ever has a Vicar and Tarts party..."

Alex, glad that Emily and Louise had taken the children back to Wishing Wells, waited for a lull in the laughter. Then he climbed up onto the pub wall. Only a few noticed initially, but the thunderous look on his face kept their attention and gradually others turned and put down their pints.

"I do not want to hijack Mr Swire's wake, but I think he would approve. He wasn't one to keep quiet, when he saw injustice."

There was curiosity and uncomfortable shuffling as Alex scanned his assembled mass.

"You may not know this, but Crystal Winterbottom was a friend of Mr Swire's. Yes, a friend. He trusted her and got to know her. You lot, on the other hand judged her on gossip. She did not murder her husband. He died in an accident.

"Most of you know she left Much Meddling and joined a circus. She and her husband, Pavel, had a knife throwing act. Unfortunately, Pavel was having an affair with another woman whose husband, Vladimir, interrupted a practice session. Pavel, shocked at the man's anger, moved as Gemma threw the knife. It severed his subscapular artery and he bled to death." He let that settle for a while, judging their faces. "As for your other accusations, she is a perfectly respectable widow."

In the silence, Mike climbed up on the wall beside Alex, "I just want to say I am sorry for my part in this. I shouldn't have repeated the gossip. I really wish I hadn't. Mr Swire would want us to 'treat as we find' and we should do that."

"To Mr Swire," said Alex grabbing a glass from Sasha, who had moved to his side.

"To Mr Swire," they chorused.

* * *

With the kids out in the woods, Emily, Louise, and Anna sat in the partial shade of an apple tree and sipped a glass of Prosecco. Louise rearranged her shoulder straps and stretched her legs out. She slipped off her black kitten heeled shoes and placed her feet on top, then hitched up her black skirt revealing her thighs. Placing her sunglasses on the garden table, she shut her eyes and tipped her head back. Anna raised an eyebrow at Emily.

"So, how goes the house hunting?" asked Emily.

"Still looking," said Anna as Louise nodded.

"Well," said Emily, "Alex and I have been talking. We would be happy to rent Fare Well to you. If you subsequently find somewhere to buy, well…"

"Really?"

"Yes. What better tenants than you!"

"I've got to tell Sasha." Anna fumbled in her bag and pulled out her phone. Several swipes and stabs later she pocketed it and set off for the pub. She didn't get far. A serious looking Violet was coming through the garden gate from the direction of the vicarage.

"Uncle James is very upset. Gemma won't talk to him."

"I'll go see him," said Anna.

"No. He said he wants to be left alone," said Violet. "I'm going to find Lily and Tansy."

So, the three women downed their Prosecco and walked round to the vicarage.

At the sight of the women James initially looked horrified but didn't take much prompting to spill his heart out. They listened and sympathised and Louise liberated some bottles from his fridge, wrinkled her nose at the use by dates, shrugged, and prised off the caps.

* * *

"Crystal, what've you done wi' me glasses."

"They are on your head."

"What did you put 'em there for?"

"I didn't mum, you did."

Gemma scanned the paper's 'vac ads' columns. There was nothing she was qualified for and nothing on a bus route or within cycling distance. She would get the bus into Barnlees in the morning and register with a couple of agencies and visit the job centre. First thing though, before anyone was about, she would drop James' keys through his door.

* * *

Having emptied James' fridge and being unable to find any further beverages, Louise headed round to Emily's. She was just emerging from the cellar with a couple of bottles of red wine when she was brought up short by an indignant Tansy made even more imposing by leather boots and a hard hat.

"Where's my mummy?"

"Round at Uncle James's."

Tansy eyed the bottles suspiciously then turned on her heels, breaking into a run as she went out the door. Louise followed trying not to giggle. When she walked through James' door, she could hear Emily apologising and Tansy shouting.

"It's not fair. Daddy promised, but he's had too many skinfuls and you've been drinking beer. I can't miss my lesson."

"I am sorry love. We just... forgot."

"Tansy, would it be alright if I took you?" asked James.

They all looked at him.

"I've only had one bottle, and I haven't finished that. I've been talking all the time."

Emily and Louise didn't say anything, but did a quick peruse of the table. They were going to have to buy James some more six packs.

Tansy threw her arms around James, which did more to cheer him up than all the chat and sympathy from the two women had. Seeing Tansy happy lifted his spirits. Before he knew it, he was being bustled out of the door.

"You'll need your booster seat," yelled Emily but Tansy was already racing home.

Seat sorted, James drove up the high street. It was only as they passed the end of Gemma's road did he realise that talking about horses had completely taken his mind off Gemma.

CHAPTER THIRTY SEVEN

J ames opened his eyes and groaned. Light streamed through his curtains. At his side his clock showed 6.25am. He might as well get up. A quick run before breakfast, and before anyone was about, might make him feel better. He worked through his warm-up routine, eager to get going. He was just about to close his door when he heard his phone ping. Hopes raised he hurried back up the hall to the kitchen table. He grabbed his phone. It was a text message telling him that changes were being made to his data tariff. Irritated he slung it onto the table. It landed, teetered on the edge, and then fell to the floor. He bent down and scooped it up, and let out a scream. The phone dropped and bounced across the floor. James grabbed the edge of the table with one hand and his back with the other, and sank to his knees.

* * *

Black wig in situ, just in case, Gemma made her way up the high street clutching James' keys in one hand and an envelope in the other. She walked: her bicycle being too conspicuous. Even though it was early, there were people about. The bakery door was open. Warm bread, with an overlay of cinnamon beckoned from across the street. It would be lovely to go in, have a browse, and buy a selection of pastries for breakfast. She gave the shop a longing glance; her entire life it seemed had been lived at a distance, excluded from things others took for granted.

On the pond the mallards chuckled, happy little family groups paddling round the reeds. As she entered the vicarage gate she fondled the keys, warm from her hand, one last time. She walked slowly, conscious of the chippings crunching under her feet. She stepped into the porch. The door was wide open. Undecided what to do, she stood, keys in hand. Then she heard a groan. She listened. Then a muffled cry. She took a step inside.

"Help!"

"James?"

"Help, help!"

Gemma ran up the hall. James was crouched in a foetal position, gripping a leg of the table.

"I can't move. My back has gone."

"Don't move."

"I can't," he snapped. "Sorry, sorry. I'm so glad you are here. Gemma it's lovely to see you." He turned his head to look at her and let out an involuntary howl.

Whilst they waited for the doctor to arrive

Gemma sat on the floor and did her best to comfort him. Her presence helped a lot but did nothing for his pain, which was tolerable provided he didn't move, but the rest of him was now protesting at the contact with the floor. As the minutes dawdled by, James expressed his delight at her presence, stating how much he had missed her, how empty his life was without her and how angry he was at the villagers for how they had treated her. His relief at her presence was apparent in every word, every limited action, every awkward breath. She couldn't find the words to tell him she wasn't staying. Instead, she rested a hand on his shoulder, her emotions torn, her regrets palpable: the words of the note in her pocket very final.

The doctor arrived, shortly followed by Alex, who, on his way to work had spotted the doctor's car. Gemma made everyone a cup of tea, whilst the doctor saw to James. She took the three mugs from his mug tree and then picked up the mug which was sitting on the table. She was about to wash it when she paused, stunned. Red lipstick adorned its rim. Her lipstick. Slowly, a lump forming in her throat, she realised that the mug hadn't been moved from where she had left it, days ago.

She handed Alex and the doctor a mug each. They sipped and waited. Half an hour after the doctor administered an injection James was able, with Alex' help, to make it to his settee. The doctor left.

"Where's Gemma," asked James as he settled, edging into a less uncomfortable position. Alex went in search of Gemma. In the kitchen there was no sign of her. On the table was a clean mug, containing a set of keys and an envelope 'To James'.

"Mate," said Alex holding out the mug.

James took the mug. The keys jangled. He rotated it and ran a thumb along the clean rim. He ripped open the envelope and read the note inside. It said simply:

Dear James,
It would never have worked between us.
We are from different worlds.
Take care of yourself.
Gemma

When Emily arrived, summoned by a call from Alex, James was still clutching the note. She went to sit next to him, but he spread out his arms on the sofa, protecting his space. "No, don't move me."

"Sorry, I'll make you a cup of tea."

"I don't want a cup of bloody tea."

"Coffee?"

His head snapped up and met her eye.

"Hot chocolate?"

Now he knew she was teasing him and attempted a wry smile. "Sorry. It is just… Why? I just don't know what to do. It could have worked between us. It should have worked between us if it wasn't for the interfering old biddies of this village."

Emily sat on the coffee table in front of James. Alex took the opportunity to slip out the door to work. James sat, hands on knees, bracing himself. Emily gently lay her hands on his. "I am so sorry."

"I love her Emily. I just don't know what I am going to do without her. We don't have to stay in Much Meddling, we could move away. I could find another parish. Her mother could come too, then neither of them would have to suffer the abuses they have." Feeling that his voice was beginning to fail him, he said, "A cuppa would be nice."

Emily stood and made her way to the kitchen. She would give him time to compose himself. She shook her head; it was so unfair. He really deserved to be happy. He was a good man. She rammed the lid back on the kettle and switched it on. The water began to boil as her anger simmered. As the tea brewed she rattled a teaspoon around each mug, pummelling the bags. Satisfied, she flung each bag in the sink along with the spoon, and turned to pick up the mugs. Emily jumped. There, in the kitchen doorway, finger pressed to her lips, was Gemma. Emily stared at her. Gemma smiled and very quietly said, "May I take those?"

"You're back?" whispered Emily. "Did you hear what he said, just now?"

"Yes, I heard."

"Are you… back to stay?"

Gemma nodded.

Tears welled in Emily's eyes. She stepped forward, threw her arms around the other woman and kissed her on the cheek. Then she stood back and agitatedly shepherded Gemma, mugs in hand, towards the living room. Just outside the door Gemma stopped and, to Emily's surprise, took a sip of tea, leaving lipstick on the mug's rim.

Emily stood in the doorway long enough to see James look up, bewilderment all over his face. He had been expecting Emily, but here was Gemma and looking like herself, no wig. Was he hallucinating? Was the injection stronger than he thought? He looked from Gemma to Emily and back again, "Gemma, how?" Not daring to hope, he held his breath.

Gemma walked into the room, sat on the coffee table in front of him and smiled. "Can we start again?"

He nodded like a scolded child given a lollipop. As Gemma handed him the mug and he saw the red rim, his happiness was complete.

Emily let herself out. Later she discovered that as Gemma had made her way home, despite the black wig, she had been recognised. Time had moved on and the high street had become busy: just what she had wanted to avoid. Ahead, she'd seen a couple of women get ready to ambush her. She had held her head high and kept going. The women had stood their ground. She'd known she wouldn't be able to sidestep them both. Oddly the women had been smiling at her. She'd braced herself, waiting for the mean sarcastic comments sure to follow. Instead, what she'd got was an apology. They were deeply sorry for the things they had said, and they hoped she could forgive them. Apparently, the blacksmith had put them straight. The vicar had done a lot of research to give them the truth but they hadn't listened: him being a goody-goody. As she'd gone on her way, others had stopped her. People had come out of shops. "Sorry, about your husband. That must have been terrible for you. If there is anything we can do to help..." Slowly, she had removed her wig and run her fingers through her hair. Then she had turned around and headed back to the vicarage, a spring in her step and hope in her heart.

* * *

It being Friday, I went to What Sup for my treat. I chose a large apricot filled pastry and a large Americano and sat with my back to the wall watching the world from the shade. I enjoyed the bustle and took pleasure in the custom that the shops were enjoying. The Ark Aid's success even spilled out onto the high street benefitting the other shops. Daniel, the owner of Heaven Scent stepped out and gave me a wave, cloth in hand. Then he turned his attention to something on his window, no doubt the work of a feathered graffiti artist. The door of Tempus chimed, and I looked across. I had grown to know the different sounds. Even though some were similar I knew which shop was which. It appeared that Jonathan had sold another wall clock, judging by the size of package that was being carried out. His work really was remarkable. At some point I would like to buy one of his pieces.

My writing had hit a bit of a brick wall. I knew what I was aiming for but was struggling to find logical ways to get the plot to work out. Maybe a walk would help. My planned walk with Emily, of the previous day, had been postponed because of Cornelius's funeral. She had planned to show me some nearby waterfalls and rock pools. I put the last piece of pastry into my mouth then surreptitiously licked a finger and wiped it round my plate, picking up the last of the crumbs. A movement at the top of my steps caught my eye. At first, I thought I was mistaken, until further movement showed me something that was almost camouflaged against the millstone grit of the walls. I downed the last of my coffee and went to investigate. From the bottom of the steps I couldn't see. But as I climbed higher, the tip of a fluffy tail and then a grey and black striped head came into view. A large, long-legged cat confronted me.

"Hello, where did you come from?"

As I reached the top step the cat rolled onto one side and stretched, playfully inviting me to stroke it. I sat on the warm stone and stretched out my hand caressing the soft multi-hewed grey fur. We sat together for a while, enjoying each others' company. The cat looked up at me and I stared into his eyes; they had such depth. I smiled and the cat purred.

* * *

Gemma and James had a long talk. She wanted to tell him everything. She had wanted to tell him everything but at first it hadn't been appropriate, she was just his cleaner. Then as they had got to know one another, it was awkward. She wanted to tell him but she didn't know how he felt about her and the truth could have been interpreted as pushing the relationship on, when he wasn't ready for that, or it could have put him off. Then, he had to go away and she didn't get the chance. Now, she told him the full story.

As a teenager she had been teased mercilessly because of her mother's occupation. Yes, it was true, her mother had worked at Nina Norton's but, as a single mother she had fed and clothed her daughter. It was only after Gemma had run off with the circus that she grew to understand what her mother must have gone

through to raise her, and she felt bad about
that. The circus had toured Europe and she had
married one of the performers. Together they
had formed a knife throwing act. Then one day,
they were practicing. Just as she threw a knife,
there was a commotion behind her and Pavel
flinched, bringing down his arm. The knife hit
him in the shoulder, severing an artery. They
couldn't stop the bleeding and he died. The
hostility of the only two witnesses caused her
to run. After three weeks she was caught and
arrested and accused of murder. Pavel had been
having an affair with the witness' wife and he
had just found out. Livid, the man had gone
to accuse Pavel, his wife close on his heels. So,
not wanting to be implicated in Pavel's death, he
testified that Crystal had killed him when she
found out. The wife, angry and upset at the death
of her lover, was also willing to blame Gemma. It
had been weeks before the woman, and then the
man, confessed to having lied.

When she was eventually freed, she left
the circus and worked her way around Europe,
taking hospitality work wherever she could find
it. Then, her mother became ill, and she came
back to Much Meddling praying that no one
would recognise her.

* * *

Over the next few days James and Gemma
spent an increasing amount of time together.

As his mobility increased and his reliance on painkillers reduced she invited him to meet her mother. Mrs Winterbottom, presented with a steady supply of drinks and biscuits, behaved herself and Gemma was relieved. Even her language, which could be quite choice at times, was acceptable. James noted the care and attention Gemma gave her mother, but also noted the strain it was taking on her. He desperately wanted to help reduce that burden and took to helping whenever he could.

CHAPTER THIRTY EIGHT

J ames put down the phone. He had a smile on his face. His conversation with the bishop had gone well. He had been a little nervous that one of Gemma's neighbours may have blabbed to him about his Chippendale impersonation, but it didn't seem so. The bishop had given him his blessing. Now it was up to him. He had some planning to do and some arrangements to make. What he proposed was risky and he had a number of reservations but hopefully his contingency plan wouldn't be needed.

* * *

With the children out somewhere Emily took the opportunity to go down into the cellar. Dustpan and brush, cloth and spray, clutched in her arms, she put all the lights on and descended. She placed her burden on the table and went to the alcove. One at a time she carried the wooden marble boxes to the table, taking care to keep them in order. At some point she planned to label them.

With the dustpan and brush she set about

sweeping out the alcove. Coughing madly, she went in search of something to cover her face. She found an old scarf and resumed her work. There were years, possibly centuries of dust and 'other stuff' amassed in the corners. When she had cleared what she could she gave the stone a quick spray and a wipe, then regretted it. Now she had a dusty sludge smeared everywhere. It took a bucket of water and lots of mopping to get the space reasonable. She was going to have to let it dry before putting the boxes back. In the cellar, that wasn't going to happen quickly. She stood back and inspected her work. The surrounding wall was streaked with cobwebs. She took her brush and swept them away. The brush hit something, and she stopped to look. Above the alcove was a lump. She gave it a good brushing but couldn't see it properly.

Returning with a torch she shone it at the wall. There, slightly recessed, was the Hag Stone, held in place by a hook. Thrilled, she reached up and took it down. Under the ceiling light she turned it in her hand. It was Sarah's stone, she was certain, but that wasn't where she'd seen it. By the state of it, the stone must have been there years, long before she moved in. She had never cleaned that area before. She couldn't possibly have seen it there; there wasn't enough light. Had she seen it in a memory? As she sat and cleaned it she racked her brains, sorting and discarding, but couldn't work out where she had seen it before.

Carefully she placed it back on its hook. She smiled, approving of its position, providing protection for the memories. She found a couple of strips of wood and placed them in the alcove; they would keep the boxes off the damp until it dried. She placed the old boxes back in order. Then, before adding the new box she lifted its lid. The marbles were still just normal marbles: her children's memories yet to be added, at the time of their deaths. She knew she would never see their memories and she didn't want to; it just wouldn't be right. Idly she lifted out the top tray and placed it to one side, caressing the odd marble, wondering which tray was for which child. She lifted out the second and then froze. Cold horror crept up her spine and her hands froze, mid-air. The bottom tray contained only 9 marbles, in 9 recesses.

There was a creak and a crash as the cellar door hit the wall. "Mummy?"

"Yes, I'm coming up. Wait there." Emily quickly put the trays in their box and placed it in the alcove. She wiped her eyes with the edge of her t-shirt and gathered her cleaning items. At the top of the steps Violet stood silhouetted. At the sight of Emily coming up, Violet backed off into the kitchen. Emily popped the cleaning items on the floor. She had a quick look at herself in the hall mirror and gave her eyes another wipe and blinked a few times. Then she went into the kitchen. Violet ran straight to her and put her arms around her. "Don't worry. All will be well." Emily wondered how she knew, but then she always did. Did she just know Emily was upset, or did she know and understand why?

* * *

At 2pm Emily knocked on my open door and called out, 'Hi'. I went out to find her stroking the large grey cat who was enjoying her attention. I expressed my delight at seeing him again and explained that he had turned up a few days previously. I asked her if she knew who owned him. She gave me an odd look and then she said the most curious thing, 'Cats in Much Meddling don't have owners. They just turn up.'

We walked across the green and down the lane by her house, then crossed the road and climbed the stile opposite. Emily seemed a little quiet. I couldn't make out why. She appeared to be making an effort to be cheerful. I asked her if everything was alright. She said it was and I didn't feel I knew her well enough, at this point, to 'pry'. We continued on our way, and I began to understand why she wanted to show me this walk. The scenery was spectacular and varied and it wasn't long before we could hear water ahead. She invited me to lead the way, through the last bit of shrubbery, wanting me to enjoy my first view of the river. I stepped onto a slab of limestone and looked around. To my right water cascaded over rocks from various points, forming a pool. It ran on a little and then fell again, the full force of the collected water gouging a larger deeper pool in front of me. I stepped forward, enjoying the cool mist it generated. To my left the water disappeared into the trees which surrounded us. Ahead and above, trees stretched up the hillside.

When I had had my fill of wandering round the edge of the rock slab, looking into the water, inspecting its different depths, we sat and enjoyed the sights and sounds. She told me that it was possible to see deer here, if you were quiet and patient enough.

We chatted, and she told me a little more of how she had come to live in Much Meddling. I sensed that there was more to this story than she was prepared to reveal. At times she hesitated, appearing to choose her words carefully. It was as if she were paving the way, judging my reaction, before telling me more.

She looked at her watch and announced that she needed to get back, Alex and the children would be home before she knew it and she needed to start getting their dinner ready.

I said goodbye to her at her gate, agreeing to meet again the following week.

As I walked through The Ark Aid I was hailed by Mary from the charity shop doorway. She had a table and 2 chairs for me. The chairs didn't match, but did I want them, at least until something better turned up. They were an odd combination but they were the right size and would, as she said, 'do'. I arranged them outside my door and then made myself a cup of tea. Mug in hand I returned to find my cat friend sitting on the table. I lifted him and placed him on the spare chair. I sat down and he stepped onto my lap and nuzzled my hand. I stroked his head a few times and he settled down on me, but not for long as we both got rather hot. He moved off onto the other chair and I decided that I was going to have to find cushions for us both. Then another thought occurred, and I spoke to my new friend, interrupting his purring.

"Am I going to have to find a name for you?"

He opened one eye and looked at me. There was a slight shuffle as he settled himself further into his seat. It very much looked that way.

* * *

This week Alex was punctual, and sober. A week was a long time for a 6-year-old and Tansy had forgotten all about Alex's misdemeanour. She climbed into the car and happily strapped herself in, tapping the heels of her boots together. Occasionally her hands held imaginary reins as she mentally practiced what she had learnt.

"I wonder which horse you will get today," said Alex.

"I hope it is Misty, or at least a different horse.

I want to ride them all."

As Alex switched off the engine Tansy said, "Uncle James parked over there. He said it was less mucky."

They walked into the stable yard. "Uncle James paid with cash, but he didn't have enough. We need to pay extra this week. I told them it was kind of him to bring me...you couldn't because of the skinfuls."

"What? You told them that?"

"It was the truth," she said, with the hint of a raised eyebrow; it was difficult to tell as her forehead movement was restricted by her helmet. "And mummy was sloshed too so Uncle James had to bring me because he'd only had one bottle. When I said he was the vicar, that seemed to help."

Once Tansy was sat on a grey mare called High Spirits Alex led her round to the door of the indoor school. "Uncle James went and sat in the gallery and watched," she said. Alex was getting a little fed up with Uncle James.

CHAPTER THIRTY NINE

When I opened my door, the cat walked in. He rubbed round my ankles, and I crouched down and stroked him. He rolled on his back and stretched out his paws inviting me to stroke his belly. I obliged, which pleased us both.

When I returned from the store my bags contained a tin of cat food: just the one, for now. No-one, during my enquiries had claimed ownership. In fact, the general concept had seemed to amuse most of Much Meddling's population, especially the older residents.

As I looked for a suitable dish, the cat sat patiently. When I put the full bowl on the floor, he tucked in. I tried a few names in my head, but none seemed right. I took a mug of coffee and sat at my new table looking down on the yard. The cat came and joined me, and we watched the world together. The boy Nathan appeared out of the charity shop carrying an armful of what looked like bunting; it was difficult to tell from where I was sitting. He waved at me and went on his way. The last time I had seen him was at Cornelius's funeral. I was glad to see that he looked much happier now. He had been devastated at the old man's death. I had barely known him, yet I missed him too. The cat nudged my hand. Cornelius was a wonderful name. I tried it out on the cat.

"Cornelius."

He purred enthusiastically and settled on my lap.

* * *

James was both excited and apprehensive. He showered, shaved and, having expressed his annoyance, stuck a little piece of tissue paper on the side of his neck. Then he said a little prayer, hoping that by the time he was dressed he would be able to remove the gory sticker. He pulled on his smart shorts and sandals. It was at this point that he noticed his feet didn't match his legs and he couldn't wear socks as they would get mucky. He eventually settled for slacks and his smart trainers and a short-sleeved shirt, open at the neck. He looked in the mirror and turned sideways, holding in his stomach. A quick comb and he was ready. He picked up his rucksack and wicker basket and set off.

At precisely 12.30pm he knocked on Gemma's front door. It opened and there was Gemma, radiant in a summer dress and canvas shoes. James held out his arm and she took it. Together they walked up the street towards the woods. He gave her his hand and helped her over the stile.

"I don't think I have been over this stile before, I usually use the one nearest the church," said James.

The path up through the woods wasn't wide enough for 2 people so they went single file, James following Gemma. As the ground rose, she slowed slightly, choosing her footing amongst the tree roots which littered the path. The ground levelled off for a while then rose again before plateauing as they neared the base of the crag: the trees at this end of the village going all the way to the rocks. Gemma paused before starting the zigzag climb up the crag and listened. Voices could be heard. It sounded like children. James stopped next to her and listened. Then from behind them came a familiar voice.

"Hi, Gemma. Hi Uncle James." Nathan appeared clutching a bundle of sticks. Then he called out to whoever was making the noise at the other side of them, "We've got an audience. We've got an audience." Then to Gemma and James, "Come and watch. Gemma, you've got to see what I can do. Please" Before she knew it Gemma was being dragged through the trees to a clearing, with James following on behind.

Gemma glanced round the clearing and took in the lines of bunting strung around the trees and the make-shift circus ring. Nathan pulled her forward and she was greeted by the triplets dressed in pink frilly leotards and glitter. The girls leapt up and down excitedly and bundled Gemma and James to a collection of upturned logs which were arranged as table and chairs. James looked at Gemma. Gemma looked at James. He smiled. She smiled back, shrugged, and sat down. Before they had got themselves settled there was a drum roll and Nathan, now wearing a top hat, announced that the Greatest Show on Earth was about to begin, whilst the triplets cantered round in circles and figures of 8 going "Naahhaayyy..."

James looked at Gemma, trying to judge her reaction, but she seemed to be okay. Nathan had said that she loved the circus, despite everything. She was smiling and seemed relaxed.

"Roll up, roll up. Come see Lily the Tie Troper." Nathan stuck out his arm and Tansy provided another drum roll. At the far side of the clearing Lily stood on her tree stump and held her pole out in front of her. Then she carefully stepped onto her tightrope. Step by careful step she made it across to the other side where she turned to her audience and took a bow.

Gemma and James clapped madly.

Next Violet was introduced as the World's Greatest Juggler. She stood in the middle of the ring and presented 3 fluorescent orange golf balls to her audience. She waited for her drum roll, which was a little late as Tansy was busy emptying a stone out of her shoe. Drum roll complete, Violet threw the first ball into the air, quickly followed by the other 2. There was the odd wild throw but the balls were all caught and she completed 9 cycles before a ball hit the floor.

The audience clapped and shouted bravo.

It was now Tansy's turn. She waited whilst Nathan arranged 3 logs inside the ring. Then she set off at the trot, before breaking into a canter and jumping the logs. After some neighing and mimed rearing and pawing of the air, she dismounted and handed the imaginary reins to Nathan. Free of her 'horse' she stepped up onto one of the logs and gave a mini gymnastic display, before taking a bow.

From her position on the log she announced, "And now the Greatest Catapulter the World has ever seen..." She held out her arm to introduce Nathan.

James took a sideways glance at Gemma. If any of this was going to upset her, this would. As far as he could tell, she seemed okay.

Nathan stepped into the centre of the ring, faced a row of pinecones set on a tree stump, and raised his catapult. Tansy provided the drum roll, and Nathan took aim. Everyone held their breath. Thwack, thwack, thwack. The pinecones vanished, blasted from their perch in rapid succession.

Gemma let out a cry. James looked at her in alarm. Nathan and the triplets all turned to look at her. She stood and started clapping her hands,

"That was incredible. Nathan, how did you do that? How did you re-load so quickly? That was just brilliant."

A pink faced Nathan smiled awkwardly back. "I practised and practised just like you told me."

"If I hadn't seen that with my own eyes, I wouldn't have believed it. I am so proud of you."

Nathan positively glowed. At his side Violet grinned and clapped in delight.

"Is that it?" asked James, knowing full well it wasn't but giving the children their cue.

Briefly the kids disappeared behind a tree then emerged wearing red noses and sets of their father's large shoes, lashed on with tape. Buckets of leaves got thrown about, planks were twirled and bottoms thwacked, feet were fallen over, and the audience laughed enthusiastically. The finale was unusual. A large flat round board was rolled out and placed on the tree stump in front of Gemma and James. Then a red and white checked tablecloth was placed over it. Before Gemma realised what was happening James' picnic basket was emptied and a table was laid out in front of her. The children took a bow. James winked at them and thanked them. Then, as one, they turned and vanished into the trees. As realisation settled on Gemma, James quietly lit the candles. Then he took hold of her hand, looked into her eyes, and cleared his throat. It was at this moment that the small piece of red soaked tissue lost adhesion and floated gently from his neck to land on their intertwined fingers. She flinched uncertainly but left her hand in his. His heart sank, but then she laughed, "Is this some bonding ritual I'm not familiar with? Do I need to provide a blood sample, too?"

"No, no, no. I am so sorry."

She grinned and gently blew the offending item aside along with his fears. She squeezed his hand affectionately and he took a deep breath.

"Gemma, before you came into my life, I thought I was happy. I had resigned myself to being single and I was okay with that. Then you turned up and that changed. Suddenly I knew that I wasn't okay with that. You made me feel joy, real joy. I was so happy. I couldn't believe it was possible to feel like that. Then you left… and I couldn't believe how bereft I felt. I had no idea I was capable of such grief."

He had been staring at her hand, taking care to deliver his speech. Now he paused and looked her in the eye. She met his gaze, her pupils dark and glistening.

He took a breath, "Gemma, I love you."

She squeezed his hand, "James, I love you too."

"It is important to me that you are happy. I would like us to get married, but only if that is what you want…"

A tear rolled down her cheek. There was a stifled, "Yes."

He stood and walked round to where he

could kneel. Then, he got down on one knee and held a tiny blue velvet box out in front him. He opened the lid. "Gemma, I want to spend the rest of my life making you as happy as I am. Will you marry me?"

There was a pause before Gemma found her voice, "Yes, James, yes. Yes, I will."

He placed the ring on her finger; it was a bit loose, but it went on despite the collective tremor. He shook slightly and she threw her arms around him, understanding how nerve-racking this had been for him. They held each other for a while then James took her head in his hands and gently kissed her on the lips...then more urgently.

14 months later

The publisher scrolled back and forth, concentrating intently, checking and re-checking. I waited nervously. She pursed her lips, giving nothing away. Emily held my hand as I gripped it tightly, the agony unbearable. The publisher looked up from her screen and smiled. I think there is not one, not two but three books here.

* * *

After our first walk together Emily and I

had spent an increasing amount of time in each other's company. The relationship was a little one sided, she talked, I listened. I didn't mind. I enjoyed her company, and I was happy to hear her story. When she eventually asked me to write it, I was delighted. The more detail she gave, as her trust in me increased, the more privileged I felt. A lot of what she said was fantastical and at first I didn't believe it. Now, having heard her full story and having lived in Much Meddling for several years, I honestly don't know, but my mind is open.

James and Gemma found their 'happy ever after' and were married in All Saints' Church, Much Meddling, the following spring. They had three bridesmaids and a pageboy. Alex was best man. The church was packed and even Mrs Winterbottom was welcomed and treated with respect by the residents of Much Meddling.

Emily eventually discovered where she had first seen the Hag Stone. She had been standing at the bar in The Three Wells, waiting to be served. Her eyes travelled along the bar and over to the door at its end. To the side of the door, above where Emily, as Sarah, had collected a candle on the night she delivered Edith's wedding present, was a hook. In the memory The Hag Stone had been hanging there, providing protection to the private quarters, back when the Wells family owned the pub. Now, it was protecting the Wells triplets' memories in

Wishing Well Cottage's cellar.

The following spring Alex bought Tansy a flaxen chestnut pony, which she named Breeze. The two of them became a familiar sight riding through the village. By the following summer Alex had constructed a series of small brightly painted jumps which occupied the far end of the field. It wasn't long before he bought a horse box to take her to various events and soon a lengthening row of rosettes decorated the wall over her bed.

Anna and Sasha moved into Fare Well Cottage and rented out their old house. Anna quickly fell back into her old role and 'girls night out' became a weekly feature, but with the addition of Gemma who was delighted to join the group of friends. Alex, James and Mike were equally delighted to include Sasha in their circle.

The cats, well, they continue to live their lives, whilst keeping watch, and their counsel.

The triplets are still young, who knows what the future has in store for them. The marbles are a concern. Emily, I know worries for her children. If the number of marbles is proportionate to their lifespans, then...

The man gave no hint of what the future was to hold, only that the girls are special and more special than previous generations. However, he did imply that they needed to be. We can only wait and ponder.

Of the earth, for the earth
Of the earth, to the earth
Of the earth, from the earth

For now, my work is done. I sit here sipping my coffee and watching the shoppers below. Cornelius sits purring contentedly on my lap and I turn my thoughts away from Much Meddling to a village on the northeast coast of England, and my next book, the ghost story I abandoned at Emily's request. I take another sip and stroke Cornelius. He opens an eye and looks at me briefly. Did he just wink? He closes his eyes and settles contentedly. I smile. All is well in Much Meddling, for now.

THANK YOU FOR READING MY BOOK

If you have enjoyed reading 'Cats' Eyes of Much Meddling', do tell your friends, and please consider leaving a review on Amazon. It is lovely to hear what people think.

Happy reading,

Pauline

COMING SOON

RIP - The Passage of Time

**Sometimes a rip appears in the veil
separating the living from the dead.
Sometimes the dead can't rest in peace.
Sometimes, the dead won't.**

She fell. Lurching, falling, grasping at air, finding only dust, choking, blinding dust. With sickening solidity, she landed and lay, unmoving, her mind numb with disbelief, her body numb with shock. Dispassionately, she examined the experience, comprehension beyond her grasp, fear scratching, clawing. There was a shuddering and she dropped again, half rotating, falling, bouncing. Through it all she was aware of the silence, an oppressive silence with an energy all of its own. Unable to control her limbs, she felt the pain as they flailed through the tumbling debris. It seemed an eternity, then merciful oblivion.

There was a hand on her face, its touch clumsy, abrasive. Fingers in her mouth, poking, gouging, and clearing. She gasped for air. Pain racked her chest, her arms, her legs. Briefly she felt relief as something heavy was lifted off her. Then the return of sickening pain and heart-thumping panic. She blinked against the grit in her eyes, desperate to see and make sense of it all. The silence persisted, surreal and enveloping and then, blessed oblivion again.

There were faces looking down at her. They looked concerned. Their mouths formed words but made no sound. Behind them the sky, dark and uncaring with stars beginning to appear through the settling dust: their existence emphasising the fleeting irrelevance of her being.

A familiar voice and an arm round her shoulders, tenderly guiding her. She was on her feet, grass between her toes. The person was hugging, half supporting her and leading her through a corridor of people, their faces all showing concern. She stared back at them. They were in dressing gowns. She was in her pyjamas. It was the middle of the night. Her guide was speaking to her, muttering soothing words. It was Natalie, yes Natalie. As a doorway loomed ahead, the bright internal lights contrasted starkly with the dark external night. Zoe stared in horror at the glow, screamed, and dropped to her knees.

ABOUT THE AUTHOR

Pauline Potterill

The author grew up in the northwest of England, on the edge of The Lake District, but has since lived in many parts of this beautiful country.

"I love local history, tradition and folklore, and believe that everyone should have a sense of their roots and be part of a community. I try to put a sense of this in my novels, hopefully in an amusing and affectionate way.

"I aim to keep readers guessing and like to surprise them. Although Wishing Wells is a romantic comedy, subsequent Much Meddling novels centre more on family life, but do include love stories. Inspiration comes from a happy fun-filled childhood, which I set against a romanticesed version of village life."

BOOKS BY THIS AUTHOR

Wishing Wells Of Much Meddling

Wishing Wells, the first of the Much Meddling novels, is a feel good, comedy romance with a touch of mystery and a fast-paced plot.

When Emily Hope is caught in a snowstorm, she has no idea how radically her life is about to change. The inhabitants of Much Meddling are plotting, individually, each with their own little scheme. Emily it seems, features in every one. Co-incidence? No! As Emily comes to learn, nothing in this beautiful little village happens by chance. Events have been managed for a long long time. Just ask the cats.

As Emily becomes embroiled in village life, and attempts to come to terms with her fate, whatever that might be, she struggles to understand her own needs: assuming of course that the mysterious periapt is just a harmless pendant, and she actually has a choice.

Fairy Rings Of Much Meddling

Another feel-good comedy romance with a bit of mystery and a lot of meddling.

In this the second of the Much Meddling novels, Emily and her family are now living happy and perfectly normal lives. Well, as normal as can be expected in any household with three baby girls. Most days are chaotic, but still normal in the traditional sense. No co-incidences are questioned. No odd occurrences go unexplained.

When the strange white cat appears Emily knows that something is not right. In fact, something is very wrong in Much Meddling. Someone, it seems, is interfering with the very fabric of its existence.

Can the Wells family fulfil their ancestral role as guardians, and save the village? The cats hope so.

Printed in Great Britain
by Amazon

31236561R00219